ELAK OF ATLANTIS
AND PRINCE RAYNOR

ELAK OF ATLANTIS
AND
PRINCE RAYNOR

Henry Kuttner

ELAK OF ATLANTIS
and Prince Raynor

For more titles in the Fiction House library,
visit our website: **www.FictionHousePress.com**

"Thunder in the Dawn", *Weird Tales*, May and June 1938.
"Spawn of Dagon", *Weird Tales*, July 1938.
"Beyond the Phœnix", *Weird Tales*, October 1938.
"Dragon Moon", *Weird Tales*, January 1941.
"Cursed Be the City", *Strange Stories*, April 1939.
"The Citadel of Darkness", *Strange Stories*, August 1939.

Published March 2022

isbn 978-1-64720-508-9

ELAK OF ATLANTIS

THUNDER IN THE DAWN

A story to stir the pulses—a tale of warlock and wizard and valiant men of might in the far-off olden time—a gripping tale of Elak of Atlantis

1. Magic of the Druid

THE tavern was ill-lighted and cloudy with smoke. Raucous oaths and no less rough laughter made the place a bedlam. From the open door a cold wind blew strongly, salt-scented from the sea that lapped restlessly against the wharves of Poseidonia. A small, fat man sitting alone in a booth was muttering to himself as he drank deeply of the wine the innkeeper had placed before him, and Lycon's quick, furtive glances searched the room, missing no detail.

For Lycon was a little frightened, and this prevented him from getting drunk as quickly as usual. His tall friend and fellow adventurer, Elak, was hours overdue from a clandestine visit to a lady of noble blood, the wife of a duke of Atlantis. This alone might not have troubled Lycon, but he was remembering certain curious events of the past fortnight—an inexplicable feeling of being trailed, and an encounter with masked soldiers in the forest beyond Poseidonia. Elak's dexterity with his rapier had saved them both, and, later, he had attributed the attack to the soldiers of Granicor, the Atlantean duke. Lycon was not so sure. Their opponents bad not been the swarthy, sinewy seamen of Poseidonia—they had been yellow-haired, fair-skinned giants such as were native to the northern shores of Atlantis. And for many moons Atlantis had been looking northward with apprehensive eyes.

The island continent is, roughly, heart-shaped, split down the middle by a waterway which runs from a huge bay or inland sea at the north down to a lake nearly at the southern extremity, thirty miles from the seacoast city of Poseidonia. For as long as men could remember the northern shores had been harried by red-bearded giants whose long black galleys had swept down from the frozen lands beyond the ocean. Dragon ships they were called, and those who manned them were Vikings—sea-pirates, plunderers who left ruin and desolation wherever they beached their craft. Lately rumors had spread of a great influx of these Northmen—and in taverns and by campfires men met and boasted and sharpened their blades.

There were two men in the brawling clamor of the inn who had attracted Lycon's intent gaze—

"The titan hand swept upward, carrying Elak and Solonola."

one, a gross, ugly figure clad in a shapeless brown robe, the traditional garb of the Druid priests. Beneath an immense bald head was a hairless, toad-like face glistening with sweat. These Druids, it was said, wielded immense power secretly, and Lycon habitually distrusted priests of any order.

Beside the Druid, Lycon watched a bearded giant whose skin showed traces of being darkened artificially, and whose hair was probably dyed, as it showed blue in the lamps' glow. Casually the small adventurer touched the hilt of his sword. Somewhat reassured by the feel of its smooth metal, he banged his cup on the table and yelled for more wine.

"What watery swill is this?" he asked the inn-keeper, a wizened oldster in a liquor-stained tunic. "It's fit for babes and women. Bring me something a man can drink, or—or——"

On the verge of uttering a grandiloquent threat Lycon subsided, muttering softly. "Gods!" he observed to himself as the innkeeper moved away, "what's got into me? These past weeks have made me a coward. I'll be jumping at shadows soon. Where in the Nine Hells is Elak?"

He paused to throw a gold piece on the table and to lift a replenished cup to his lips. That was but the first of many cups, and presently Lycon's apprehension and worry had crystallized into belligerency. The bearded giant was watching him, he saw.

Lycon drained his cup, set it down with a crash—and sprang to his feet, overturning the table. Dark faces were turned to him; wary eyes gleamed in the lamplight.

FOR all his fatness Lycon was agile. He leaped over the table and headed for the giant, who had not moved, save to set down his liquor.

Lycon was, by this time, very drunk indeed. He paused to drag his sword from its scabbard, but unfortunately it stuck, marring the impressiveness of the gesture. Nevertheless Lycon persisted, and pulled out the weapon at last. He flourished it beneath the other's nose.

"Am I a dog?" he demanded, glaring malevolently at the giant, who shrugged.

"You should know," he said gruffly. "Go away

4

before I slice off your ears with that toy."

Lycon gasped inarticulately. Speech returned with a rush.

"Misbegotten spawn of a worm!" he snarled. "Unsheathe your sword! I'll have your heart out for this——"

The blackbeard cast a swift glance around. He did not look frightened, but, oddly, annoyed, as though Lycon had interrupted some important project of his own. Yet he stood erect, and his blade came out flashing. The innkeeper hurried up, clucking his annoyance. In one of his hands was a bungstarter, and watching his chance he brought this down toward Lycon's head.

From the corner of his eye the little man saw the movement. He ducked, whirled, felt his shoulder go numb beneath the blow. The giant's sword swept out at his unprotected throat.

Something hit Lycon, sent him sprawling back, while razor-sharp steel raked his chest. He fought frantically to regain his footing. He came upright with his back to the wall, sword in hand—and stood staring.

Elak had at last arrived. It was his blow that had hurled Lycon from the path of the giant's steel, and now the lean, wolf-faced adventurer's rapier was engaging the blackbeard's weapon in a dazzling flash and shimmer of clanging metal, while Elak's laughter brought fear to his opponent's eyes. The innkeeper crouched near by, the bungstarter gripped in his hand, and swiftly Lycon caught up a heavy flagon and crashed it down on the man's head. He fell, blood spurting, and Lycon turned again to watch the battle.

The blackbeard was being forced back by the rapidity of Elak's onslaught. Few could stand successfully against the electric speed with which the adventurer wielded his rapier; already the giant was bleeding from a long cut along the forehead. He cried, "Wait! Wait, Elak——"

And his sword came down, leaving his throat unprotected.

But Elak also lowered his rapier. His wolfish face cracked in an ironic grin.

"Had enough?" he taunted. "By Ishtar, but you've little courage for your size."

The giant fumbled with the fastenings of his tunic. Abruptly he brought out something thin and dark and writhing coiled about his arm. He flung it at Elak.

The rapier screamed through the air, but missed its mark. Elak sprang aside just in time; the dark thing shot past him and arched up to avoid the swinging cut of Lycon's sword. For a brief moment it hung in empty air, while the silence of stupefaction stilled the tavern's clamor.

It was a serpent—but a winged serpent! A snake, with two webbed, membranous wings sprouting from its body. Beady eyes glittered in the triangular head as the monster hung aloft. Then down it came, swift as an arrow's flight.

Chairs and tables crashed over, and the thunder of frantic feet sounded. Lycon's thrust almost spitted Elak. The winged snake, unhurt, flashed away, but its fangs had grazed Elak's shoulder. The brown leather of his tunic darkened swiftly, while a stench of foul corruption was strong in his nostrils.

"Bel!" he ground out. "I can't——"

Suddenly a bulky figure loomed before him— the Druid, huge arms lifted, shielding the adventurer with his own body. Elak made to thrust him aside. Then, staring, he paused.

From the upthrust hands of the Druid a pale flame was rising, twin fires that burned fiercely, dwarfing the yellow glow of the lamps. Incredibly the flames swelled and grew and abruptly took flight. The winged serpent twisted in midair, its wings whirring. But inexorably the flames raced down upon it.

They spread out lambent fingers, interlacing, till around the monster revolved a sphere of silently glowing fire. The serpent was hidden from view by a globe of flame.

And it swiftly diminished, shrank to a tiny glowing point—and vanished. Where flame and serpent had been was nothing. A gray dust filtered slowly to the rough planks of the floor. . . .

2. Northmen in Cyrena

"SO MAY all traitors die!" the Druid said harshly.

He was staring at an outsprawled giant figure that lay broken across a splintered table, a man whose black-bearded, swarthy face was upturned to the lamplight. On his brow a circle of reddened skin was burned and blistered, and blood bubbled in his throat.

Before either Lycon or Elak could move, the Druid had bent above the dying man, gripping his hair with rough fingers.

"Who sent you?" he snarled, his toadlike face aglisten with sweat. "Tell me, you dog—or I'll——"

"Mercy!" the wretch gasped, blood gushing from his mouth.

"I'll give you such mercy as will send your soul screaming down the Nine Hells! Who sent you? Tell these men!"

The man croaked, "Elf! He——"

Callously the Druid turned away. A frown creased Elak's brow as he saw the fear-glazed eyes roll up in death. "Elf?" he repeated. "I know that name."

"You should," the Druid growled. "Perhaps you know mine, then—Dalan. Come on, we've no time to talk. The guards will be here in a moment."

Lycon hesitated, shrank back. But Elak gripped his arm and urged him in the wake of the Druid.

"We can trust him," he whispered. "I've heard tales of this Dalan. And I think——" There was a wry smile on Elak's lean face. "I think we'll be safer with him than anywhere else."

A wan moon hung low over Atlantis. Keeping in the shadows, the three cautiously made their way along the waterfront. Once they shrank back into a doorway while a troop of guards clattered past. And at last they came to a low hut into which Dalan ushered them, barring the door carefully before he turned to take a lantern from a peg on the wall.

Even then he paused to lift a trap-door in the floor before setting the lantern on the rough table in the center of the bare, gloomy room. "In case of surprize," he explained; "though I think we're safe enough here."

"In Bel's name, what's this all about?" Lycon demanded. The drink was wearing off, and he was trembling a little with reaction. Gratefully he sank down in a chair the Druid indicated. "Did you kill that bearded swine? Winged snakes—magic fires—haven't you anything to drink in this cavern?"

"You'll need a clear head for what I'm going to tell you," Dalan said. "There's magic in it, yes, or at least a science you can't understand. I slew that traitorous dog with a power we Druids have had for ages—a power over fire. And thus I slew Elf's messenger."

"The snake? Who is this—Elf?"

Dalan sent a somber glance toward Elak, whose face was grim and cold. He asked, "This man—does he know nothing? Have you told him of Cyrena?"

Elak shook his head. "Tell him, Dalan."

"Cyrena? The northermost kingdom of Atlantis?" Lycon asked. "I know Orander rules it, but that's all."

"A dozen years ago Norian ruled Cyrena," the Druid said. "He had two stepsons, Orander and Zeulas. Zeulas killed him."

Elak moved uneasily.

"Zeulas killed him," Dalan repeated, "in fair fight, and both men had provocation. Because of this, Zeulas, though he was the elder, did not assume the crown. He left Cyrena to wander, a homeless vagabond, through Atlantis."

Lycon turned to stare at Elak. "By Ishtar! You don't mean——"

"He is Zeulas," the Druid said. "His brother, Orander, rules over Cyrena. Or—did rule."

"The Vikings?" Elak asked.

"Yes. They've invaded the land, with the aid of Elf the warlock. Elf has always hated your brother, who would never give him the freedom he wanted for his black sorcery and human sacrifice. So Elf made a pact with the Northmen to destroy Orander, in exchange for power and for the victims he needs for his necromancy."

"Did he——" Elak did not finish, but a cold fire blazed in his eyes.

"He couldn't kill Orander; my magic was too strong for that. But he has taken him captive and left the armies of Cyrena without a head. So the chiefs argue and battle among themselves, and the Vikings slay them at leisure."

Lycon was nearly sober now. A smoking oath came from his throat. "Your kingdom, Elak? This is your kingdom? And the Northmen and this stinking wizard rule it? Dalan"—he stood erect, teetering a little—"we head north tomorrow— tonight! I'll slit this Elf's throat like a pig's."

Elak pulled him down. "Wait a moment. Dalan—you want me to return to Cyrena? To lead the armies against the Vikings?"

The Druid nodded. "That's why I'm here. Elf caught me unawares, and he has your brother captive. But if you'll come north, you'll give Cyrena the leader it needs. My magic will aid you."

"To free Orander?"

"Yes. And to destroy Elf, to drive out the Northmen!" The toad face grew hideous with rage. "They desecrate the Druid altars, crucify our priests! They worship Loki and Thor and Odin, devils of the blackest abyss—and they worship Elf's evil gods, as well. By Mider!" Dalan's hand moved in a strange quick gesture as he named the Druids' greatest deity. "You'll come—you must come, Zeulas—Elak—whatever you name yourself now!"

Elak stood up. "Yes, I'll come. I'd sworn never to enter Cyrena again, but this is a different thing."

"And I'll go with you," Lycon put in. "You'll need a strong sword in the forests. It's a far distance to Cyrena."

"Good!" Dalan's great hands swept down, gripped Lycon's shoulders. "You have courage—and you'll need it. But we'll not go through the forests. Look."

He bent to scrawl, with a bit of charcoal, a rough map on the table's top. "Here we are at Poseidonia. We go inland thirty miles to the Central Lake, where I've a ship waiting. Then north, down the river through the heart of Atlantis, into the Inland Sea that touches Cyrena. We'll go with the current, and my oarsmen are strong."

"And we start——" Lycon's face was eager.

"Tomorrow, at dawn. You'll stay here with me tonight."

ELAK hesitated. "Dalan, we may not return. And I promised—well, there's a girl I'll have to see tonight."

"Velia?" Lycon asked. "Duke Granicor's wife? I should think you'd had enough of her by now. And, by the way, what kept you tonight?"

"Her kisses," Elak said frankly. "I told her I'd see her before leaving Poseidonia."

Dalan grunted, "The guards——"

"I can evade them."

"What about the man I killed in the tavern tonight—and Elf's messenger? I tell you, Zeulas—or Elak—Elf fears you. He knows I came to Poseidonia to bring you north to fight him, and he knows, too, that if you're dead, the Vikings will sweep unopposed over Cyrena. He has servants besides the Northmen—renegades, traitors!"

"I see Velia tonight," Elak said stubbornly. He turned toward the door.

"Wait." Dalan's huge hand spun him about. "There's no need to take unnecessary risk. We'll leave tonight—and, on the way, you can stop for a kiss or two with this wench. But you're a fool to do it."

"It isn't the first time women have made a fool of Elak," Lycon said, grinning. "But Dalan's right. We'd better leave Poseidonia now. I'll feel safer in the forest."

Elak shrugged and waited while the Druid hastily erased the map from the table. That done, the three cautiously let themselves out into the moonlit alley. . . .

THE palace of Duke Granicor shone whitely, towering on a hillock above Poseidonia. To the southeast the ocean swept out to a dim horizon. In the other direction was the forest, dark, menacing. In the shadow of a gate Lycon and Dalan waited while Elak dextrously mounted the wall. He moved quietly through the perfumed blossoms of the garden till he reached the trellis beneath Velia's window.

He had climbed it often before, and it gave no trouble now. The girl came upon the balcony as he softly called her name. He was briefly silent, studying her golden beauty in the moonlight.

Her transparent robe concealed little; she seemed like an amber statue draped in gauze. Bronze hair fell disheveled about an oval, elfin face; amber eyes were upturned questioningly to Elak's. Without a word he drew her close.

"I'm leaving Poseidonia," he said after a time. "I may not see you again for a while."

She clung to him. "Elak, I wish—I'll go with you!"

"No. You——"

"I will! I can't stand it here with Granicor. He's a beast, Elak—a devil. You know how he bought me from my father—I'm little better than a slave to him. I—I'd have killed myself if I hadn't met you."

"Don't be a little fool," Elak said gruffly. "You'll get used to him in time. Though, by Ishtar, his face is enough to frighten babies! Well——"

"You're frank, at least, vagabond," a new voice growled. "And you'll be franker on the rack, with this harlot beside you!"

Elak released the girl and swung about quickly to face the man who came on to the balcony from the shadows. Duke Granicor was smiling, baring stained, discolored teeth through a gray-shot beard. In his silks and velvets he looked incongruously bedecked, a huge ape masquerading in borrowed finery. Bloodshot small eyes glared at Elak from little pits of gristle.

"You skulking dog!" Duke Granicor roared, lifting a dagger. "Your face'll frighten soldiers when I'm through with you!"

From the garden below came the clash of armor, and the swift thud-thud of racing feet.

3. Through the Black Forest

ELAK had no time to draw his rapier before Granicor was upon him. He twisted lithely beneath the dagger's blow, felt the blade tear and scrape along his ribs. Then he closed with his opponent, grimly silent.

Granicor's arm rose up, blade red and dripping, but before it could descend Velia had gripped it. Before the duke could wrench his weapon free the girl had bent swiftly, set her teeth in hairy flesh. Granicor roared on oath; but the dagger dropped, went clattering over the rail to the garden below.

Someone was climbing the trellis. Elak dropped swiftly beneath Granicor's encircling arms, and his own sinewy arms went about the duke's knees, gripping them tightly. With one swift movement he hurled himself up and back, sent his opponent crashing over the marble balustrade, hurtling down into the shadows. A yell of alarm and a scrambling in the foliage, ending in a smashing thud, told of a guard wrenched from his perch by Granicor's descending body.

Elak seized Velia's hand. "Come on," he snapped, and dragged her from the balcony within the room. A glance told him that there were no enemies here. Apparently the duke had been alone, save for his cohorts in the garden.

Now Velia took the lead. "I know the palace," she said swiftly. "There's a door Granicor may have overlooked. If there's no guard——"

They sped along dimly-lit halls, draped with tapestries and rugs of somber magnificence. Faintly there came to Elak's ears the sound of men's voices shouting. Into a narrow hall—down a steep winding staircase. . . .

Elak gripped a heavy iron door, flung it open. Someone rose up before him, startled and menacing; armor glinted in the moonlight. But the slim rapier sheathed itself in flesh, and blood spurted from a pierced throat as the guard sank down groaning. They hurdled his body and raced into the garden.

Blades shimmered frostily; shadows closed in

on them. Elak saw Granicor, his face blood-smeared and horrible, one arm dangling use-lessly, bellowing commands to his men. But surprize was in their favor, and they made the gate safely.

To their surprize it was open. Elak pushed the girl through and turned to find the pack yell-ing at his heels.

Huge hands gripped him; he was drawn through the gateway. Metal clanged. The gross figure of the Druid stood briefly between him and the soldiers. Then, without warning, a tongue of fire licked up from the ground. It spread and lifted, filling the gateway with its red blaze. Dalan turned.

"That will stop them," he grunted, "for a time, anyway. Hurry!"

Lycon came out of the shadows, and the four raced into the dimness, seeking shelter in a near-by grove of trees before Granicor remem-bered to use arrows. As they came panting among the shielding trunks a menacing roar came from the palace, and a rout of men, armor glittering, came pouring down the hill.

"More than one gate," Elak muttered. "Well, shall we fight—or run?"

"Run," Lycon advised. "I'll stay here and hold them, for a while, at least. You can——"

The Druid whispered, "Come. I know the for-ests. Follow me—and they'll never find us. You too, Lycon."

VELIA'S hand was warm in Elak's as they silently trailed Dalan. Like a shadow for all his gross bulk the Druid slipped from tree to tree, taking advantage of every bush and shrub, till at last the noise of pursuit died in the distance. Only then did he pause to wipe the sweat from his ugly face.

"No enemy can find a Druid in the forests," he informed the others. "If necessary, our magic can send the trees marching against those who follow."

Elak grunted skeptically. "Well, I've let us in for something now. Velia's coming with us. I'm not going to leave her here to be skinned alive by Granicor."

She pressed closer to him, and Elak's arm went about her warm slimness.

"It's no hardship," Lycon said, glancing slyly at the girl. "And my sword is yours to command."

Velia thanked him with a glance, and the little man expanded visibly. Elak's expression was none too cordial.

"Let's get started," he said. "We've a long march to the Central Lake and your ship, Dalan."

The Druid nodded and took the lead. They set out through the moonlit forest. . . .

Presently the moon sank, but Dalan guided them unerringly, even in the vague starlight, where they would have been separated had they not joined hands. Weird noises came out of the night; the shrill calling of birds and the rustle of underbrush. Once the ground shook beneath the tread of some giant beast that lumbered past unseen in the gloom. And once Elak spitted with his rapier a spider as large as his hand, which squirted venom a dozen feet as it writhed and died.

As dawn came they reached the Central Lake, a chill blue expanse whose depths had never been plumbed. Zones of sapphire and aquamarine and deeper blue lay across its surface. Floating at anchor not far away was a long galley, sails furled, waiting.

Sand crunched beneath their sandaled feet as the four hurried to the water's edge. Dalan made a speaking-tube of his hands and bellowed lustily till a small boat left the galley, heading shoreward.

"That's done, at least," Lycon said with satisfaction. "My poor feet!"

He sat down and rubbed them tenderly. His own sandals had gone to protect Velia's feet, but the girl's flimsy nightrobe had been ripped to shreds by thorns and branches. She kicked off the sandals, slipped out of her garment, and ran into the lake, laughing with pleasure as the cool water caressed her aching muscles.

Lycon eyed her enviously. "I'd join her, if I had time," he observed. "Well, a few buckets of water will do the trick on deck. Here's the boat."

Two oarsmen rowed it; Dalan greeted them and quickly clambered aboard, his brown robe fluttering in the breeze. The others joined him; Lycon and Elak and Velia, who, after a few abortive attempts to adjust her robe, gave up the effort and made it into a brief kirtle.

"You may swim along the shore," the Druid warned her, "but not out where the waters are deeper. This lake goes down to hell itself, I think, and there are devils below its surface."

Lycon stared curiously around, apparently disappointed because no devils appeared. Then he fell to polishing his sword. . . .

In the galley's pit men lounged on benches. Brawny, half-naked oarsmen, not slaves, for they were not shackled to the benches. Dalan shouted an order as he climbed on board. Men scrambled to obey, settling in disciplined order, gripping their oars. A tall, broad-shouldered man with a golden collar mounted a platform. He gestured, cried a command.

The oars swept down, cleaving the blue waters of Central Lake. The galley sprang forward, plunging north.

North to Cyrena!

4. Power of the Warlock

SO THE strong oars dipped and plunged, and the galley ran northward to where two shores converged in the river that cleft the heart of Atlantis, rushing between granite precipices, lazing through sunlit meadows, thundering swiftly and more swiftly toward the Inland Sea and Cyrena. And these days seemed the happiest of all to Elak and Velia; while Lycon divided his time between drinking steadily and arguing with the overseer about navigation, a subject of which he knew nothing. Only over Dalan a shadow seemed to hang, and this grew darker as they swept north. When the sails were unfurled they hung loose and useless, though stormclouds gathered each night to the southward. At last Dalan called Elak to the cabin.

"Elf works magic," he said grimly. "Duke Granicor has not given up the pursuit. He sails after us, with Elf's wizardry helping him."

Elak whistled between his teeth. "That's not so good. How do you know?"

Dalan lifted a dark cloth from a pedestal; light glinted from a crystal sphere large as Elak's head. "Look," he said. "I've known this for days. . . ."

At first Elak saw only the transparent depths of the crystal, and very slowly, very gradually, they clouded and became translucent. Light images began to flash before his eyes, a vague succession of darting colors . . . and these crystallized into a scene, a tiny picture within the sphere: a galley, sails set and straining, racing between shores which Elak remembered passing only a day before. He looked up quickly.

"Wind? But our sails——"

"Calm follows our galley, but Elf's magic speeds Granicor's. We're nearly in the Inland Sea now, though, and—wait!"

Something was happening within the crystal. The sharply-defined image shook and wavered, like a reflection in water. It misted and faded and changed—and a face swam into view: the face of a youth, rounded as a child's. Blue eyes, clear with candor, met Elak's; soft flaxen hair fell about the man's shoulders. And, for all the innocence of that cool gaze, Elak subtly sensed an ageless, malefic evil that dwelt within the blue eyes, a black horror utterly incongruous with the beauty of the face.

"Mider!" the Druid snarled. "Elf—watches us! He——"

The red lips parted in a singularly sweet smile. Dalan thrust his face down close to the crystal.

"Elf!" he roared. "Hear me! Ho, you stinking spawn of devils—hear me! Not all your foul wizardry can keep me from Cyrena, or the man I bring with me. Tell Guthrum that! Let him pray to Odin and Thor—and I'll grind their faces in the dust as I'll grind yours." He cursed the warlock bitterly, foully, while Elak watched fascinated.

The smile did not leave Elf's face. The crystal dimmed, grew cloudy—and was transparent. The vision had gone before Dalan paused in his tirade.

Sweating, he mopped at his gross face. "Well, you've seen Elf now. For the first time, eh?"

Elak nodded.

"What do you think of him?"

"I—scarcely know. He has my brother captive?"

"He holds Orander. And Guthrum, the Viking king, does as Elf wishes. You must fight Guthrum, Elak, as I Elf. And Granicor's galley comes swiftly."

"I don't see why you fear him," Elak said.

"Your own powers——"

"Are limited. And Mider knows what magic aids Granicor. D'you see that storm?" He gestured toward a port-hole. Black clouds were drifting up from the south. "All the winds of hell are there—yet our sails hang without a breeze to lift them. Look."

He turned to the north. "See that land, far distant? It's Crenos Isle, a place best shunned. We go past Crenos to Cyrena—but I think Granicor will find us first."

DALAN was right. The long galley of the duke swiftly drove before the storm, and just off the southern extremity of Crenos Isle the two ships met.

"One thing's in our favor," Dalan grunted, issuing weapons to the oarsmen. "Slaves man their oars. But ours are men, and warriors—men from Cyrena who'll not ask for quarter. But we have no fighting crew, and Granicor has."

"It's my fault," Elak said morosely. "If I hadn't got the duke on our trail——"

"Forget it!" Lycon swaggered up, brandishing his sword and exuding a strong aroma of spirits. "We'll run that dog up by the heels at his own masthead. Besides, Velia's a girl worth fighting for, by Ishtar!"

Velia, looking like a slim youth in her soft tunic, laughed almost gayly. "Thanks, Lycon. At least I'll not have to go back to Granicor. There are many ways to die here—to die easily."

"None o' that," Elak told her; "though I suppose you're right. You can't enjoy life with your skin off. And that's the duke's favorite torture."

The sky darkened. Wind buffeted them. The oarsmen bent to their oars, swords at their sides. Granicor's ship lowered sail, but double banks of oars propelled it swiftly forward.

"They mean to ram," Dalan muttered. "Well, two can play at that game. Ready, now——"

He roared an order into the gale. Oars were lifted; the ship came around, and timbers cracked and groaned and shuddered at the shock as the galleys scraped almost prow to prow.

"Up oars!" Dalan bellowed. "Cast off grappling-irons!"

His intention had been to cripple Granicor's galley by smashing one bank of oars, but he was too late. A dozen hooks snaked out, were drawn taut. The ships were locked together—and a wave of shouting, blood-hungry men came pouring over the gunwales.

"Get in the cabin," Elak commanded Velia, but she did not heed; there was a slim blade in her hand, and she stood coolly at his side. Dalan and Lycon flanked the two. The oarsmen seized their weapons, met the invaders. Swords clashed blindingly.

"Stay here, Lycon," Elak said suddenly. "Guard Velia." He sprang down into the pit among the mob of yelling swordsmen. A few arrows fell, but the galleys swayed and pitched so that accurate marksmanship was impossible. Still stronger came the storm wind, darker grew

ELAK OF ATLANTIS

the clouds.

"'Ware, Elak!" Lycon's voice.

The tall adventurer ducked a sweep of steel that came out of nowhere, saw a grinning swarthy face rise up behind him. The rapier danced into a dazzling shimmer and the man went down coughing blood. Then Elak caught sight of Granicor fighting his way toward him, gray beard blood-spattered, shouting furious oaths. He sprang to meet the duke.

The ships heeled, rocked sickeningly in the trough of the waves. From the corner of his eye Elak saw a flicker of red fire, realized that Dalan was battling too. The Druid's magic turned the tide.

Cold steel men could battle, but not this searing flame that sprang out of empty air to leave blistered corpses in its wake. The struggle went back to the gunwales, back and back to Granicor's galley, carrying Elak and the duke with it. Dimly Elak heard Dalan's exultant shout, the shrill cry of Velia. . . .

Without warning disaster struck. A blast of frigid, resistless air, a maelstrom of wind that smashed down on the two craft and ripped them asunder, sent them plunging through waters gone insane. Elak saw Dalan's galley being swept away, heard Granicor roaring in triumph as he plunged forward. He tensed for a leap, realizing as he sprang that he would fall short.

Salt water drove into his nostrils, choking him. He went down like a plummet, clinging grimly to his sword. Somehow he held his

24

breath, fighting up toward a dim, hazily translucent green light. And somehow he kept afloat in
a madness of racing seas, hanging to the frag-
ment of an oar that drifted within his reach . . .
but at last darkness took him, and he went
down into the shadows.

Shadows that whispered, mocking him. Dim
shadows, with cool blue eyes of Elf, moving
swiftly in errands of mystery . . . vague visions of
strangeness and of magic . . . and the faces of
Velia and Lycon and the Druid, anxious and
afraid. They were searching for him, he knew,
and he tried to call a reassuring message. But
the dreams faded and were gone. . . .

5. The Dwellers on the Isle

ELAK awoke very slowly, conscious of a dull
pain in his chest. A sullen gray sky lowered
above him as he opened aching eyes. Near by
waves crawled up whispering on a slate-dark
beach. He tried to sit up, and discovered that his
arms were bound tightly.

He turned to see tall rocks hemming him in,
monolithic eidolons that rose up in all directions
save seaward. His attention was drawn by a
flicker of movement to a slab of rock that towered twenty feet above him; there was a very
narrow crevice splitting it, and from it came a
man.

Elak could not repress a start. Before him
was a Pikht—a member of the almost legendary
race that had held Atlantis so many eons ago

that their very existence had almost been forgotten. White men from the east had warred upon the Pikhts, exterminating them ruthlessly, until, on Crenos Isle, there dwelt what was probably the last survival of the race.

The man was dark-skinned and very short—scarcely five feet in height—and hairless. Not even his pale eyes were fringed by lashes. He wore no more than a loin-cloth, and great muscles crawled beneath the smooth skin. His somber face had an indefinably bestial cast—and Elak thought suddenly of tales he had heard of the kinship of Pikhts to the beasts—that these men were the first beings who had possessed the true human form, and who had possessed powers lost to those of a higher stage of evolution.

The Pikht bent over Elak, a knife in his hand. His voice was thick, guttural, and Elak could scarcely understand the Atlantean tongue he spoke. "Get up, stranger. Slowly!"

Elak, with some effort, got to his feet, careful to make no hasty movement. His rapier, he saw with regret, was gone. Also his legs were bound together by a thong about a foot long.

The Pikht urged him toward the crevice in the rock. It narrowed until his broad shoulders scraped the sides, then widened as he led down. Elak debated the advantage of trying to take his captor unaware, but, bound and unarmed as he was, he knew only death would result. Presently he felt stairs beneath his feet, invisible in the shrouding darkness.

"'Ware!" It was the Pikht's harsh voice. "Not

too fast!"

Obediently Elak slackened his pace. Before him a slit of light widened, and he looked down a corridor cut out of solid rock.

Perhaps two hundred feet long it was, lit by bronze lamps that stood in niches in the wall. Iron doors, with barred windows set in them, broke the monotony of gray rock on one side; the other side was blank, roughly chiseled stone. Elak paused.

The Pikht's blade gouged skin from his captive's back. Glancing around, Elak saw that behind the dark-skinned dwarf were two other men, replicas of his captor, hairless and smooth-skinned and dark. They carried long blades, longer than themselves.

Elak let himself be prodded along the passage. As he passed the barred doors he realized that they guarded captives, Atlanteans all, some clad in leather or armor, others in furry skins. In the silent faces that watched him Elak saw fear—fear so great that none spoke aloud. In whispers men cursed the Pikhts, and the dwarfs smiled mockingly, their eyes coldly alight with malicious amusement.

At a door near the end of the tunnel the Pikht halted. He gestured, and one of his companions lifted a great metal bar that locked the panel. The iron door was swung open, and Elak was thrust across the threshold.

Metal clanged; the bar was thrust into its socket. The cell, cut from solid rock, held nothing; but in the further wall was another door—

an iron slab whose smooth surface was feature-less and unbroken.

Elak heard the Pikhts go padding along the passage. And, very slowly, the iron slab began to swing outward.

A man crept into the cell. His emaciated body was clad in a tattered jerkin, and tangled, yellow hair hung about a bearded, pain-ravaged face. His eyes were vacuous, filmed with a blue glaze. Spittle drooled from the slack mouth. Behind him the door swung silently shut as Elak sprang forward. He had only a flashing glimpse of a gray corridor—no more.

The man huddled in a corner, shuddering and moaning. Elak looked down at him with pity.

"Who are you?" he asked. "Can you under-stand me?"

"Yes . . . yes, I can understand. The Shadow took Halfgar, my son. The Shadow on the pool . . ."

The bearded face was contorted with grief and horror. Elak cast a swift glance at the iron door, cryptically shut. What talk was this of—a Shadow?

The blue stare focussed on Elak. "Elf the war-lock gave me to the Pikhts, and my son Halfgar went with me because he fought at my side against Elf's men. They——"

Elak leaned forward tensely. "Elf? These dwarfs—Pikhts—know him?"

"Yes; they serve him. They give him magic in return for strong men whom they sacrifice to their god. For ages they've dwelt on Crenos Isle worshipping——" The man's voice dropped to a thin reedy whisper, and madness crept into his eyes. "The Shadow took my son. The door opened, and I went out into the passage where the pool was. I saw water below me, and a Shadow lying upon it. The Shadow leaped up at me, and as I drew back it touched my brow . . . it was not hungry then. It had just fed on Halfgar . . . it took him from my side as I slept . . . there are doors which are not to be opened. . . ."

The whisper stopped. The man's eyes widened. He sprang to his feet, clawing at his breast with ripping fingernails, tearing away skin and flesh in long ribbons. He screamed, a frightful, agonized shriek that resounded through the cell.

And he fell, a boneless huddle in the corner. His bearded face stared up blindly, and Elak saw that he was dead.

A soft rustling made him turn. Very slowly, very gently, the iron door was swinging outward. From the vagueness beyond the portal a misty gray light crept into the cell.

Elak heard the lapping of water . . .

DALAN'S black galley lay beached on Crenos Isle, battered and bruised by the storm. The same gale that had flung the ship ashore had sent Duke Granicor's craft driving northward till it had been lost to view in the scud. Now the oarsmen were busy calking seams, mending the ruin the tempest had wrought.

But Dalan, in the cabin, crouched over his crystal globe, his ugly face set in harsh lines.

Velia and Lycon stood beside him, curiously eyeing the sphere, watching the flashing images
that swept through its depths.

"Elf's magic is strong," the Druid muttered.
"He battles me at every step. But——"

"Is Elak alive?" Velia asked anxiously. "Why
won't you tell me?"

"Because I don't know. Keep quiet, girl! Elf's
spells war with mine, and I see nothing—yet."

He peered into the shimmering sphere. Lycon
squeezed Velia's arm reassuringly. And, suddenly, Dalan expelled a long breath of relief.

"So! He lives—see?"

Within the crystal a picture grew, a tiny image of a beach flanked by towering gray rocks.
On the slope a man lay bound and unconscious.

"Praise Ishtar!" Lycon said. "Is he far? I'll go
after him——"

"Wait," the Druid commanded. "I know that
beach. Elf's allies, the Pikhts, have an underground temple there. And—look!"

Velia gave a soft little cry. There was movement
within the crystal; a man emerged from a cleft in
one of the tall rocks and approached Elak's prostrate figure. As they watched they saw Elak prodded to his feet by the Pikht, urged into the darkness of the fissure. For a second the sphere was a
ball of jet; then it brightened and showed a long
corridor cut out of solid rock. Three dark-skinned
dwarfs thrust Elak forward. . . .

"Mider!" Dalan said tonelessly. "He's in the temple! And that means he's to be sacrificed to——"

"Not if I know it!" Lycon snapped. "How far is

this temple? The crew have swords, and know how to use them. Tell me how to go, Dalan—north or south?" He was at the door, grinning unpleasantly as he fingered the hilt of his blade. "I'll butcher those little devils for you!"

"Good! Go south, Lycon—and swiftly. You'll know the place?"

"I'll know it. How far have we to go?"

"Half an hour's march, if you travel fast." The Druid turned to his globe. "I'll stay here. You must fight the Pikhts—but I battle Elf. And——" His huge hands swept down, gripped the crystal. "Hurry, Lycon! Elak's in danger now—deadly danger!"

Lycon thrust the door open, sprang on deck. His shrill voice shattered the morning calm. And in response the crew leaped to obey, dropping oar and hammer, taking up sword and ax, dropping over the rail to the beach. A half-naked, villainous-looking band, they trotted south, urged on by Lycon's searing oaths and the flat of his blade.

And with them came Velia, keeping always at Lycon's side, eyes flashing with battle-hunger, lips parted in a smile that was not pleasant to see. They went so swiftly that they reached their destination before the time Dalan had allotted. Recognizing the black cleft in the stone, Lycon halted his men to take the lead.

He stepped into the darkness with a strange crawling of uneasiness, sword bared, blinking in an attempt to pierce the gloom. Something moved, and he cut at a menace he sensed rather than heard. Steel gashed his thigh, but he felt his blade rip through flesh and grind against bone. A squealing, scarcely human cry sounded. In a frenzy of loathing he struck and struck again, cutting his way forward against soft bodies that resisted briefly and then broke and retreated under his onslaught.

The oarsmen poured into the cleft, led by Velia, and in the darkness the Pikhts rallied and came at them, snarling rage. For a little while there was a black madness of battle, a chaos of yells and oaths and death cries. In the end Lycon won through, and the Pikhts scattered like rats before the sweep of thirsty blades.

Before Lycon now was a dim-lit corridor, one wall set with barred doors. He cut down a screaming dwarf that plunged at him, dagger bared, and left the rest to Velia and the crew. Swiftly he raced along the passage, casting hasty glances into each cell as he passed. Captives stretched out imploring hands, begging for release, but Elak was not among them.

Near the end of the corridor, one door was open. Lycon sprang over the threshold, saw a bare, empty cell with an iron slab ajar in the opposite wall. He went forward, sword dripping red on the stones as he lifted it.

Water was lapping softly near by. . . .

6. The Night of Gods

ELAK stepped through the portal and found himself in a narrow passage. Gray light bathed him. In the distance he saw a sparkling surface that rippled in the cold glow.

And suddenly he heard Dalan's voice. It came softly from empty air, urgent, peremptory, calling his name.

"Elak! *Elak!*"

Searching the bare walls with incredulous eyes, Elak whispered, "Dalan? 'Where are you?"

The Druid's voice rang out sharply. "No time now, Elak—the Shadow comes as I speak. Leap into the pool—dive into it, now! At the end of the passage——"

Still Elak hesitated. "But where are you——"

"There's no time to talk now! Hurry——"

The stark urgency of Dalan's words spurred Elak to action, sent him racing along the corridor. He checked himself sharply on the brink of a square basin. Little menace in that, or in the blue-green water that filled it. But within the pool dwelt horror. A Shadow lay upon it.

The shadow of a man, cast by—nothing! An opaque outline that lay incredibly on the surface of the pool. And it darkened into blackness, while the gray luminescence of the corridor dimmed.

"'Ware, Elak!"

Dalan's voice, loud in warning! Elak whirled, saw a dark-skinned dwarf almost upon him, pale eyes blazing, bestial face menacing. In the Pikht's hand was a dagger.

The two men smashed together on the pool's brink, went down, clutching and tearing, the oily body of the dwarf squirming like a snake in

Elak's grasp. Steel grated on the stones. Elak's fingers closed relentlessly on his opponent's knife-wrist.

With a powerful lunge the Pikht brought his dagger down, its point touching Elak's chest. The two rolled over, snarling oaths, and— dropped into emptiness!

The pool took them—dragged them down into water icy as polar seas, blue as turquoise. Elak could see nothing but that illimitable blueness as he went down, choking for breath, battling against blinding panic. Was the pool bottomless?

The sapphire tint deepened to indigo, foamed in fantastic patterns before Elak's eyes. He realized abruptly that this was not water surrounding him—could not be, or he would have drowned minutes ago. There was a swift accelerating rush, and abruptly frightful cold, incredible agony, tore at the citadel of Elak's brain. He was conscious of a change.

Air rushed into his lungs—air stale and dead, as though it had never been breathed, yet curiously refreshing. Dim, flickering shadows were all about him. And the swarthy devil-mask of the Pikht's face swam into view from the vagueness.

Pale eyes glared into Elak's; the dagger came down viciously and buried itself in the ground as he writhed aside. He clutched at the dwarf's wrist, missed, and flung himself bodily upon the Pikht, bearing the smaller man down by his weight. But he could not maintain a hold upon the muscular, oily body.

Snarling, the dwarf lunged forward, teeth

bared. Elak smashed his forehead into the Pikht's face, felt blood spurt into his eyes, blinding him. He shook the scarlet drops away.

Abruptly he released the Pikht's wrist. His hands shot up and gripped the dwarf's throat—sinewy hands that had been trained on battle-ax and rapier. The knife hit into his body, ripped flesh from his breast as he twisted desperately. But the Pikht had struck too late.

Elak's tapering brown fingers almost met in oily flesh. Tendons stood out like rigid wires; there came a brittle cracking sound. A bubbling scream of agony died in the dwarf's throat before it could emerge.

The pale eyes glazed. The stunted body went limp.

Elak stood up, bracing himself. He stared in sheer astonishment.

It was no earthly landscape which he saw. Obscure color-patterns, shifting and dancing strangely, weaved in the cool air all about him. He thought of the shadows of trees painted on white rock, flickering arabesques of dancing leaves fluttering in the wind. Yet the weird pattern was not only on the pale clay-colored plain on which he stood, but rather all about him in the air. He stood alone in a fantastic weave of somber shadows.

Colorless shadows, dancing. Or were they colorless? He did not know, nor was he ever to know, the color of the grotesque weavings that laced him in a web of magic, for while his mind told him that he saw colors, his eyes denied it.

SUDDENLY darkness swept down, engulfing him. And very faintly a thudding sounded, and swiftly grew louder. With a giant pounding of cyclopean feet something strode past Elak in the blackness, something that shook the plain with the thunder of its passing. There was no other sound save for the tremendous booming thuds of the titan feet.

They died in the distance; the darkness lifted. Again the flickering shadow patterns grew in the air. And again they darkened into blackness.

The sound of wings came to Elak. Something was flying far overhead, something that wailed endlessly and mournfully, keening the cry of one lost and wandering in eternal night. A sense of overpowering awe touched Elak, and horror beyond all imagination—the horror one feels in the presence of a thing, so alien that the flesh of mankind instinctively shrinks and shudders. Elak knew, somehow, that he had entered a land in which men had not been intended to exist.

"Elak . . ."

Faintly, from very far away, the thin whisper came—Dalan's voice. Elak whispered the Druid's name as the darkness changed into the vague shadow-patterns. The distant voice came again.

"You are in a perilous place, Elak, but you live. Lycon's swordsmen slay the Pikhts now, the crystal tells me . . . you are very far away, Elak, but I come swiftly. Mider aids me. . . ."

Blackness again, and a roaring as of great winds. Power unimaginable shuddered through Elak's body like a spear shattering on a shield.

And it passed, and the darkness lightened to the crawling shadows.

"You are with the gods, Elak," came Dalan's far whisper. "You are no longer in Atlantis, or even on earth. You are in a far land. And with you are those the Shadow has engulfed—the gods! Not the gods of Atlantis, nor the Viking gods, but the gods that have died. Around you move those whose flesh is not our flesh, whose lives are alien to ours. I come, Elak. . ."

Piercingly sweet, throbbing almost articulately, a harp-string murmured through the gloom. Dalan's voice faded into silence, and again the note sobbed out. Above it a soft-toned song lifted in the words Elak knew were in no earthly language.

Startled, apprehensive, the Druid called, "Elak! Elf's magic battles mine—he——"

Then silence, till a gentle voice spoke.

"Dalan," it whispered. "Dalan, Elak . . . my enemies. Now you shall die, Elak, for the Druid cannot reach you. The power of my harp keeps him from your side."

Very faintly Dalan called Elak's name. Once again he called, and was silent. Shifting shadows moved through the dim air. Elak's hand went involuntarily to his side. Remembering that he was weaponless, he stooped and pried the dagger from the Pikht's cold fingers. But despair was mounting within him. How could he fight Elf, alone in this lost hell, without Dalan to aid him?

"Your doom comes," Elf murmured, and the

harp-string twanged eerily, laden with bitter sweetness. "You live, Elak, and there is no life in Ragnarok. Only the dead gods, and the dust of the souls of men."

The dancing shadow-patterns slowed their fluttering and became motionless. The sound of Elf's harp died; it was utterly silent.

And, far in the distance and gigantic, towering above the horizon, a Shadow began to form in the air. In form it was human, but from its darkening nucleus there breathed chill horror that made Elak grip his dagger with desperate fingers. Fear shook him—the fear that attacks the citadel of man's soul when it faces the Unknown.

7. Solonala—and Mider

A SOUND behind him made Elak turn swiftly, his weapon ready. What he saw made him pause in wonder. Even in the shadowy gloom he sensed something fantastically unreal about the figure that came stealing out of the dusk with curiously rocking gait.

But there was friendliness in the gesture with which the half-seen being beckoned. It glanced beyond Elak to where the Shadow grew and darkened on the horizon, and then swiftly bent above the dead Pikht. Dark hands moved quickly—and suddenly the dwarf moved, raised himself stiffly to his feet and stood motionless as an automaton!

The Pikht had died—that Elak knew. Even

now the bald, misshapen head lolled monstrously on one sagging shoulder. Elak could scarcely see the dwarf's face, but he knew intuitively that the shallow eyes held no life. An icy shudder shook him.

The Pikht turned. Swaying, the squat figure raced forward, past Elak, toward the Shadow that loomed in black horror in the distance. A soft hand was thrust in Elak's, and he looked down to see a white girl-face peering anxiously up at him.

He felt himself being tugged along, and yielded, smiling a little wryly. After all, into what worse hell could he be guided? The patterns flickered all around them as they moved, and presently Elak heard a low voice say:

"We should be safe now."

"You speak Atlantean?" he asked involuntarily, and quiet laughter mocked him.

"I speak my own tongue. All languages are one here. Just as the Shadow appears differently to everyone, and yet is the same to everyone after being—taken—so do all tongues seem alike here. The world from which I came is far from yours. How are you named?"

"Elak. The—Shadow?"

"It has faded. See?"

Elak glanced over his shoulder, but could make out nothing but the dancing patterns of alien color. The invisible girl went on, "I put life into the dead being and sent him to the Shadow, so that we could escape while the Shadow fed. We are safe for a little while, Elak."

She paused as the air lighted; they stood before a cave that opened into the side of a rampart which towered up until it was lost in the dimness. A misshapen, flat-topped boulder guarded the entrance of the tunnel mouth, and behind this Elak's companion stepped swiftly.

"Come," she urged. "We can hide here—for a time at least."

But Elak had reached her side—had gripped her slim arms with fingers rendered cruel by his amazement. He stared at the girl in wonder, knowing that she sprang from no earthly race.

A satyr-girl! A faun-maiden, slender and white and virginal as cool marble, round-breasted, with red-golden hair that hung in velvet coils about the smooth shoulders. To her waist she was human. Below that all semblance of humanity ended, and sheer fantasy began.

Her legs were golden-furred and crooked like those of a beast—not ungainly goat-legs, but rather the limbs of some graceful deer, ending in tiny hoofs that glinted golden in the dim light. Her face was as unearthly as her nether limbs, for all its classic beauty. No earth-girl had ever possessed *golden* eyes—eyes like flaky pools of pure gold, without white or pupil, that stared at Elak as unwinkingly as those of a cat. Her face was curiously feline in contour as she smiled at Elak, looking up at him fearlessly.

"I am strange to you?" she asked. "But you are strange too. There are many worlds besides your own, Elak."

"So it seems," the Atlantean gasped. "By Bel!

This must be some mad dream I'm having!"

The girl urged him further into the cave. A dim light irradiated its further recesses, which were draped with violet samite that hid the rough rock walls. Cushions carpeted and hid the ground.

"I am Solonala," the faun-girl told Elak, relaxing gracefully in a little nest of soft pillows. "Has Elf's magic sent you here, too?"

Elak did not answer; his eyes watched the eery golden-furred legs in fascinated wonder. Solonala glanced down, smiling, and clicked her hoofs gently together.

"We are made in different patterns, you and I."

Elak nodded. "Yes. Though—Elf, you say? D'you know him?"

"I know him, and I fought him. The land where I once ruled is far from here, and far from your own earth. But Elf's powers enable him to go from world to world, and when he came to mine I saw that he was evil, and tried to destroy him. He was the stronger."

She shrugged slender shoulders. "So I came here, or rather Elf exiled me here. He couldn't kill me, for I'm not human, as you are—decay cannot touch my flesh, as it will touch yours in time. But he imprisoned me in this land, where in time I'll be taken by the Shadow. . . ."

"What is this Shadow?"

Golden eyes watched Elak, luminous in the glow. "You saw it as a man's shadow—eh? A man such as yourself? But I saw it as Solonala's shadow. Every being sees the Shadow as his own. For it is his own. It is the ultimate death. It is destruction. This land is its home, but it can come to other worlds when gateways have been opened."

Gateways—such as the pool in the Pikhts' underground den!

"And it is here that the gods come when they die, Elak." Her voice was hushed. "You heard them pass, I think. Darkness always comes when the dead gods go by, for they wander this lost land alone in eternal night. . . ."

FAINT, infinitely far away, there sounded a thin murmur—the hum of a plucked harp-string. Dim and drowsy, it stole into Elak's mind until, scarcely aware he heard it, he realized that he was nodding sleepily. Solonala watched him alertly out of great golden eyes.

"I hear magic," she said.

The harp-string throbbed on, blanketing Elak in drowsiness. As he went down into slumber he was conscious of Solonala leaning toward him, cat-face puzzled . . . and then darkness. . . .

He dreamed. He dreamed of the black galley's cabin, and of Dalan, crouching over his crystal globe. Within the sphere a flame rose up like a blossoming flower. It grew and lifted till it towered above the Druid's glistening bald head.

Its scarlet tip bent down, expanded into a lambent rose of fire. It swayed and trembled in midair. Dalan prayed.

"Mider, hear me. God of the Druids, Lord of

Flame, let your hand draw back this man from the Shadow——"

The vision faded. The dim murmur of a harp-string put a period to it. Vaguely Elak saw Solonala's face swimming in silver mistiness, her lips parted.

Again the harp sent its sorcerous whispering into Elak's sleeping mind—Elf's harp, fraught with deadly magic!

"Elak!"

Dalan's voice!

The harp-string twanged angrily. Above its noise came a harsh cry.

"Elak! Mider aid me—Elak! Hear me!"

The tall adventurer sprang to full wakefulness, his hand racing to the dagger at his belt. A low murmuring sounded from without the cave. Elak got quietly to his feet and moved toward the portal.

There he paused, his eyes wide. On the flat rock before the cave mouth crouched Solonala, her white body gleaming in the shifting shadow-patterns, and all about her, genuflecting and abjecting themselves in ghastly worship, was a horde of tiny, hideous white things that moved so swiftly Elak could not clearly define their outlines. Indeed, he had no chance, for as he appeared Solonala lifted her head, saw him, and flung out a slim arm commandingly. The white beings streamed away and were lost in the distance.

Now Elak saw what had previously escaped him. Towering to the sky beyond Solonala, menacing and terrible, loomed—the Shadow!

The girl let her arm drop to her side. Without moving she watched Elak.

"Elf's magic brought the Shadow here while you slept," she said. "I could not waken you, though I tried. Those little ones—I made them. Living things, to appease the Shadow's hunger while we flee. Perhaps we can escape." She paused doubtfully.

From empty air roared the voice of Dalan.

"Courage, Elak! I come—and with aid!"

And the voice of Elf, disembodied, gentle—mocking.

"What can Mider do against the Shadow, Druid? Your god lives—and there is no life in Ragnarok."

The immense Shadow on the horizon grew darker. The flickering patterns in the air seemed to weave faster, troubled.

Without warning Elak saw the Shadow fold down tremendously and swoop upon him. He felt Solonala's soft body shuddering against his, and his arms went instinctively about her. The faun-girl cried out—and her voice was clipped off into utter silence. Blackness abysmal and unearthly smothered them.

They were one with the Shadow. They were nothingness—annihilation, complete and final emptiness. And yet Elak was dreadfully conscious of a feeling of power—cosmic power, terrible in its illimitable vastness. Aside from this, nothing existed for him. Solonala's body no longer pressed against his. He felt the fortress of his soul, his mind, crumbling under the assault of the Shadow.

And, suddenly, hope came. How it first manifested itself Elak did not understand, but he realized that no longer was he being absorbed into the Shadow. Something was pulling him back—lifting him from the sucking void that was annihilation.

He heard the Druid's voice, strained, triumphant. "Mider! Save him, Mider—god of oak and fire——"

Light flashed out all around—warm, rose-tinted, luminous flame. In its fierce glow was revealed the figure of Solonala, unearthly in her beauty—and also the incredible thing on which the two stood. It was a hand.

Eight-fingered, colossal, it was no earthly hand. The hand of Mider himself, reaching down into the hell of the Shadow at the Druid's prayer. The titan hand swept upward, carrying Elak and Solonala. . . .

It checked itself. Blackness crept back, dimming the rosy flame-walls. A sea of shadow rose like a tide, and the hand began to sink down, slowly at first, and then with ever-increasing speed.

Dalan's cry came, despairing, inarticulate. And Elf's soft laughter.

Solonala knelt beside Elak. She put her arms around his neck; tender lips brushed his. Then, before he could move, she sprang away and flung herself into the void. For an intolerable, agelong second her white-and-gold-figure loomed against blackness—and was gone. A cry, gull-plaintive, drifted to Elak's ears as he started forward.

He was too late. The hand of the god swept up. Elak fell to his knees, struggling to drag himself to where Solonala had vanished . . . and then there was only darkness around him, and the howling and shrieking of great winds. . . .

8. They Come to Cyrena

"ELAK." It was Lycon's voice.

Elak opened his eyes. Gray light bathed him.

He was in the corridor of the pool, in the underground Pikht temple. Above him hovered the small fat figure of Lycon, round face alight with anxiety.

"Are you alive, Elak? Did those damned dwarfs——"

Elak drew a deep breath, got painfully to his feet, water cascading from his hair and garments. He looked down to where, beside him, the surface of the sunken basin lay blue and calm, untroubled by the Shadow that had once darkened it.

"I've just dragged you from there," Lycon said, following his gaze. "You shot up from the water like a cork."

"There was no other?" Elak asked. "You saw no one else, in the pool?"

Lycon was silent for a time, watching his friend's eyes. Presently he shook his head.

"No," he said softly. "There was no other."

And then there was no more talk for a while, because Velia led in the blood-smeared oarsmen, who had just slain the last of the Pikhts; and Lycon was noisy about the number of dwarfs he had cut down, and was, he said, almost thirsty enough to drink water.

"But not quite," he added. "Let's get back to the galley. It wasn't damaged much by the storm, Elak, and we can launch it in two days. . . ."

SO AGAIN the black galley drove northward through the Inland Sea, skirting the western shores of Crenos Isle, on through the swirling waters until white cliffs loomed on the horizon. And there, when it was least expected, Duke Granicor's ship came down on them as the galley was beached.

"Mider rot him!" the Druid growled, climbing ponderously over the rail, his brown, sea-stained garment flapping in the wind. "There's no time to fight him now, Elak. We've got to get the chiefs together, lead them against the Northmen."

"My brother," Elak said. "Don't forget him."

"I know. But that must come later. You can't help Orander till the Vikings are driven from Elf's fortress, where they have their headquarters, and where your brother's a prisoner."

Lycon swaggered up, a flagon swinging against his side. "By the Nine Hells and a dozen more," he observed, "are we afraid of Granicor? Go on ahead, Elak, and take Dalan with you. Give me two oarsmen and I'll stay here and——"

"You're drunk," Elak said without rancor. "Go

away." He turned to stare at the long galley that was rapidly growing larger as it swept shoreward. Elak's spirits had been dampened since his adventure with the Pikhts, and the image of Solonala could not be dimmed even by Velia's caresses. Her self-sacrifice had shaken him more than he knew. And within him had crystallized a burning desire to cross blades with Elf, to slay the warlock minstrel—and swiftly!

So he agreed with Dalan. "We'll head inland, eh?"

"To Sharn Forest. The chiefs will gather there, with their men. I've sent a messenger, and the word will go through Cyrena. When the armies have gathered at Sharn, we'll move north on Elf's fortress."

"Good! I wish I had my rapier, though—this sword's too heavy." Elak made the tempered blade hiss through the air, and Dalan chuckled.

"You can spill blood with it, though. Come. Granicor is almost within bowshot."

Dalan in the lead, the band set out to climb the white cliffs, reaching the summit as the Duke of Poseidonia beached his galley. Granicor wasted no time in threats; grimly silent, he led his crew in pursuit.

But the duke was soon left behind. This was familiar country to Dalan, and swiftly the party marched through a tangled forest wilderness, even Velia touched by eagerness that enabled her to keep pace easily. That night they camped in a little valley by a stream that chuckled pleasantly as it wound among furze and bracken.

Elak, sitting by the fire, idly plaited Velia's bronze hair. "It's good to be in Cyrena again," he told her. "I never thought I'd walk this land again. Do you like it, Velia?"

She nodded, the firelight bronze on her face. "It's rough and wild and—and honest, somehow. Strong men must live here, Elak."

"The Northmen are stronger," Dalan growled. "At least, until Cyrena has a leader." He reached out a huge hand and retrieved Lycon, who was reeling dangerously close to the fire. "Bah, this drunken dog! But he's a faithful one, at least."

"Only the gods know my true worth," Lycon said surprizingly, and collapsed in an inert heap, muttering faintly. Suddenly he sat up, his eyes bright. "Listen, Elak!"

As he spoke feet came trampling through the underbrush. Granicor's voice bellowed a raucous command. Yelling men charged down the slope.

"Gods!" Elak snapped. "He's trailed us, somehow. To arms!" His sharp cry cut icily through the night; swords gleamed redly; and the next moment Granicor and his crew were within the circle of firelight.

Dulled by the heat of the flames, not expecting attack, yet Dalan's men met the charge bravely. The two forces came together, crashed and mingled, and then it was a whirling firelit madness of blood and steel. Granicor headed directly for Elak, and, nothing loath, the tall adventurer sprang to meet him, sword hissing. The blades shrieked together in midair, were sent fly-

49

ing by the power of the blows, and, weaponless, Elak and Granicor closed, the duke snarling oaths, the other watchful and silent. They went down, scattering embers from the fire's edge.

SUDDENLY a shrill, warning cry came, above a low thunder of hoofs that boomed out from near by.

"Vikings! 'Ware—*Vikings!* The Northmen!"

And down into the valley rode red-bearded giants, roaring, spears driving, swords hewing, driving resistlessly over the campfire as they had swept down on Cyrena. Men screamed and died beneath trampling hoofs, and those who lived fled into the forest. In a moment the encampment was empty, save for the Northmen, the dead, and two men who lay locked in furious struggle on the ground.

Elak's arm was locked about Granicor's throat, but the duke's bull-thewed legs were slowly crushing his ribs, forcing the breath from his body, when the Vikings prodded the two apart with ungentle blades.

"Thunder of Thor!" a harsh voice grunted. "What madmen are these? Guthrum, they——"

Guthrum! At that name Elak tore free, sprang to his feet, heedless of the steel points that pricked him. His stare found a red-bearded giant in chain-mail and brimless helmet, a man whose face had once been strong and powerful and valorous—a man whose eyes were dead!

Blue eyes, dull and cold and bitterly ferocious, watched Elak. This was Guthrum, leader of the Northmen, whose pact with Elf had resulted in the imprisonment of Orander, King of Cyrena.

"Guthrum?" It was Granicor's voice. "The Viking? My people aren't at war with yours. I am from Poseidonia!" The duke stood squarely facing Guthrum, looking up defiantly at the somber figure on horseback.

Without replying the Northman lashed out with a mail-shod foot, sent it driving into Granicor's face. Blood spurted as the duke reeled back. He caught himself, fumbled for a weapon that was not there—and hurled himself forward, up at Guthrum's throat, snarling a blazing oath.

The Viking's horse reared; Granicor went down under driving hoofs. Bitter laughter shook Guthrum, but the dull rage in his eyes was unchanged as he looked down on the prostrate Atlantean, turned to eye Elak. The tall adventurer felt a shudder course down his spine as he met that dreadful blue gaze. Something had been drained from the Viking chief, and there sit in his eyes that which was not human.

Granicor staggered upright, and Guthrum wheeled his mount to face the gory figure. In silence he listened while the duke choked out furious curses born of agonizing rage and shame. And then:

"Do you think I fear such as you? Do you think I fear anything on earth—after what a warlock has shown me?" The dull stare of the Viking was utterly horrible in its cold ferocity. "I, who have come sane from the vaults of Elf's citadel—

shall I fear your curses?"

He clapped spurs to his horse, went thundering into the darkness. From the gloom his voice came roaring back:

"Crucify those men!"

9. The Chiefs in Sharan

SPURRED by the menace of Guthrum's words, Elak tore free momentarily from his captors, but as he turned to the forest they were upon him. He fought furiously, desperately—uselessly. He was born down, held powerless in the grip of red-bearded, mail-clad giants, as Granicor, his face a bloody ruin, was also held.

Working swiftly, the Vikings stripped Granicor of his armor, dragged him to where a great oak grew near by. He cursed them, striving to break away, his tiny eyes flaming with rage and fear. But thongs lifted the duke's ape-like body, binding him inexorably against the tree's bole. His arms were drawn up behind him, circling the trunk—and with iron spikes and improvised hammers the Northmen went about their crimson work.

Elak watched, white-faced, as iron tore through flesh and bone, listening to the frightful cries that burst through Granicor's mangled lips. The Vikings left him at last, letting him hang by his hands, shoulders wrenched almost out of their sockets. They turned to Elak.

He tensed for a hopeless struggle. And abruptly he sensed astonishment in the craggy faces about him. The Vikings had turned, staring, to where a gross brown figure stood just within the circle of firelight.

Dalan—his toad face hideous with fury, huge hands lifted. He made no sound, but so dreadful was the menace in his expression that the Northmen were held motionless for a moment. Then a cry went up; they surged forward, blades ready.

The Druid flung out his arms in a strange gesture—as though he hurled a curse at his enemies. From his thick lips a word came, unfamiliar, alien. There was power in the gesture, power in the word Dalan spoke. The air seemed to quiver, charged with electric force.

Thunder burst in Elak's ears. He was flung back, blinded by a sheet of white flame that washed the clearing in stark brilliance. For a second he lost consciousness.

Then the Druid was lifting him, muttering curses. Feebly Elak freed himself, stared around. The place looked as though lightning had struck it. The grass and trees were seared and blackened, and of the Northmen only charred corpses in half-melted armor remained.

"Ishtar!" Elak whispered, his voice unsteady. "What—what happened, Dalan? Is this more of your—magic?"

The Druid nodded. "A fire-magic I cannot work often. We have power over flame, Elak—and there's flame in the sky as well as on earth. With Mider's aid, I drew down the lightning. Those barbarians died by their own god's thunderbolt." Vicious laughter shook the huge bulk. "Lucky for you I wasn't cut down when the Vikings rode in. Look, their horses have stampeded—those that aren't blasted to death."

Elak touched his singed eyebrows. "I don't see how I escaped. Can you direct this wizard lightning of yours, Dalan?"

"Perhaps. Also the Northmen wore armor, and you have none. That may have accounted for it. See—the man they crucified, Granicor—he wears no armor, and he's still alive. Barely, I think."

Elak's gaze went to where the tortured body of the duke hung from the oak. He hesitated, then went forward purposefully.

"Lycon?" he asked over his shoulder. "Velia? Are they safe?"

The Druid nodded. "Yes, they're waiting not far away. But the rest of the crew are dead or scattered. We'll have to move quickly to reach Sharn Forest—I didn't know the Vikings had come this far south, and four of us can't very well fight an army. In Sharn we'll meet the chiefs—what are you doing, you fool? Freeing that dog?"

"He's an Atlantean, at least," Elak said, wrenching at one of the iron spikes that transfixed Granicor's hand. "And this is no way for any man to die."

The duke had apparently lost consciousness. As the last spike came free, his body slumped down in a bloody huddle at the tree's foot. Elak paused.

"He can't live long. But I don't like to leave him here to be tortured by the Northmen if they come. Yet——"

"We can't take him with us! Gods, will you feed him pap and nurse him after he's just tried to slit your throat?—while Elf rules Cyrena and holds your brother captive? I tell you we must get to Sharn—and quickly!"

"Very well," Elak agreed, turning toward the forest. "He can't live till morning—no man could, with those wounds. To Sharn, then—and after that we march on Elf's fortress."

"We march on Guthrum's army," Dalan grunted, "wherever it may be. But it won't be far from the warlock's citadel. Guthrum's headquarters is there."

His ungainly figure vanished in the shadows, Elak at his side. And at the foot of a great oak tree a frightful figure dragged itself half erect, an ape-like man, seared and bloodstained and wounded on hands and feet. Mangled lips writhed and opened.

"Elf's—fortress," a harsh voice whispered, cracked with agony. *"And Guthrum!"* A gout of blood spewed from the man's throat, and a paroxysm of coughing shook him. He clung to the oak, dragged himself upright, grinning with abysmal pain.

"So I won't live till morning?" he mumbled. "I'll live—till I find Guthrum!"

Duke Granicor staggered a few steps and collapsed, but he lay inert for only a moment. Then, very slowly, wheezing and groaning between clenched teeth, he began to drag himself into the forest.

ELAK stood before the Druid altar in Sharn Forest, a great gray stone, its top hollowed out into a shallow basin that was stained darkly by countless ages of sacrifice. It was dawn. A day and a night had passed since the encounter with Granicor and the Northmen, and for a few hours Elak had slept in the shadow of the Druid stone, while the chiefs gathered, drawn to Sharn by swift messengers. Lycon and Velia had slept beside him, and Dalan had watched, greeting each newcomer as he arrived. Now nearly all the chiefs were here, a grim half-circle in the cold light of dawn, their strong faces betraying little of their thoughts. Yet somehow Elak sensed hostility in the eyes watching him, and their gaze was suspicious as well as appraising. Dalan realized something of this, for his ugly face was set in an appalling snarl.

A young chieftain pushed forward, bull-necked, ruddy-cheeked. He advanced till he stood only a few feet from Dalan, and halted with folded arms.

"Have I your leave to speak, Druid?" he asked mockingly.

Somber eyes watched him. "Ay, Halmer. Since Cyrena chooses a cub for spokesman—speak."

Halmer's laugh was scornful. "My words are those of all, I think. Well—listen, then. The Northmen are still on the coasts. They will not come south. If they do, we can drive them back."

"What of Orander?" Dalan asked. "What of your king?"

The young chief hesitated. Then, gathering courage from the Druid's calm, he snapped, "We'll fight for our own holdings, if need be. But Elf's magic—who can fight that? I say, let the Northmen hold the coast, if they want it. They've not troubled my lands yet. If they do, I'll know how to drive them away."

"And one by one you will go down beneath Guthrum," Dalan said. "Halmer speaks for you all? You'll let your king rot in Elf's power, you'll let the Northmen hang like a cankerous sore on the coast—by Mider! but you need a king's strong hand to rule you! Without Orander you squabble among yourselves like a pack of snarling curs."

Some looked shamefaced at that, but none spoke.

Finally:

"Who is this Elak?" one asked. "You say he's Zeulas, the king's brother. Perhaps. But you ask us to bow down before a man who killed his stepfather—a man who may, then, kill his brother and rule Cyrena!"

Elak growled a curse. He pushed past the Druid.

"It wouldn't take much of a man to rule you, I think," he snapped harshly. "There were not so many fools and cowards here when I left Cyrena. I killed Norian, yes—but in fair fight, and most of you remember that my stepfather had no great love for either Orander or me. But as for my wanting to rule this land of women—bah! I've asked your aid. If you won't give it, I'll go to Elf's fortress alone and find my brother."

At his words there was a stir. One man, a tall, lean oldster in dented armor, came to cast his sword at Elak's feet.

"Well, I'll go with you, at least," he said. "And my followers are not few. I remember you in the old days, Zeulas—and I know you speak true words now."

With antique courtesy Elak gravely retrieved the fallen sword, touched his forehead with the hilt, and returned it to the oldster.

"Thanks, Hira. I remember you, too, and that you were always ready to fight for Cyrena. These other dogs——"

Hira's lean face twisted wryly. "No, Zeulas—or Elak. They are not dogs; they're brave men all—but fear of Elf's magic and hatred of each other have made them less noble."

Brawny Halmer laughed, "Go with Hira, stranger—and you too, Druid, since he's a madman too. I go back to my own holding now—and send me no more messengers." He turned on his heel, to be halted by the curt voice of Dalan.

"Wait."

He turned. "Well?"

"You fight among yourselves, you follow cubs like Halmer—and you fear Elf's magic. Now for ages on uncountable ages the Druids have dwelt in Cyrena, and they will not go down now before the gods of the North—not for the lack of a few strong sword-arms. So I tell you this: Druid magic may protect you against Elf's wizardries. And it may not. But, by Mider!"—the toad face was a venomous devil mask; Dalan spat the words at the chiefs—"By Mider! Elf won't protect you against the power of the Druids! And we have not lost our power!"

Some shrank back, and there were pale faces among those turned to Dalan. But Halmer laughed scornfully, shrugging broad shoulders.

"Old men and children may fear you," he mocked. "But I do not."

The Druid lifted a huge hand, pointed upward. His voice came sonorously, laden with menace.

"Then listen, Halmer. And—watch! Should it not be dawn now?"

At his words a little movement of apprehension shook the chiefs. None had noticed before, but over the brightening vault of the sky an iron-gray cope of cloud had been drawn. Heavily it lay above Sharn, growing darker as they watched. A shadow fell on the clearing. The trees loomed strangely ominous in the dimness.

Yet Halmcr laughed again. "Do we fear clouds? Your magic is feeble—charlatan!"

DALAN said nothing; his black eyes, half hidden by sagging lids, watched Halmer. A cold wind blew through Sharn; whispers rustled the forest. Steadily it grew darker.

From the chiefs a low murmur of fear went

up.

Elak felt Velia creep close to him, put his arm protectingly about her slim waist. For once Lycon was silent, looking up apprehensively. Before the altar Dalan's misshapen figure towered, arms raised in menace.

Halmer's voice was not quite steady, his face a little less ruddy, as he barked, "I'll not stay here longer. I——"

"Go," the Druid said. "If you dare."

Halmer clapped hand to sword, turned, pushed through the group of chiefs. None followed as he moved to the edge of the clearing. Then, about to step into the dark shadows beneath the trees, he paused and drew back a step.

It seemed to Elak that, far in the gloom, something was watching—something infinitely horrible, avid for prey. And Halmer must have sensed something of this. He wavered, without taking step forward or back.

"Druid magic is feeble," Dalan whispered. "What holds you, Halmer? There is nothing in the wood."

Nothing—but a soft soughing, a nameless rustle in primeval, shadow-darkened forest. The dark dawn lowered over Sharn.

"Old men and children fear me," the Druid mocked. "But *you* do not, Halmer. No."

Snarling a furious curse, the young chief leaped forward into the gloom as though casting off unseen shackles. The murmuring deepened, grew to a low, sullen roar. Halmer was a dim shadow plunging forward between towering trunks.

Men saw him pause, casting a startled glance upward. His sword flashed out—and the roar of the forest grew deafening. From above something came hurtling down, a great branch, torn from its parent tree, sent plunging through foliage, upon a man who screamed once in frantic fear and died. Men saw Halmer borne down, broken, under the terrible impact. The roaring died to a faint murmur, lessened almost to nothing.

"Druid magic is feeble," Dalan said softly. "Does Halmer think that now?" He swung to face the chiefs, bellowing. "Follow Halmer if you dare! Leave Sharn without swearing fealty to Elak— and you walk the forests under the Druid curse. By Mider! Go—and see how long you live!"

But none dared face the Druid's wrath. One by one the Chiefs came forward and cast their blades before Elak.

So Elak took command of Cyrena's armies— and from Sharn Forest the word went forth like flame: Gather! Sharpen steel! The land is risen against the Northmen—and the king's brother leads Cyrena against Elf and Guthrum!

Gather! Gather to march against the Viking hordes!

10. In the Valley of Skulls

LYCON swilled wine from a goatskin, set it down, and wiped his mouth with the back of a pudgy hand. His sharp eyes drifted over serried ranks of armored man, flashing steel, horses snorting hungry for battle. It had taken twelve days to draw the last fighting-man from the mountains and far places of Cyrena; three days more of steady marching to reach the Valley of Skulls, named for a bandit who, long ago, had littered the slopes with the heads of his enemies. But the Northmen had drawn together swiftly, and had made their stand, too, in the Valley of Skulls. A river separated the two armies, safely beyond bowshot of each other:

"When do we attack?" Lycon asked Elak, who stood beside him on a little knoll.

"Soon," the lean adventurer said. "The sun will rise in a few minutes. At sunrise we cross Monra River." He tested the metal of his rapier. "It's good to have a weapon like this again. I'll give this blade its baptism today."

"And I'll give mine," Velia broke in, coming lightly up the hill toward them. Her slim armor-clad body gleamed in the gray light of false dawn. Her bronze hair foamed out from a helmet that was too small to prison its bright masses. "This is different from Poseidonia, Elak. This was the life I was meant for—not a perfumed harem in Granicor's palace."

"Yes, it's different from Poseidonia," Lycon said glumly. "They have good liquor there. It's next to impossible to get wine in this barbarian land, and the bitter ale your countrymen drink is too much for me, Elak. Gall and wormwood!" He spat and reached for the goatskin again.

Elak drew Velia close to him, kissed her

swiftly. "We may meet death today," he told the flushed girl. "I'd rather you'd stay in camp."

Velia smiled and shook her head. "I've tasted war, and I like the draft. Listen!"

Far along the valley trumpets blew a call; they grew louder, closer, till the tocsin resounded from slope to slope. Across the river the armies of the Northmen waited. . . .

"They mean to use arrows as we cross," Elak said. "But I think they'll be disappointed. My plans are made."

Trumpets shouted, drums groaned, banners lifted, streaming in the chill dawn wind, and the army of Cyrena moved forward. Brawny, fair-skinned, yellow-haired warriors, following their chiefs, riding their chargers into the foaming current of Monra River—and, watching, Elak smiled.

"Hira and Dalan have led men to the Vikings' flanks," he told Velia. "The Northmen think we'll ford the river near the center of their front. But—look!"

The first rank of Elak's army were in the river, dashing across in the face of a storm of arrows. On the opposite bank waited pikemen, and behind them, armored redbeards with swords and axes. The men of Cyrena seemed suddenly to surge forward in the wake of the advance guard, hurling themselves toward Monra River, down the valley's slope. But in their rear ranks a concerted movement was taking place; whole troops and companies were racing to left and right, slanting toward the river, attempting to outflank the Northmen.

"What's this?" Velia asked. "The Vikings can ride as fast as our men. Why——"

Across the river the enemy had seen Elak's move, and their flanks moved outward—but not far. A great shout arose far to the left, and, a moment later, a thunderous roar came from the right. Over the ridge, on both wings of the Viking army, rode warriors, streaming down the slopes, swords and lances gleaming in the sunlight.

"Hira—and Dalan!" Lycon said. "They outflanked the Northmen in the night. They'll give us a chance to cross Monra."

Now the strategy was evident; a thin line of warriors held the bank of the river, their bowmen keeping the enemy engaged. And the rear ranks of Cyrena galloped to left and right, racing into Monra River, plunging across it and up the steep shores in the face of a hail of arrows and steel. They could not have succeeded had it not been for Hira and Dalan, whose warriors spread ruin and confusion in the Viking flanks.

"We've crossed," Elak barked, eyes agleam. "Now we're on equal ground—it's strength, not strategy, that counts now we've crossed Monra. Come on!" He turned to a great white charger that stood near by, stamping his impatience, his hoofs striking fire from the rocks underfoot. With one leap Elak was in the saddle.

Upright in the stirrups, shouting, rapier unsheathed, he thundered down the slope, and behind him rode Lycon and Velia—down to the water's edge, into Monra River, foam splashing high as they charged across. A roar went up from the warriors—and the next moment, driven back by the impetus of Elak's forces, slashing and thrusting at his heels, the Northmen gave way up the slope, desperately contending each inch of ground lost.

Then there was nothing but a red maelstrom of hewing and cutting, ax and sword and strongly-driven spear; screaming of horses that galloped by with riders clinging with one hand and warring with the other; horses plunging and dying in a welter of thunderous crimson ruin— giant men fighting and falling and slaying as they fell.

Raven banners toppled. Shouts of *"Odin! Thor with us!"* mingled with roars of *"Cyrena! Cyrena!"* Elak thrust and thrust again, guiding his steed with one hand as it stumbled and leaped over knots of prostrate, struggling men and still, bloody bodies. Above the ranks that surrounded him he saw the Druid's head nodding and swaying far to the right, and a great sword hewed steadily about Dalan, cutting a wide swath of corpses. And ahead, in the front rank of the Viking army, rode Guthrum, red beard flaming, moving like a towering pestilence among men whose helms and heads were crushed by his bloody ax.

"Thor! Thor with us!"

"Cyrena!"

Sweat and blood smeared Elak's face. He tried to find Lycon and Velia, knew it was impossible in the mêlée. A Viking rode at him yelling, spear leveled; the white warhorse leaped forward and aside at Elak's urging. The spear-point grazed his cheek as he swayed aside, and his blade sank deep into the Northman's hairy throat. He whipped it out, steel singing, thrust at a new foe.

THE sun rose higher, and the reek of spilled gore mingled with the stench of sweat. At the top of the ridge the Vikings rallied, knowing that if they were driven past it they were lost. And like a massacre King Guthrum raged among his enemies, his ax rising and falling steadily, rhythmically, dreadful as the hammer of the Northmen's god Thor. The army of Cyrena was checked—driven back a little down the slope.

"Forward!" Elak spurred his charger, sent it leaping against the mad horde that swept down Skull Valley. *"Cyrena! Ho, Cyrena!"* His rapier darted out like a snake striking, and its touch was as deadly. A Viking fell, screaming his deathcry.

And Elak's voice caught his army as it hesitated on the brink of retreat that led to destruction. One man, mad with valor, facing an army—and then Cyrena held, held and resisted and charged to meet the Northmen as they poured down.

"Slay!" A voice screamed—Dalan's, hoarse, trumpet-loud. "Slay the Vikings! For Cyrena!"

Men dazed and exhausted with battle felt new life pulse within them; blood-drunken, murder-hungry, they flooded against their enemies in a blasting charge that could have only one result. Fighting bitterly, insanely, hopelessly, the Northmen were overwhelmed, pushed up to the crest—beyond it, down the slope, while from the Valley of Skulls the armies of Cyrena came like a consuming flame. It was the day of doom for the Vikings—their Ragnarok, and the raven banners fell in the dust and were trampled by racing hoofs.

"Slay! Slay the Vikings!"

Upright in his stirrups Elak shouted, seeing in the defeat of the Northmen the ruin of Guthrum, the end of Elf—the freeing of his brother Orander. Cyrena had conquered—that he knew. Beside him Lycon reined up, his round face flushed and bleeding.

"Ho, Elak! They run like rabbits!" Even now Lycon could not refrain from his habitual exaggeration. For the red-bearded giants were not fleeing; they fought on, hopelessly, slaying as they died.

Resolution flared in Elak's eyes. "Lycon—stay here. Lead our men." He whirled his horse.

"Where are you going, Elak?"

"To Elf's fortress! Now! I'll take him by surprize——"

The rest was lost as Elak clapped spurs down, galloped up to the ridge—along it, skirting the edge of the battle. Lycon's shout was unheard in the roar.

But another had seen Elak's flight. A horse broke from the uproar, raced in pursuit. Astride it sat Dalan, brown robe streaming. Not even in this battle had he donned armor, and strangely no weapon had touched him. But few could venture alive within the deadly sweep of the Druid's sword. The runes carved on its blade ran red now, dripping along the horse's flank as it raced after Elak.

And behind them rose the death cry of the Vikings in Cyrena, while after Elak, after the Druid, rode vengeance. Guthrum on his huge black charger, grimly silent, leading a little band of Northmen—and there was cold murder in the Viking king's bitter eyes!

11. How Granicor Died

ELF'S fortress rose, a great grim castle of stone, flanked by the sullen waters of the Inland Sea. It was empty now, or nearly so, for the Vikings had gone to meet Elak's army in the Valley of Skulls, and Elf kept few servitors. Men whispered that not all of these were human.

In the dimness of early morning a man had come down from the hills and entered the citadel, hoisting himself painfully from stone to jagged stone of the wall that guarded Elf's privacy. But the rivet-studded, iron barbican that blocked the inner gate he could not pass; and so he waited, skulking in the shadows, caressing the edge of a long sword he carried in one maimed hand. The face of Duke Granicor was like that of one of the gargoyles that grinned from the roofs of the fortress. Incredibly he had lived, had made his way north in search of

Guthrum, and now, knowing nothing of the battle in the Valley of the Skulls, he sat on his haunches, a malignant fire glowing in his eyes. His clothing was in rags, and he more than ever resembled some monstrous shaggy ape lying in wait for its prey.

The sun was high when at last he heard the clatter of hoofs, and swiftly drew back into a shadowy niche. Elak and the Druid reined to a halt before the door of iron let into the outer wall, and the tall adventurer swung from his horse, his gaze examining the rough stones. The other's voice halted him.

"Wait, Elak. We won't have to climb. I'll open this door for you."

Dalan, without dismounting, reached into the folds of his robe, drew forth something which he hurled at the barrier. Immediately a sheet of blinding white flame sprang up, hiding the wall momentarily, setting the horses lunging and prancing in terror. Elak was nearly jerked from his feet as he fought to hold his steed.

Then the flames died. Where the door had been was a white-hot puddle of melted iron, and the stones of the portal were blackened and cracked by the intense heat. The Druid spurred forward his horse, and it hurdled the searing liquid iron easily. Elak followed, just in time to see fire burst out from the grill of the barbican.

"So far so good," Dalan grunted, watching the iron melt and drip to the stones of the courtyard. "But Elf doesn't depend on doors and walls alone."

Elak, looking up, did not answer. On the summit of the inner wall a gargoylish figure was carved seemingly of rugose dark stone, a creature that might have sprung from any of the Nine Hells. Stunted and huge and hideous it seemed to crouch above the courtyard, glaring down menacingly. Wide wings swept out from its gnarled shoulders. Somehow Elak sensed evil in the posture of the thing, the tiny eyes that seemed to watch him.

"Come! The barbican's down

THE Druid's black warhorse stepped forward—and simultaneously Elak caught a flicker of movement from above, sensed rather than saw a great figure that hurtled down, wings sweeping, talons clutching murderously. He clapped spurs into the stallion, sent him driving against Dalan's steed. With the same movement he unsheathed his rapier, thrust up almost without aim.

A flapping of wings buffeted him. The weapon was torn from his grasp, and he crashed down on the stones, battling for his life with a monster that clawed and bellowed and ripped with vicious tusks—the thing he had thought carved from stone, the gargoyle, brought to evil life by Elf's dark sorcery. Exhausted as he was, Elak was no match for the creature. The fangs drove toward his throat; a foul breath was strong in his nostrils.

Then the weight on Elak's body was gone; gasping for breath, he saw the monster gripped by the Druid, lifted above the bald, gleaming head. There was tremendous strength in Dalan's gross frame. He crashed the struggling monster down on the flags, leaped on it with crushing feet. His sword swung redly. . . .

"By Bel!" Elak murmured, retrieving his rapier. "Is that a devil? I've never seen beast or man like that before, Dalan."

"Nor has anyone else," the Druid informed him, staring down at the monster's still body. "It's an elemental, and devil's a good name for it. Elf set it to guard the gate. Well"—he swung his blade—"if I can cut through the warlock's neck as easily—good! Leave your horse, Elak. We must go on foot from here."

Hidden in a niche near by, Duke Granicor watched, wondering. But when Dalan and Elak passed the threshold, vanishing from sight in the depths of the fortress, Granicor sprang out and followed them.

And down from the hills rode a half-dozen horsemen, led by King Guthrum, spurring and yelling as they galloped. Only the Viking chief was silent, gripping his war-ax on which blood had dried in dark red splashes. . . .

"To the vaults," Dalan said, hurrying swiftly along empty stone corridors. "I know the way. I've seen it often in my crystal. Hurry!" The Druid almost seemed to sense the danger that followed at their heels.

Elak's quick gaze searched the depths of side passages that led into enigmatic depths of the fortress. They raced on, through high-vaulted tunnels, down winding stairs dimly lit or in darkness, across great rooms that housed the magnificence of a king's palace.

They met no one. The vast citadel was deserted, or seemed so. And at last, when Elak guessed they had penetrated far underground, they came to a metal door, strangely figured with cabalistical signs, before which Dalan paused.

"This is the heart of Elf's castle," he said softly. "Here he holds your brother captive. Elak——" The Druid fumbled under his robe, drew out a long object wrapped in cloth. He unwound the casing, revealing a short dagger, apparently carved out of crystal.

"There is strong magic in this," Dalan said, handing the weapon, hilt first, to Elak. "And it will slay the warlock where no earthly steel can spill his blood. It is the Druid knife of sacrifice."

Nodding, Elak slipped it into his belt. Dalan turned to the metal door, pushed it open. A flame of amber light blinded the two momentarily. Then their vision cleared; they stepped across the threshold. . . .

They stood on a platform that thrust out from a wall of sheer rock that towered up and to both sides and down into a fathomless immensity of golden blaze that hurt the eyes with its fires. Ahead they saw nothing but clouds—amber clouds billowing and shifting continually, drifting like the sea all about them; flame-bright, yet cool as fog in its clinging mistiness. Elak shrank back involuntarily before the strangeness of the spectacle.

"Steady!" The Druid's huge hand gripped him. "Steady, now. We've a perilous road here— watch!"

Something swam into view from the mists to the left, a black object that seemed like a huge flat-topped globe as it slipped silently closer. Hanging unsupported in the amber fog it emerged, drifting forward until it hung not a foot from the edge of the platform on which the two men stood. Now Elak saw that it was indeed a globe, like an orange with its top sliced off, hollowed out into a great cup.

"We ride that chariot!" Dalan whispered. "Follow me."

He lumbered forward a few steps and sprang. The brown-robed, gross figure hurtled above the golden depths, plunged down safely within the hollow globe. It did not even sway beneath the impact.

"Elak!" The Druid had turned, was beckoning. "Hurry!"

The tall adventurer dared give himself no time to think; he leaped, his heart hammering. Almost he overshot the mark, but Dalan's hands clutched him, lifting him to safety. White-faced, Elak stood erect on legs which were not quite steady.

The rim of the globe was waist-high. The diameter of the circular floor was about four feet, made of some unfamiliar jet-black substance he did not recognize.

The weird chariot swung in its orbit, skirting bare rock walls. The platform from which they had leaped was lost in the golden haze. They drifted through an endless sea of cool fire. . . .

AS GRANICOR followed Dalan and Elak through the fortress he had soon come to realize that he, too, was being followed in his turn. Not guessing that the man he sought was among those who pursued him, he pressed on more swiftly—and the metal door that led to the platform above the abyss swung open under his hand as Elak leaped to the hollow globe. Guthrum stared in astonishment, not realizing until the black sphere had been lost in the mists that the noise of his pursuers was growing louder. Then he stepped across the threshold and flattened himself against the rock wall, sword lifted.

Thus Guthrum's men did not at first see the duke. They came in a mob through the doorway, yelling like wolves. One nearly went over the platform's edge as he twisted in midair, trying to halt his plunging rush. He reeled against a companion, clutching his shoulder—and neither one of them saw their slayer!

For Granicor lunged forward roaring. The sweep of his great sword toppled one Viking against the other, and they went over the brink in a flurry of arms and legs and a knife-edged shriek of despair. Before the other Northmen knew death was among them Granicor had struck again, shouting as he caught sight of Guthrum's hated face. A helm was crushed like paper, and bone shattered under the rush of the duke's steel; then blades licked out, and a cry went up from the Vikings. Three had died already—and there were more to die that day.

For Granicor moved like a pestilence, iron muscles in his great-thewed body toughened by his hatred of King Guthrum. His brand fell and swung and murdered in a crash of ringing steel there above the golden abysses, and though he was unarmored no thrust or cut seemed to have power to hurt him. Three he killed, and was wounded in breast and back and thigh. Blood gushed out through his tattered rags. Then even the hardy Vikings felt a shudder of horror go through them, for this madman, his body warped with torture, wounded almost to death—laughed! Granicor shouted with laughter, the insane glee that rose resistlessly within him as he cut his way toward Guthrum. Blood gushed from the half-healed wounds on hands and feet, mingling with the crimson welter that flooded the platform.

One man's head leaped from his shoulders; and on the back sweep of the sword Granicor drove steel deep into a Viking's side, slicing through chain-mail like cardboard. He dashed blood and sweat from his eyes with a shapeless paw—saw one giant figure before him, a huge redbeard whose ax was driving down, screaming through cleft air. The duke leaped in, blade slashing.

The ax bit deep into Granicor's back. He shouted, stiffened. The sword dropped from his hands. In the bitter eyes of Guthrum a black laughter rose.

But the duke was not yet dead. He swayed, face contorted, clawing emptiness. He looked up and saw Guthrum, standing alone above corpses, the only Northman left alive.

Roaring, he sprang.

Steel fingers locked in Guthrum's hairy throat. Weaponless, Granicor made of his body a human projectile that drove the red-bearded giant back and down—back to the platform's edge—and beyond!

The two men plunged into the abyss, locked in a death-grip, Duke Granicor shouting mad triumph.

But from the Viking king came no sound as he fell through the golden mists to death.

12. *Warlock and Druid*

SWINGING through empty space went the hollow globe with Elak and Dalan within it, on and on in a great curve till at last something loomed out of the dimness ahead. The Druid drew in his breath sharply.

"Leap after me, Elak—and swiftly."

A pinnacle, a tower, a jagged eidolon of granite swam into view, lifting from amber fog-clouds. Dalan climbed laboriously on the sloping, waist-high rim, crouching there. The steep crag drifted closer. And the Druid sprang—scrabbled with hand and foot to cling to the dangerously angled rock. Elak followed, knowing a sickening instant of cold horror as he felt beneath him incredible depths of emptiness. Then they stood together on the slope—and Dalan pointed to a tunnel mouth just above them.

"There's our road, Elak. Come."

They stumbled cautiously toward the cryptic opening in the rocks. It led to a short tunnel, leading downward, very dimly lighted by the amber glow that filtered from the mouth. At the end of the passage was a door. It was unlocked; Dalan swung it open. Just beyond the threshold, on the rock floor, was a lamp, its bright flame illuminating every detail of the cave that lay before them.

It was empty save for a small square altar of dark stone, and the figure of a man who knelt before it, staring into the coldly yellow depths of a jewel he clasped in stiff hands.

"Orander!" Elak almost shouted. There was no answer.

Orander of Cyrena, Elak's brother, knelt as though carved from stone, his intent gaze riveted upon the jewel he gripped. He was younger than Elak, yet, somehow, he seemed older. Golden hair, unbound, grew in a leonine mane over the well-shaped head. There was strength in the king's face—power, and something of nobility.

But the man was—*veiled!*

Over his features there lay, like the shadow of death, an impalpable darkness, intangible, yet conveying a definite air of *withdrawal.* It seemed to Elak that, strangely, his brother was very far away, though his body was only a few feet distant. And even as he called again he knew that Orander would not hear.

"The king is lost to Cyrena," Dalan said quietly. "There is strong sorcery in the yellow jewel."

"I'll waken him, then," Elak grunted, moving forward. Suddenly he paused. Amazement flooded his lean face. For a second he seemed to strive futilely against empty air. His hands went out, seeming to slide across an invisible wall that blocked his way.

"Strong sorcery!" the Druid said. "No—don't use your rapier. You'd shatter it. There's only one way to reach Orander—and it's a perilous one."

At Elak's impatient gesture Dalan turned to the lamp. Swiftly he extinguished it, and shut the door so that the yellow glow could not filter in. Intense blackness darkened the cave.

"There's only one road by which we can reach the king, Elak—a road I've never traveled. Watch."

Elak obeyed. He could see nothing. Flashing light-images played before his pupils, but gradually these faded and vanished. They were alone in darkness.

Then he saw a tiny pin-point of yellow light.

"Do you see it?" Dalan muttered. Elak grunted assent.

"Then follow it. Keep the light constantly before your eyes. Walk forward slowly until— until——"

The Druid's voice faded oddly and was lost in silence. Without hesitation Elak stepped toward the tiny yellow light. He expected to crash into the invisible barrier that had blocked his path, but it did not materialize. After he had advanced a dozen paces he paused. Orander should now be almost at his side.

Urgently came Dalan's hoarse voice. "Go on! Quickly!"

The yellow light had vanished. For a moment Elak searched for it vainly; then, dimly, he saw it, winking like a tiny star. He moved on again, and as he did the light grew brighter.

Yet it was only a pin-point; guiding him through utter blackness. As he went on he realized that he had traversed the length of the cave, and should crash against the rock wall. Yet he did not. And the rock beneath his feet had a different feel—softer, more elastic.

Suddenly there was a moment of frightful vertigo, a wrenching jar that tore at every atom of his body. He felt utterly disoriented—strangely lost, curiously conscious of movement he could not analyze.

The darkness fled away and was gone. Cool yellow light was all around him. At Elak's side was the Druid—but no longer were they in the cave.

They stood on a glowing plain of amber, under a golden sky that was sunless and luminous. All around them was a featureless, coldly blazing expanse, stretching endlessly into infinity.

"Ishtar!" Elak's voice was hushed. "Where are we, Dalan? This isn't—earth."

"No. We are in a far place now, and a dangerous one. We passed through a door into another world."

"A door?"

"The yellow jewel," Dalan said. "It is the bridge between our land and this world. More than that——"

THE Druid broke off, staring. The distant glowing plains seemed to be undergoing an incredible transformation—lifting, rising like great waves, marching forward from the horizons toward the two men.

Elak caught a glimpse of Dalan's face, startled and apprehensive, and then the two were jerked apart. A gap widened in the earth between them. Elak caught a flashing glimpse of abysmal depths where red-orange fire glowed. He seemed to be spinning through empty space, rocketing across the great plain with furious speed. Briefly the world seemed to close about him, as though he were being crushed between the vast plains which had somehow been folded in around him. He clutched his rapier-hilt in hopeless desperation.

And then he stood alone on the great shining plain. Nothing else was visible but the brazen amber sky; the Druid had vanished. It was utterly silent.

"Elak," a soft voice called. The tall adventurer turned. He saw no one.

Then, from empty air, there sprang—a shadow! Two-dimensional, unreal, it grew darker, took on form and substance. As Elak gazed, a man grew into visibility and stood watching him, a slim, blueeyed youth with soft flaxen hair. He wore a doeskin tunic, his only weapon a dirk girded at his belt. In his hand he gripped a harp.

Elak remembered the face he had seen in Dalan's crystal globe on the galley—the face of Elf the warlock, the same on which he looked now. And again he sensed the ageless, incredible evil that lurked in the depths of the candid blue eyes, watching as a devil might peer through a mask.

"I am Elf," the warlock said. "But I think you know that." He did not move as Elak unsheathed his rapier, crouching menacingly, one foot forward.

"Yes, I know it," the tall adventurer answered warily. "Where's Dalan? Bring him here—or I'll let blood flow from your throat before you can move to cast a spell."

Elf smiled. "No, my business is with you. Elak—you have spoiled my plans. But I have no wish to kill you. Instead, I'd rather see you on the throne of Cyrena."

"Eh?" Elak did not lower his blade. "What are you trying now? Bring Dalan here, I say!"

"Dalan has lied to you. He said I had your brother captive——"

"And I saw him! Your lies won't help."

"He's here, yes," Elf admitted. "But not a captive. In Cyrena he was a king. But in this land of mine he is more. I have made him—a god!"

"What are you talking about?" Elak snapped. "You're playing for time. Bring——"

The warlock swept his hand over the harp's strings. Throbbing sweetness, with a poignant undertone of bitterness, rang out. Instantly they were in utter blackness.

And at that moment Elak thrust with his rapier, thrust at empty air. Cursing, he slashed blindly about. Suddenly the darkness lifted.

For an instant Elak saw his brother's face hovering gigantically above him, the weird veil of alienage still shrouding the strong features. In the king's eyes Elak saw withdrawal—a withdrawal so awe-inspiring that he felt momentarily cold, as though some breath of the unknown had touched him.

The voice of Elf came softly. "I have shown you Orander," the warlock murmured. "Now I shall show you more. You shall see the worlds over which the god who is Orander rules."

Again the dark veil fell.

GREAT vistas of flashing light, orange, scarlet, yellow, glittering with amazing beauty, down which fled cyclopean shadows. Slowly the vision faded and became distinct. Elak seemed to be hovering in empty air above a huge city, many-tiered and gardened, that rose on the summit of a mountain beneath him.

Fantastic splendor ruled the city. Shining domes and minarets rose high above the wide marble streets, and arches and bridges spanned the lakes and canals where water—glowing with yellow radiance—moved sluggishly between its banks. The inhabitants of the city were not human.

They were beasts—and yet more than beasts. Elak was reminded of giant colossi of stone, winged monsters, bearded and talc-winged, lion-bodied, sleekly beautiful. Smoothly powerful muscles rolled beneath the satin pelts. And wise, wise and ancient beyond all imagination, were the faces that Elak saw. The plumes of the vari-colored wings fluttered in the gentle breeze that swept over the mountain-top, honey-sweet, spiced with odors redolent of Eastern lands.

"It is Athorama," Elf's voice murmured from empty air. "Over all this splendor Orander rules."

Blackness fell again, and, lifting, disclosed a sea-girt city, where the yellow light was tinged with a dim green glow—a white city clothed in green and scarlet, blue and purple. Vegetation wound up the towers, and serpentine trees writhed and twisted in the streets. Very slowly moved the men and women of this city—clad in flowing garments that trailed behind them eerily in the dimness. And there were vague shadows swimming to and fro. . . .

"It is Lur," said Elf. "It is sunken Lur. And over this also is Orander a god."

Darkness fell, and lifted to disclose the am-ber-glowing plain on which Elak stood. Beside him was the warlock, smiling gently. He lifted a hand as Elak's blade flickered.

"Wait. You have seen these worlds which I made for Orander's pleasure, in which all moves and is ordered as he desires. Now I shall show you the king again."

The harp hummed eerily. In the ochre glow of the sky, clouds grew, shaping themselves in oddly patterned order. Slowly the vague outline of a face began to appear above them—the face of Orander, King of Cyrena. The eyes seemed to dwell on something infinitely far away. The titan face hung in the sky, fantastically huge and distant.

"Orander," the warlock said. "Here is Elak."

There was no change in the giant face, nor did the lips move; yet a voice said distinctly and coldly:

"I hear."

Elak felt an icy shock go through him at the sound of that voice. It belonged to something which was no longer human. But because he knew that it was also Orander's voice, he fought back his horror and called the king's name.

"I hear," the voice said again. "I know why you have come. It is useless. Go back."

"You're putting words into the mouth of a phantom," Elak snarled, swinging round to face Elf.

"It is I, once Orander. Elf has made me a god, and he has built me worlds for my pleasure. Go back."

"You see," the warlock said, his gaze meeting Elak's frankly. "Would you rob a god of his worlds? I put no enchantment on Orander. The king asked me to grant him this boon, and with my magic I did so—made worlds over which your brother rules. Would you drag him back to

Cyrena—a place from which he fled?"

Elak did not answer. A frown darkened his face. Elf went on slowly.

"Dalan was jealous of my power; that was all. He tried to lead Cyrena against me, and in self-defense I sought the Northmen's aid, for I could not call on Orander. Join me, Elak—you can sit on Cyrena's throne, and my magic will serve you. Forget the Druid's lies!"

Doubtfully Elak lowered his rapier. "I don't want to rule," he said. "I seek no crowns. I came here to win back Cyrena from invaders, and to free my brother. But——"

"But Orander does not wish to be freed——"

"You lie!"

Dalan's voice! Elak's head jerked up. He stared at the sky—to where, beside the titan face of Orander, hung another face, hog-fat, toad-ugly, glaring down at Elf.

"Mider!" roared the Druid. "By Mider—you seek to stuff Elak's head with lies? Your spells won't aid you now—you spew of serpents!"

The warlock looked up unmoving. And the voice of Dalan thundered on from the sky.

"My magic is stronger than yours—else I'd not be here now. Ay, you seek to enlist Elak's aid, for you dare not fight him—not while he carries the Druid knife of sacrifice."

Elf's lips were twisted in a venomous snarl. But the Druid ignored him, bellowed:

"Elak! There's foul enchantment on Orander. He's glamored by the damned witchery of Elf's poison, by the spell cast on him unawares—but he can be called back to Cyrena, and he'll thank you for it. No man is made to be a god, and there'll be a fearful doom on Orander unless he's called back. Speak to him of Cyrena—of his people, Elak!"

FOR a second the adventurer hesitated, staring up at the cyclopean face of the king. Then, suddenly, he lifted his rapier with a shout. He had seen something change in the god-face, and the veil of horror had lifted from the alien eyes.

"Orander!" Elak cried. "Orander—come back to Cyrena! The sea cliffs are harried by Northmen, and dragon ships bring invaders with torch and sword. The chiefs have risen—but they need a king, else Cyrena will fall again.

"Orander, remember your kingdom—remember the fields of your land, green in the warm sunlight, silver under the moon. Remember the steadings and the cattle of your people—Sharn Forest, and the Druid altars.

"The mountains and plains of Cyrena, your warhorse and your sword, remember all these! Remember those who held the throne before you without failing—remember the blood and steel that make up your kingdom. Orander—come back to Cyrena!"

The titan face was no longer that of a god. It looked down on Elak, the face of Orander, Cyrena's king. His pulses surged with triumph as he heard the Druid shout:

"Shatter the jewel, Orander—shatter the demon jewel you hold!"

Simultaneously there came a thunder and a crashing as of riven worlds, and the ochre light vanished from the sky. The tumult roared all about Elak, the darkness broken by flashing, brief lightimages. The ruins of sunken Lur sank down in thunder; the huge and splendid city of Athorama crashed in terrible destruction down the mountain, while the mitered beasts flew screaming, beating the air with frantic pinions. All around Elak was the death-cry of a ruined universe, and it swelled and rose to a dreadful crescendo of terror.

He saw Elf's face, twisted into a Gorgon mask of hate and fury, rushing toward him; something like the coil of a great serpent swept about his body. The rapier was gone, but he remembered the crystal dagger in his belt, clawed out the Druid blade. He drove it again and again into the cold, scaly thing that gripped him, unseen in the darkness that had fallen. Chill flesh seemed to shrink from beneath his attack.

Then he felt fangs closing on his throat, ripped out desperately with the dagger. There was a single frightful scream of deathly agony, and in a moment of blazing light Elak saw the body of Elf falling into a fathomless gulf that loomed below him. As he watched, the warlock's figure seemed to be wrenched asunder by some unseen power that waited in the abyss. And again darkness fell—and silence.

There was a low wheezing and scrambling near by, and light flickered up dimly. Elak saw the Druid bending over a lighted lamp, and realized with incredulity that he stood in the cave of the black altar. Swiftly he turned.

A man was rising to his feet—and on the stones around him lay splintered yellow shards. Orander—no longer tranced by Elf's magic, no longer under a spell. The king's eyes met Elak's.

The adventurer leaped forward, gripped his brother's arms. "Orander! Ishtar be praised!"

"Praise Mider, rather," Dalan said dryly. "And praise Orander for shattering the jewel and breaking the spell." An expression of malevolent triumph came over the ugly face. "But you've slain Elf, Elak, and for that you have my thanks. May his soul be tortured through eternity in the Nine Hells!"

FROM a turret of King Orander's castle Dalan watched three figures ride south weeks later. His heavy shoulders lifted in a shrug. Beside him Orander smiled a little sadly.

"He wouldn't stay, Dalan. And I'm sorry for that."

"He was wise," the Druid said. "A country should have but one hero, its king. Best let him go in peace, lest quarrels come if he had stayed."

"No. There would be no quarrels. But Zeulas—Elak, as he calls himself—is a wanderer. He will not change now, though I urged him. So he rides south again, with Lycon and Velia at his side."

The figures on horseback grew small on the plain—two who rode very close together, and one who followed at a little distance, reeling in his saddle and keeping his balance only by occasionally gripping the beast's mane. Elak and Velia talked, with soft laughter and high hearts, as they cantered onward—and behind them, Lycon, in his own fashion, was happy also.

"Wine," he murmured thickly to himself. "Goatskins of it. Good wine, too! The gods are very good. . . ."

SPAWN OF DAGON

An eldritch, fearsome tale of the worship of the
fish-god in the ancient world, and the prowess
of a doughty swordsman in old Atlantis

Under all graves they murmur,
    They murmur and rebel,
Down to the buried kingdoms creep,
And like a lost rain roar and weep
    O'er the red heavens of hell.
                        —Chesterton.

TWO streams of blood trickled slowly across the
rough boards of the floor. One of them emerged
from a gaping wound in the throat of a prostrate,
armor-clad body; the other dripped from a chink
in the battered cuirass, and the swaying light of
a hanging lamp cast grotesque shadows over the
corpse and the two men who crouched on their
hams watching it. They were both very drunk.
One of them, a tall, extremely slender man
whose bronzed body seemed boneless, so supple

91

was it, murmured:

"I win, Lycon. The blood wavers strangely, but the stream I spilt will reach this crack first." He indicated a space between two planks with the point of his rapier.

Lycon's child-like eyes widened in astonishment. He was short, thick-set, with a remarkably simian face set atop his broad shoulders. He swayed slightly as he gasped, "By Ishtar! The blood runs uphill!"

Elak, the slender man, chuckled. "After all the mead you swilled the ocean might run uphill. Well, the wager's won; I get the loot." He got up and stepped over to the dead man. Swiftly he searched him, and suddenly muttered an explosive curse. "The swine's as bare as a Bacchic vestal! He has no purse."

Lycon smiled broadly and looked more than ever like an undersized hairless ape. "The gods watch over me," he said in satisfaction.

"Of all the millions in Atlantis you had to pick a fight with a pauper," Elak groaned. "Now we'll have to flee San-Mu, as your quarrels have forced us to flee Poseidonia and Kornak. And the San-Mu mead is the best in the land. If you had to cause trouble, why not choose a fat usurer? We'd have been paid for our trouble, then, at least."

"The gods watch over me," Lycon reiterated, leaning forward and then rocking back, chuckling to himself. He leaned too far and fell on his nose, where he remained without moving. Something dropped from the bosom of his tunic and fell with a metallic sound to the oaken floor. Lycon snored.

Elak, smiling unpleasantly, appropriated the purse and investigated its contents. "Your fingers are swifter than mine," he told the recumbent Lycon, "but I can hold more mead than you. Next time don't try to cheat one who has more brains in his big toe than you have in all your misshapen body. Scavenging little ape! Get, up; the innkeeper is returning with soldiers."

He thrust the purse into the wallet at his belt and kicked Lycon heartily, but the small thief failed to awaken. Cursing with a will, Elak hoisted the body of the other to his shoulders and staggered toward the back of the tavern. The distant sound of shouting from the street outside grew louder, and Elak thought he could

"Ishtar!" Elak breathed. "What wizardry's this?"

hear the querulous complaints of the innkeeper.

"There will be a reckoning, Lycon!" he promised bitterly. "Ishtar, yes! You'll learn——"

He pushed through a golden drapery and hurried along a corridor—kicked open an oaken door and came out in the alley behind the tavern. Above, cold stars glittered frostily, and an icy wind blew on Elak's sweating face, sobering him somewhat.

Lycon stirred and writhed in his arms. "More grog!" he muttered. "Oh gods! Is there no more grog?" A maudlin tear fell hotly on Elak's neck, and the latter for a moment entertained the not unpleasant idea of dropping Lycon and leaving him for the irate guards. The soldiers of San-Mu were not renowned for their soft-heartedness, and tales of what they sometimes did to their captives were unpleasantly explicit.

However, he ran along the alley instead, blundered into a brawny form that sprang out of the darkness abruptly, and saw a snarling, bearded face indistinct in the vague starlight. He dropped Lycon and whipped out his rapier. Already the soldier was plunging forward, his great sword rushing down.

Then it happened. Elak saw the guard's mouth open in a square of amazement, saw horror spring into the cold eyes. The man's face was a mask of abysmal fear. He flung himself back desperately—the sword-tip just missed Elak's face.

The soldier raced away into the shadows.

WITH a snake-like movement Elak turned, rapier ready. He caught a blur of swift motion. The man facing him had lifted quick hands to his face, and dropped them as suddenly. But there was no menace in the gesture. Nevertheless Elak felt a chill of inexplicable uneasiness crawl down his back as he faced his rescuer. The soldiers of San-Mu were courageous, if lacking in human kindness. What had frightened the attacking guard?

He eyed the other. He saw a medium-sized man, clad in voluminous gray garments that were almost invisible in the gloom—saw a white face with regular, statuesque features. A black hollow sprang into existence within the white mask as a soft voice whispered, "You'd escape from the guards? No need for your rapier—I'm a friend."

'Who the—but there's no time for talk. Thanks, and good-bye."

Elak stooped and hoisted Lycon to his shoulders again. The little man was blinking and murmuring soft appeals for more mead. And the hasty thunder of mailed feet grew louder, while torchlight swiftly approaching cast gleams of light about the trio.

"In here," the gray-clad man whispered. "You'll be safe." Now Elak saw that in the stone wall beside him a black rectangle gaped. He sprang through the portal without hesitation. The other followed, and instantly they were in utter blackness as an unseen door swung creakingly on rusty hinges.

Elak felt a soft hand touch his own. Or was it a hand? For a second he had the incredible feeling that the thing whose flesh he had touched did not belong to any human body—it was too soft, too cold! His skin crawled at the feel of the thing. It was withdrawn, and a fold of gray cloth swung against his palm. He gripped it.

"Follow!"

Silently, gripping the guide's garment, bearing Lycon on his shoulders, Elak moved forward. How the other could find his way through the blackness Elak did not know, unless he knew the way by heart. Yet the passage—if passage it was—turned and twisted endlessly as it went down. Presently Elak had the feeling that he was moving through a larger space, a cave, perhaps. His footsteps sounded differently, somehow. And through the darkness vague whisperings came to him.

Whispers in no language he knew. The murmurous sibilants rustled out strangely, making Elak's brows contract and his free hand go involuntarily to the hilt of his rapier. He snarled, "Who's here?"

The invisible guide cried out in the mysterious tongue. Instantly the whisperings stopped.

"You are among friends," a voice said softly from the blackness. 'We are almost at our destination. A few more steps——"

A few more steps, and light blazed up. They stood in a small rectangular chamber hollowed out of the rock. The nitrous walls gleamed dankly in the glow of an oil lamp, and a little stream ran across the rock floor of the cave and lost itself, amid chuckles of goblin laughter, in a small hole at the base of the wall. Two doors were visible. The gray-clad man was closing one of them.

A crude table and a few chairs were all the furnishings of the room. Elak strained his ears. He heard something—something that should not be heard in inland San-Mu. He could not be mistaken. The sound of waves lapping softly in the distance . . . and occasionally a roaring crash, as of breakers smashing on a rocky shore.

He dumped Lycon unceremoniously in one of the chairs. The little man fell forward on the table, pillowing his head in his arms. Sadly he muttered, "Is there no mead in Atlantis? I die, Elak. My belly is an arid desert across which the armies of Eblis march."

He sobbed unhappily for a moment and fell asleep.

ELAK ostentatiously unsheathed his rapier and laid it on the table. His slender fingers closed on the hilt. "An explanation," he said, "is due. Where are we?"

"I am Gesti," said the gray-clad one. His face seemed chalk-white in the light of the oil lamp. His eyes, deeply sunken, were covered with a curious glaze. "I saved you from the guards, eh? You'll not deny that?"

"You have my thanks," Elak said. "Well?"

"I need the aid of a brave man. And I'll pay

well. If you're interested, good. If not, I'll see you leave San-Mu safely."

Elak considered. "It's true we've little money." He thought of the purse in his wallet and grinned wryly. "Not enough to last us long, at any rate. Perhaps we're interested. Although——" He hesitated.

"Well?"

"I could bear to know how you got rid of the soldier so quickly, back in the alley behind the tavern."

"I do not think that matters," Gesti whispered in his sibilant voice. "The guards are superstitious. And it's easy to play on their weakness. Let that suffice!" The cold glazed eyes met Elak's squarely, and a little warning note seemed to clang in his brain.

There was danger here. Yet danger had seldom given him pause. He said, "What will you pay?"

"A thousand golden pieces."

"Fifty thousand cups of mead," Lycon murmured sleepily. "Accept it, Elak. I'll await you here."

There was little affection in the glance Elak cast at his companion. "You'll get none of it," he promised. "Not a gold piece!"

He turned to Gesti. "What's to be done for this reward?"

Gesti's immobile face watched him cryptically. "Kill Zend."

Elak said, "Kill—Zend? *Zend?* The Wizard of Atlantis?"

"Are you afraid?" Gesti asked tonelessly.

"I am," Lycon said without lifting his head from his arms. "However, if Elak is not, he may slay Zend and I'll wait here."

Ignoring him, Elak said, "I've heard strange things of Zend. His powers are not human. Indeed, he's not been seen in the streets of San-Mu for ten years. Men say he's immortal."

"Men—are fools." And in Gesti's voice there was a contempt that made Elak stare at him sharply. It was as though Gesti was commenting on some race alien to him. The gray-clad man went on hurriedly, as though sensing the trend of Elak's thoughts. "We have driven a passage under Zend's palace. We can break through at any time; that we shall do tonight. Two tasks I give you: kill Zend; shatter the red sphere."

Elak said, "You're cryptic. What red sphere?"

"It lies in the topmost minaret of his palace. His magic comes from it. There is rich loot in the palace, Elak—if that's your name. So the little man called you."

"Elak or dunce or robber of drunken men," Lycon said, absently feeling the bosom of his tunic. "All alike. Call him by any of those names and you'll be right. Where is my gold, Elak?"

But without waiting for an answer he slumped down in his chair, his eyes closing and his mouth dropping open as he snored. Presently he fell off the chair and rolled under the table, where he slumbered.

"What the devil can I do with him?" Elak asked. "I can't take him with me. He'd——"

"Leave him here," Gesti said.

Elak's cold eyes probed the other. "He'll be safe?"

"Quite safe. None in San-Mu but our band knows of this underground way."

"What band is that?" Elak asked.

Gesti said nothing for a time. Then his soft voice whispered, "Need you know? A political group banded together to overthrow the king of San-Mu, and Zend, from whom he gets his power. Have you more—questions?"

"No."

"Then follow."

Gesti led Elak to one of the oaken doors; it swung open, and they moved forward up a winding passage. In the dark Elak stumbled over a step. He felt the cloth of Gesti's garment touch his hand, and gripped it. In the blackness they ascended a staircase cut out of the rock.

Half-way up, Gesti paused. "I can go no further," he whispered. "The way is straight. At the end of the stairway there is a trap-door of stone. Open it. You'll be in Zend's place. Here is a weapon for you." He thrust a tube of cold metal into Elak's hand. "Simply squeeze its sides, pointing the smaller end at Zend. You understand?"

Elak nodded, and, although Gesti could scarcely have seen the movement in the darkness, he whispered, "Good. Dagon guard you!"

He turned away; Elak heard the soft rush of his descent dying in the distance. He began to mount the stairs, wonderingly. Dagon—was

HENRY KUTTNER

Gesti a worshipper of the forbidden evil god of ocean? Poseidon, a benignant sea-god, was adored in marble temples all over the land, but the dark worship of Dagon had been banned for generations. There were tales of another race whose god Dagon was—a race that had not sprung from human or even earthly loins. . . .

GRIPPING the odd weapon, Elak felt his way upward. At length his head banged painfully against stone, and, cursing softly, he felt about in the darkness. It was the trap-door of which Gesti had spoken. Two bolts slid back in well-oiled grooves. And the door lifted easily as Elak thrust his shoulders against it.

He clambered up in semi-darkness, finding himself in a small bare room through which light filtered from a narrow window-slit high in the wall. A mouse, squeaking fearfully, fled as he scrambled to his feet. Apparently the room was little used. Elak moved stealthily to the door.

It swung open a little under his cautious hand. A corridor stretched before him, dimly lit by cold blue radiance that came from tiny gems set in the ceiling at intervals. Elak followed the upward slant of the passage; the red sphere Gesti had mentioned was in the topmost minaret. Up, then:

In a niche in the wall Elak saw the head. The shock of it turned him cold with amazement. A bodiless head, set upright on a golden pedestal within a little alcove—its cheeks sunken, hair lank and disheveled—but eyes bright with in-

101

credible life! Those eyes watched him!

"Ishtar!" Elak breathed. "What wizardry's this?"

He soon found out. The pallid lips of the horror writhed and twisted, and from them came a high skirling cry of warning.

"Zend! Zend! A stranger walks your——"

Elak's rapier flew. There was scarcely any blood. He dragged the blade from the eyesocket, whispering prayers to all the gods and goddesses he could remember. The lean jaw dropped, and a blackened and swollen tongue lolled from between the teeth. A red, shrunken eyelid dropped over the eye Elak had not pierced.

There was no sound save for Elak's hastened breathing. He eyed the monstrous thing in the alcove, and then, confident that it was no longer a menace, lengthened his steps up the passage. Had Zend heard the warning of his sentinel? If so, danger lurked all about him.

A silver curtain slashed with a black pattern hung across the corridor. Elak parted it, and, watching, he froze in every muscle.

A dwarf, no more than four feet tall, with a disproportionately large head and a gray, wrinkled skin, was trotting briskly toward him. From the tales he had heard Elak imagined the dwarf to be Zend.

Behind the wizard strode a half-naked giant, who carried over his shoulder the limp form of a girl. Elak spun about, realizing that he had delayed too long. Zend was parting the silver curtain as Elak raced back down the corridor.

At his side a black rectangle loomed—a passage he had overlooked, apparently, when he had passed it before. He sprang into its shielding darkness. When Zend passed he would strike down the wizard and take his chances with the giant. Remembering the smooth hard muscles that had rippled under the dead-white skin of the man, Elak was not so sure that his chances would be worth much. He realized now that the giant had seemed familiar.

Then he knew. Two days ago he had seen a man—a condemned criminal—beheaded in the temple of Posedion. There could be no mistake. The giant was the same man, brought back to life by Zend's evil necromancy!

"Ishtar!" Elak whispered, sweating. "I'd be better off in the hands of the guards." How could he slay a man who was already dead?

Elak hesitated, his rapier half drawn. There was no use borrowing trouble. He would keep safely out of sight until Zend was separated from his ghastly servitor—and then it would be an easy matter to put six inches of steel through the wizard's body. Elak was never one for taking unnecessary risks, as he had a wholesome regard for his hide. He heard a shuffling of feet and drew back within the side-passage to let Zend pass. But the wizard turned suddenly and began to mount the steeply sloping corridor where Elak lurked. In Zend's hand was a softly glowing gem that illuminated the passage, though not brightly.

Elak fled. The passage was steep and narrow,

ELAK OF ATLANTIS

and it ended at last before a blank wall. Behind
him a steady padding of feet grew louder in the
distance. He felt around desperately in the dark.
If there was a hidden spring in the walls, he
failed to find it.

A grin lighted his face as he realized how narrow the passage was. If he could do it——

HE PLACED his palms flat against the wall, and
with his bare feet found an easy purchase on the
opposite one. Face down, swiftly, with his muscles cracking under the strain, he walked up the
wall until he was safely above the head of even
the giant. There he stopped, sweating, and
glanced down.

Only an enormously strong man could have
done it, and if Elak had weighed a little more it
would have been impossible. His shoulders and
thighs ached as he strained to hold his position
without moving.

The trio were approaching. If they should
glance up, Elak was ready to drop and use his
blade, or the strange weapon Gesti had given
him. But apparently they did not notice him,
hidden as he was in the shadows of the high
ceiling.

He caught a glimpse of the girl the giant carried. A luscious wench! But, of course, Zend
would undoubtedly choose only the most attrac-
tive maidens for his necromancy and sorcery.

"If that dead-alive monster weren't here," he
ruminated, "I'd be tempted to fall on Zend's
head. No doubt the girl would be grateful."

She was, at the moment, unconscious. Long black lashes lay on cream-pale cheeks, and dark ringlets swayed as the giant lurched on. Zend's hand fumbled out, touched the wall. The smooth surface of stone lifted and the gray dwarf pattered into the dimness beyond. The giant followed, and the door dropped again.

With a low curse of relief Elak swung noiselessly to the floor and rubbed his hands on his leather tunic. They were bleeding, and only the hardness of his soles had saved his feet from a similar fate. After a brief wait Elak fumbled in the darkness and found the concealed spring.

The door lifted, with a whispering rush of sound. Elak found himself in a short corridor that ended in another black-slashed silver curtain. He moved forward, noticing with relief that the door remained open behind him.

Beyond the silver curtain was a room—huge, high-domed, with great open windows through which the chill night wind blew strongly. The room blazed with the coruscating brilliance of the glowing gems, which were set in walls and ceiling in bizarre, arabesque patterns. Through one window Elak saw the yellow globe of the moon, which was just rising. Three archways, curtained, broke the smooth expanse of the farther wall. The chamber itself, richly furnished with rugs and silks and ornaments, was empty of occupants. Elak noiselessly covered the distance to the archways and peered through the curtain of the first.

Blazing white light blinded him. He had a

flashing, indistinct vision of tremendous forces, leashed, cyclopean, straining mightily to burst the bonds that held them. Yet actually he saw nothing—merely an empty room. But empty he knew that it was not! Power unimaginable surged from beyond the archway, shuddering through every atom of Elak's body. Glittering steel walls reflected his startled face.

And on the floor, in the very center of the room, he saw a small mud-colored stone. That was all. Yet about the stone surged a tide of power that made Elak drop the curtain and back away, his eyes wide with fear. Very quickly he turned to the next curtain—peered apprehensively beyond it.

Here was a small room, cluttered with alembics, retorts, and other of Zend's magical paraphernalia. The pallid giant stood silently in a corner. On a low table was stretched the girl, still unconscious. Above her hovered the gray dwarf, a crystal vial in one hand. He tilted it; a drop fell.

Elak heard Zend's harsh voice.

"A new servant . . . a new soul to serve me. When her soul is freed, I shall send it to Antares. There is a planet there where I've heard much sorcery exists. Mayhap I can learn a few more secrets. . . ."

Elak turned to the last alcove. He lifted the curtain, saw a steep stairway. From it rose-red light blazed down. He remembered Gesti's words: "Shatter the red sphere! His magic comes from it."

Good! He'd break the sphere first, and then, with no magic to protect him, Zend would be easy prey. With a lithe bound Elak began to mount the stairs. Behind him came a guttural cry.

"Eblis, Ishtar, and Poseidon!" Elak said hastily. "Protect me now!" He was at the top of the staircase, in a highdomed room through which moonlight crept from narrow windows. It was the room of the sphere.

Glowing, shining with lambent rose-red radiance, the great sphere lay in a silver cradle, metallic tubes and wires trailing from it to vanish into the walls. Half as tall as Elak's body it was, its brilliance soft but hypnotically intense—and he stood for a moment motionless, staring.

BEHIND him feet clattered on the stair. He turned, saw the pallid giant lumbering up. A livid scar circled the deadwhite neck. He had been right, then. This was the criminal he had seen executed—brought back to life by Zend's necromancy. In the face of real danger Elak forgot the gods and drew his rapier. Prayers, he had found, would not halt a dagger's blow or a strangler's hands.

Without a sound the giant sprang for Elak, who dodged under the great clutching paws and sent his rapier's point deep within the deadwhite breast. It bent dangerously; he whipped it out just in time to save it from snapping, and it sang shrilly as it vibrated. Elak's opponent seemed unhurt. Yet the rapier had pierced his heart. He bled not at all.

The battle was not a long one, and it ended at a window. The two men went reeling and swaying about the room, ripping wires and tubes from their places in the fury of their struggle. Abruptly the red light of the globe dimmed, went out. Simultaneously Elak felt the giant's cold arms go about his waist.

Before they could tighten, he dropped. The moon peered in at a narrow window just beside him, and he flung himself desperately against the giant's legs, wrenching with all his strength. The undead creature toppled.

He came down as a tree falls, without striving to break the force of the impact. His hands went out clutchingly for Elak's throat. But Elak was shoving frantically at the white, cold, muscular body, forcing it out the narrow window. It overbalanced, toppled—and fell.

The giant made no outcry. After a moment a heavy thud was audible. Elak got up and recovered his rapier, loudly thanking Ishtar for his deliverance. "For," he thought, "a little politeness costs nothing, and even though my own skill and not Ishtar's hand saved me, one never knows." Too, there were other dangers to face, and if the gods are capricious, the goddesses are certainly even more so.

A loud shriek from below made him go quickly down the stairway, rapier ready. Zend was running toward him, his gray face a mask of fear. The dwarf hesitated at sight of him, spun about as a low rumble of voices came from near by. At the foot of the stairway Elak waited.

From the passage by which Elak had entered the great room a horde of nightmare beings spewed. In their van came Gesti, gray garments flapping, white face immobile as ever. Behind him sheer horror squirmed and leaped and tumbled. With a shock of loathing Elak remembered the whispering voices he had heard in the underground cavern—and knew, now, what manner of creatures had spoken thus.

A race that had not sprung from human or even earthly loins. . . .

Their faces were hideous staring masks, fishlike in contour, with parrot-like beaks and great staring eyes covered with a filmy glaze. Their bodies were amorphous things, half solid and half gelatinous ooze, like the iridescent slime of jellyfish; writhing tentacles sprouted irregularly from the ghastly bodies of the things. They were the offspring of no sane universe, and they came in a blasphemous hissing rush across the room. The rapier stabbed out vainly and clattered to the stones as Elak went down. He struggled futilely for a moment, hearing the harsh, agonized shrieks of the wizard. Cold tentacles were all about him, blinding him in their constricting coils. Then suddenly the weight that held him helpless was gone. His legs and arms, he discovered, were tightly bound with cords. He fought vainly to escape; then lay quietly.

Beside him, he saw, the wizard lay tightly trussed. The nightmare beings were moving in an orderly rush toward the room in which Elak had sensed the surges of tremendous power, where lay the little brown stone. They vanished beyond the curtain, and beside Elak and the wizard there remained only Gesti. He stood looking down at the two, his white face immobile.

"What treachery is this?" Elak asked with no great hopefulness. "Set me free and give me my gold."

But Gesti merely said, "You won't need it. You will die very soon."

"Eh? Why—"

"Fresh human blood is needed. That's why we didn't kill you or Zend. We need your blood. We'll be ready soon."

An outburst of sibilant whispers came from beyond the silver drape. Elak said unsteadily, "What manner of demons are those?"

The wizard gasped, "You ask him? Did you not know——"

GESTI lifted gloved hands and removed his face. Elak bit his lips to choke back a scream. Now he knew why Gesti's face had seemed so immobile. It was a mask.

Behind it were the parrot-like beak and fish-like eyes Elak now knew all too well. The gray robes sloughed off; the gloves dropped from the limber tips of tentacles. From the horrible beak came the sibilant whisper of the monster:

"Now you know whom you served." The thing that had called itself Gesti turned and progressed—that was the only way to describe its method of moving—to the curtain behind which its fellows had vanished. It joined them.

Zend was staring at Elak. "You did not know? You served them, and yet did not know?"

"By Ishtar, no!" Elak swore. "D'you think I'd have let those—those—what are they? What are they going to do?"

"Roll over here," Zend commanded. "Maybe I can loosen your bonds."

Elak obeyed, and the wizard's fingers worked deftly.

"I doubt—no human hands tied these knots. But——"

"What are they?" Elak asked again. "Tell me, before I go mad thinking hell has loosed its legions on Atlantis."

"They are the children of Dagon," Zend said. "Their dwelling-place is in the great deeps of the ocean. Have you never heard of the unearthly ones who worship Dagon?"

"Yes, But I never believed——"

"Oh, there's truth in the tale. Eons and unimaginable eons ago, before mankind existed on earth, only the waters existed. There was no land. And from the slime there sprang up a race of beings which dwelt in the sunken abysses of the ocean, inhuman creatures that worshipped Dagon, their god. When eventually the waters receded and great continents arose, these beings were driven down to the lowest depths. Their mighty kingdom, that had once stretched from pole to pole, was shrunken as the huge landmasses lifted. Mankind came—but from whence I do not know—and civilizations arose. Hold still.

These cursed knots—"

"I don't understand all of that," Elak said, wincing as the wizard's nail dug into his wrist. "But go on."

"These things hate man, for they feel that man has usurped their kingdom. Their greatest hope is to sink the continents again, so that the seas will roll over all the earth, and not a human being will survive. Their power will embrace the whole world, as it once did eons ago. They are not human, you see, and they worship Dagon. They want no other gods worshipped on Earth. Ishtar, dark Eblis, even Poseidon of the sunlit seas. . . . They will achieve their desire now, I fear."

"Not if I can get free," Elak said. "How do the knots hold?"

"They hold," the wizard said discouragedly. "But one strand is loose. My fingers are raw. The—the red globe is broken?"

"No," Elak said. "Some cords were torn loose as I fought with your slave, and the light went out of it. Why?"

"The gods be thanked!" Zend said fervently. "If I can repair the damage and light the globe again, the children of Dagon will die. That's the purpose of it. The rays it emits destroy their bodies, which are otherwise invulnerable, or almost so. If I hadn't had the globe, they'd have invaded my palace and killed me long ago."

"They have a tunnel under the cellars," Elak said.

"I see. But they dared not invade the palace

while the globe shone, for the light-rays would have killed them. Curse these knots! If they accomplish their purpose——"

"What's that?" Elak asked—but he had already guessed the answer.

"To sink Atlantis! This island-continent would have gone down beneath the sea long ago if I hadn't pitted my magic and my science against that of the children of Dagon. They are masters of the earthquake, and Atlantis rests on none too solid a foundation. Their power is sufficient to sink Atlantis for ever beneath the sea. But within that room"—Zend nodded toward the curtain that hid the sea-bred horrors—"in that room there is power far stronger than theirs. I have drawn strength from the stars, and the cosmic sources beyond the universe. You know nothing of my power. It is enough—more than enough—to keep Atlantis steady on its foundation, impregnable against the attacks of Dagon's breed. They have destroyed other lands before Atlantis."

Hot blood dripped on Elak's hands as the wizard tore at the cords.

"Aye . . . other lands. There were races that dwelt on Earth before man came. My powers have shown me a sunlit island that once reared far to the south, an island where dwelt a race of beings tall as trees, whose flesh was hard as stone, and whose shape was so strange you could scarcely comprehend it. The waters rose and covered that island, and its people died. I have seen a gigantic mountain that speared up from a waste of tossing waters, in Earth's youth, and in the towers and minarets that crowned its summit dwelt beings like sphinxes, with the heads of beasts and gods and whose broad wings could not save them when the cataclysm came. For ruin came to the city of the sphinxes, and it sank beneath the ocean—destroyed by the children of Dagon. And there was—"

"Hold!" Elak's breathless whisper halted the wizard's voice. "Hold! I see rescue, Zend."

"Eh?" The wizard screwed his head around until he too saw the short, ape-featured man who was running silently across the room, knife in hand. It was Lycon, whom Elak had left slumbering in the underground den of Gesti.

The knife flashed and Elak and Zend were free. Elak said swiftly, "Up the stairs, wizard. Repair your magic globe, since you say its light will kill these horrors. We'll hold the stairway."

WITHOUT a word the gray dwarf sped silently up the steps and was gone. Elak turned to Lycon.

"How the devil——"

Lycon blinked wide blue eyes. "I scarcely know, Elak. Only when you were carrying me out of the tavern and the soldier screamed and ran away I saw something that made me so drunk I couldn't remember what it was. I remembered only a few minutes ago, back downstairs somewhere. A face that looked like a gargoyle's, with a terrible great beak and eyes like Midgard Serpent's. And I remembered I'd seen Gesti put a mask over the awful face just before you turned there in the alley. So I knew Gesti was probably a demon."

"And so you came here," Elak commented softly. "Well, it's a good thing for me you did. I—what's the matter?" Lycon's blue eyes were bulging.

"Is this your demon?" the little man asked, pointing.

Elak turned, and smiled grimly. Facing him, her face puzzled and frightened, was the girl on whom Zend had been experimenting—the maiden whose soul he had been about to unleash to serve him when Elak had arrived. Her eyes were open now, velvet-soft and dark, and her white body gleamed against the silver-black drape.

Apparently she had awakened, and had arisen from her hard couch.

Elak's hand went up in a warning gesture, commanding silence, but it was too late. The girl said,

"Who are you? Zend kidnapped me—are you come to set me free? Where——"

With a bound Elak reached her, dragged her back, thrust her up the stairway. His rapier flashed in his hand. Over his shoulder he cast a wolfish smile. "If we live, you'll escape Zend and his magic," he told the girl, hearing an outburst of sibilant cries and the rushing murmur of the attacking horde. Yet he did not turn. "What's your name?" he asked.

"Coryllis."

"'Ware, Elak!" Lycon shouted.

Elak turned to see the little man's sword

flash out, shearing a questing tentacle in two. The severed end dropped, writhing and coiling in hideous knots.

The frightful devil-masks of monsters glared into Elak's eyes. The children of Dagon came sweeping in a resistless rush, cold eyes glazed and glaring, tentacles questing, iridescent bodies shifting and pulsing like jelly—and Elak and Lycon and the girl, Coryllis, were caught by their fearful wave and forced back, up the staircase.

Snarling inarticulate curses, Lycon swung his sword, but it was caught and dragged from his hand by a muscular tentacle. Elak tried to shield Coryllis with his own body; he felt himself going down, smothering beneath the oppressive weight of cold, hideous bodies that writhed and twisted with dreadful life. He struck out desperately— and felt a hard, cold surface melting like snow beneath his hands.

The weight that held him down was dissipating—the things were retreating, flowing back, racing and flopping and tumbling down the stairs, shrieking an insane shrill cry. They blackened and melted into shapeless puddles of slime that trickled like a little gray stream down the stairway. . . .

Elak realized what had happened. A rose-red light was glowing in the air all about him. The wizard had repaired his magic globe, and the power of its rays was destroying the nightmare menace that had crept up from the deeps.

In a heartbeat it was over. There was no trace of the horde that had attacked them. Gray puddles of ooze—no more. Elak realized that he was cursing softly, and abruptly changed it to a prayer. With great earnestness he thanked Ishtar for his deliverance.

LYCON recovered his sword, and handed Elak his rapier. "What now?" he asked.

"We're off! We're taking Coryllis with us—there's no need to linger here. True, we helped the wizard—but we fought him first. He may remember that. There's no need to test his gratefulness, and we'd be fools to do it."

He picked up Coryllis, who had quietly fainted, and quickly followed Lycon down the steps. They hurried across the great room and into the depths of the corridor beyond.

And five minutes later they were sprawled at full length under a tree in one of San-Mu's numerous parks. Elak had snatched a silken robe from a balcony as he passed beneath, and Coryllis had draped it about her slim body. The stars glittered frostily overhead, unconcerned with the fate of Atlantis—stars that would be shining thousands of years hence when Atlantis was not even a memory.

No thought of this came to Elak now. He wiped his rapier with a tuft of grass, while Lycon, who had already cleaned his blade, stood up and, shading his eyes with his palm, peered across the park. He muttered something under his breath and set off at a steady lope. Elak stared after him.

"Where's he going? There's a—by Ishtar! He's

going in a grog shop. But he has no money. How——"

A shocked thought came to him, and he felt hastily in his wallet. Then he cursed. "The drunken little ape! When he slashed my bonds, in the wizard's palace, he stole the purse! I'll——"

Elak sprang to his feet and took a stride forward. Soft arms gripped his leg. He looked down. "Eh?"

"Let him go," Coryllis said, smiling. "He's earned his mead."

"Yes—but what about me? I——"

"Let him go," Coryllis murmured. . . . And, ever after that, Lycon was to wonder why Elak never upbraided him about the stolen purse.

BEYOND THE PHOENIX

A tale of Elak of Atlantis, and an evil priest who was more than human and who worshipped a foul god—a tale of perilous sorcery and thrilling action

1. A King Dies

And the torchlight touched the pale hair
  Where silver clouded gold,
And the frame of his face was made of cords,
And a young lord turned among the lords
  And said: "The King is old."
                                    —G. K. Chesterton.

"I WON'T kill you quickly," said Lycon, a fierce grin of satisfaction on his round face. "No. I've suffered your insults too long. I must bring an offering each day to the altar of your stinking god, eh? An ear for that!"

He brought down his sword in a vicious sweep.

"Good! Now your nose, Xandar—you've sniffed out too many victims with it already. Thus——" Again steel flashed.

"And an eye, Xandar—see? I remove it with the point. Very carefully. For a copper coin I'd make you eat it."

"Drunken little fool," Elak said, coming over to the table. "Leave that roasted pig alone. It won't be fit to eat after you've finished carving it."

Lycon looked down at the succulent brown carcass on the great wooden platter. "I've not hurt it," he said sullenly.

"You'll be having us swinging by our necks if you keep yelling threats against Xandar. I don't like him any more than you do. But—under the king—he rules Sarhaddon."

This, unhappily, was true. Since the two adventurers had come to Sarhaddon, a little-known city in western Atlantis, they had risen high in the service of King Phrygior, eventually attaining posts in his personal bodyguard. But they had more than once incurred the dislike of the high priest, Xandar, perhaps because they were outlanders who had come from the seaport city of Poseidonia. At any rate, Xandar disliked the two, and took pains to make this clear. It was within his power to levy tribute from any citizen, and therefore Lycon's purse was usually empty. He stole as much as was safe from Elak, but the latter had lately become suspicious.

"I don't like this," Elak said now, his dark wolf-face set in harsh lines. "We're supposed to be with the king now., Always, when he's asleep, his men guard him. Yet the captain sends us down here to the kitchen to wait for—eh? A message, he said."

"This is as good a place as any," Lycon observed, draining a huge drinking-horn. "What foul mead! Twelve cups and I can still walk. It

"The two figures moved in a grotesque saraband to the tune of the evil drumming and the pipes."

was not like this in Poseidonia."

Elak turned away in disgust. He went to a mullioned window and stared down at the lights of the city, spreading over Sarhaddon Valley. Gaunt granite cliffs rose all about them, and a silver tracery near by marked the course of Syra River. It flowed under the castle, to disappear, so the tales went, into the Gates of the Phœnix, a place in which Elak did not believe, but in which every other inhabitant of the city did. He knew, of course, the traditional death-ceremony of the kings. Their bodies were placed aboard a royal barge, and set adrift on Syra—and returned, as the tavern stories went—to the land of their fathers beyond the Phœnix Gates.

Elak grunted softly and touched the hilt of a slim rapier that hung at his side.

"I'm going back," he said. "Wait if you want. I've a feeling——"

Without finishing, he hurried into the hall and up a winding stone stairway, followed by Lycon, who was gulping mead from a horn as he came. The staircase was a long one, for King Phrygior slept in a high tower that rose above the gray stone battlements of the castle. And the sound of furious battle came to Elak and made him whip out his rapier, snarling a bitter oath.

"Curse Lokar for a traitor!" he whispered, blade ready as he bounded up. Behind him the drinking-horn dropped from Lycon's hand and went clashing and ringing down; but the noise it made could not be heard above the tumult in the king's apartments. Elak gained the anteroom and stood for a moment staring.

At his side and below him the deep well of the tower dropped down, bounded by the winding staircase. Yet, somehow, it seemed to Elak that as he stared into the room a dozen feet away he was looking into the abyss of a pit even deeper— a bottomless well that stretched beyond infinity.

A blackness lay beyond the threshold, almost tangible in its tenebrous intensity. It was as though a jet curtain had been stretched across the doorway, barring entry.

Yet from beyond came the sound of battle, and abruptly the king's voice in a shout of agony.

Impulse rather than reason sent Elak forward, plunging across the threshold, breaking through the dark veil. For a brief instant the chill of polar lands clawed at his flesh, and he was blind. Then Elak was in the midst of a shambles, his sight restored, and as he saw from the corner of his eye the black curtain behind him had disappeared completely.

THE room was a wreck. Priceless tapestries had been torn down and lay in sword-ripped tatters, smeared with blood. Not a piece of furniture was upright. Above the familiar smell of incense rose the acrid odor of sweat and blood, and at Elak's feet a man lay with his throat torn open, rags of cartilage protruding from the ghastly wound. A dozen corpses were here—few men survived. One of these was Lokar, captain of the guard, who was just swinging his sword down in a stroke that would have decapitated Phrygior, who was clawing at an overturned table in a desperate endeavor to regain his feet.

Elak moved with lightning speed. His rapier, sword-arm and body formed one incredibly swift thrust of movement, and Lokar shouted and let go his sword, which clashed harshly on the stones as it fell. The giant soldier whirled, clutching an impaled wrist from which red spurted. He saw Elak, and bellowed wordless rage.

Ignoring his wounded arm, Lokar sprang for Elak. And Elak made a motion of giving ground, his rapier hanging loose. At the last moment the adventurer leaned forward, bracing one foot on the flagging, and whipped around the rapier-point with flashing, deadly speed. Lokar saw the danger too late. The slender blade ground into his eye, burst through the thin shell of bone, and sheathed itself in the man's brain.

"Look out—'ware, Elak!" Lycon shouted from the doorway. Elak swung about, teeth bared. One living enemy faced him—an unarmed man. Yet, inexplicably, Elak felt an icy shudder crawl down his spine at sight of this man—Xandar the priest.

He was a hunchback—yet no dwarf. His body, though warped and twisted hideously, was gigantic, and great muscles surged beneath the swarthy skin. Above the flattened, hairless head rose the hump, its horror strangely enhanced by the rich gold cloth that draped it. One side of the creature's face was a mangled, featureless slab of scar tissue, remnant of some long-past battle. The red lips, singularly shapely on the left side, widened into a shocking lipless hole on the other.

The monster roared, "Ho, you fool! Back! Swiftly!"

"I serve the king, not you, gargoyle," Elak

grunted, and lifted his weapon. At his feet Phrygior stirred, his white beard all slobbered and
bespattered with blood. And now Elak saw a
dagger's hilt embedded in the king's bare breast,
center of a widening crimson stain.

Again the priest bellowed, "Back! Back!"

And Elak, moving forward on cat-like feet,
hesitated. An indefinable warning tingled within
his brain. He paused, staring at Xandar.

Was it illusion? The monster's warped body
seemed to be growing larger, impossibly increas-
ing in bulk till it seemed to tower within the
room. Elak shook his head, cursing. What madness was this? He tried to peer at Xandar, and
found himself blinking through a dark, hazy
mist that slowly grew thicker. Wavering in the
dimness stood the shapeless pillar that was
Xandar, now shrinking, now swelling to Elak's
warped vision. Whence the fog had sprung he
did not know, but the subtle evil of it tore at the
fortress of his mind with warning fingers. There
was danger here—deadly danger. Strong in his
nostrils was a sickly-sweet smell, musky, somehow reminiscent of the odor of growing things—
but not things that grew in any healthy manner.
Rather the disgusting miasma of life that sprang
from foul corruption, fungi and lichen bursting
from spores and feeding on rotten carcasses. . .

He heard Lycon's hoarse breathing behind
him, and the sound brought back his courage.
Xandar was a vague shadow—but at that
shadow Elak lunged, rapier leveled. He felt himself smothered suddenly by a blacker darkness,

and found his breath stopped by the horrible, miasmic stench. Then there was the familiar feeling of flesh ripping under his steel, the grinding jar of metal clashing on bone, rippling up the rapier to his hand. From the priest burst a bellow of agony.

And the shout changed to words—a frantic cry in syllables Elak did not recognize, though their unearthly sound made him wonder. Grinning harshly, he once more sent steel arrowing through the shadow—vainly, this time.

And the darkness lifted, faded as though a veil had been withdrawn. Elak stood staring in the center of the room, gasping with amazement. He whirled.

"Lycon! Did he get past you?"

The little man shook his head, glancing at his heavy sword. "Ishtar, no! I'd have split him from pate to groin——"

"There must be a hidden passage in the wall," Elak said, and dropped beside the king. Phrygior's bearded lips parted to swallow the wine Elak forced between them. Eyes cold as gray stone looked into the adventurer's—and a blazing spark leaped into them.

"The priest! Kill him!"

"He's gone," Elak said. "The others——"

PHRYGIOR looked down, touched with weak fingers the dagger-hilt in his breast. He said hoarsely, "Leave it. To unsheathe it now would kill me in a moment. First I must——" He fumbled toward the wine-flask. "Esarra—my daughter—summon her."

Elak made a quick gesture. "Get the princess, Lycon. I'll guard the king."

"No need—now. Xandar has—accomplished his design." Elak held the flask to Phrygior's lips while the dying man drank deeply, and soon, strengthened, he began again.

"The priest has plotted against me for long, Elak. Some of his dogs were in my guard, and tonight they killed the ones who remained faithful. He has long desired the throne—and Esarra. But he dared not defy the Phœnix—the god of Sarhaddon's kings. Thus he sought aid—more wine, Elak. My blood drains fast. . . .

"So. Baal-Yagoth—you know not the name. Few remember, yet ages and ages ago when the gods dwelt on earth, Baal-Yagoth was the power of evil, the embodiment of dark lust. He sought to establish his dominion over the world, but in a great battle Assurah, the Phœnix, overthrew him, imprisoned him in the land of the gods . . . and now Assurah sleeps, and Xandar has called Baal-Yagoth out of the dark lands to rule Sarhaddon. Only a man crazed with venom and hatred would have dared, for the black god can have no power on earth till a human willingly opens up his soul and brain for Baal-Yagoth's dwelling-place. Within Xandar dwells his god."

Now Elak remembered what had happened when he had attacked the priest.

The king drank more wine. "My strength goes fast. Unless Esarra arrives speedily——" He stiffened in a spasm of agony. "Elak! I cannot wait!

Your arm——"

Elak extended his hand, and Phrygior seized it. From his own wrist he took a bracelet of black stone, on which were carved symbols Elak did not recognize. But on the largest lozenge was the outline of a Phœnix, eagle-shaped, rubies and gold aping the mythical bird's coloring. Swiftly the king snapped the bracelet on Elak's sinewy arm. It felt curiously cold.

Phrygior touched the phcenix with grotesque, archaic gestures. He murmured a phrase—and his grim face, already shadowed with death, lightened. "Only the Phœnix may unloose the sacred bracelet from your wrist now," he said quietly. "You must go to Assurah—beyond the Gates of the Phœnix. Listen well, Elak, for my strength ebbs.

"At the foot of this tower a tapestry is on the wall, with a dragon battling a basilisk. Touch the basilisk's eyes thrice. Once press the dragon's eyes. A door will open, and you must go through it with your companion, taking Esarra so she will not fall into Xandar's hands. A barge has long waited at the end of the passage you'll find—waited for my corpse. I would have you— take me with you. Esarra will guide you. She is of the Phœnix blood——"

Quite suddenly the indomitable will that had kept Phrygior alive failed. He gave a convulsive shudder, arching his back in agony, while froth bubbled on the white beard. Then he fell back and so died, scarcely an instant before Esarra and Lycon crossed the threshold.

The girl flew to her father's side, while Elak arose, eyeing Lycon's reddened sword. The small adventurer nodded briefly.

"More of Xandar's dogs. I killed 'em. The girl helped, too—her dagger drew blood as often as my sword. What now?"

There was little time to explain. A few words told Esarra how matters stood, and she hastened down the stairway, while Elak followed, bearing the corpse of the king. After him Lycon descended warily.

THE tower's floor seemed deserted, though from not far away came the clash of ringing steel and the shouts of men. The great tapestry stretched across one wall. Elak saw that the eyes of the basilisk and the dragon were gems, and he pressed these as Phrygior had commanded. With scarcely a sound one of the stone flags lifted, revealing a staircase leading down to blackness.

Lycon snatched a flambeau from its socket and led the way, while Elak, after a futile attempt to close the secret trapdoor, followed the girl. He eyed her curiously as her profile was from time to time outlined against the torchlight. A beauty, he thought. The regal cast of her face was softened by its warm humanity, and brown curls clung damply to her pale forehead. The slender, delicate curves of her body were scarcely hidden by the silken night-dress, ripped in more than one place so that ivory flesh shone through.

Behind him Elak heard the pound of foot-

steps; he called a warning, and the three hastened their pace. The stairs gave way to a corridor, stone-walled and dank, and this in turn
opened into a low-roofed, broad chamber. A narrow ledge ran around its base; below the ledge
was water, blackly ominous. A barge floated in
the huge pool.

Elak had but a glimpse of dark silks and velvets, a jewel-studded canopy that was a fitting
covering for a king's corpse. He leaped aboard
the barge, put down his burden, and whirled,
rapier out. A hasty glance around showed that
the cavern had but one other opening—metal
gates, corroded and green with verdigris, that
descended from the roof to below the water's
surface. Then from the tunnel-mouth burst the
pursuers—Xandar's men, swords red, baying
like hounds as they ran.

"Lycon! To me!" Elak shouted, but the little
man did not answer. The tall adventurer
bounded back to the ledge, spitting the foremost
attacker through the throat, and deftly wrenching the rapier free as the man fell to splash into
the water. He caught sight of Lycon and Esarra
working desperately at a great bar of metal—a
lever—that hung from the roof. Then Elak forgot
all else in a red blaze of battle.

Three men he slew, and was himself wounded
in the shoulder, while a flung blade missed his
jugular by an inch and sliced his cheek. There
was a grinding roar of hidden machinery, and
Elak heard a frantic shout from Lycon. He
turned to see the barge plunging away on the

breast of a descending torrent.

Ignoring the men who were now pressing in to the kill, Elak leaped. A spear screamed past his head as he jumped, and he saw it thud into the barge's side.

Ironically, that weapon saved him. He fell short, and his clutching fingers found the haft of the spear. For a second it held, and then Lycon's hands were on his wrists, tugging him to safety.

Above the barge rose the gaunt gray stones of the castle. Already the swift current had carried the craft beyond the door, and the three were safe from pursuit. It was, however, impossible to land, for there were neither poles nor oars. They drifted into a steadily deepening gorge, with the roar of the Syra rising into a thundering madness in their ears.

2. The Opening of the Gates

No growth of moor or coppice,
  No heather-flower or vine,
But bloomless buds of poppies,
  Green grapes of Proserpine,
Pale beds of blowing rushes,
Where no leaf blooms or blushes
Save this whereout she crushes
  For dead men deadly wine.
                        —Swinburne.

THE river raced into the heart of the mountains that surrounded Sarhaddon, till the blue sky was a brilliant narrow path above, jaggedly outlined by the towering scarps. The three on the barge could do nothing; it was impossible to talk below a shout. Nevertheless Elak explained to his companions what had happened.

"Ishtar!" Lycon screamed above the torrent's roar. "I never trusted that devil Xandar! Did you kill him, do you think?"

Elak shook his head. "Got his arm, I think. That's all." Reminded of his own arm, he began to dress it, while Esarra went to stand in the barge's prow, peering ahead into the mists beneath a pale, shading hand. It was her cry that brought the others.

"The Gates! The Phœnix Gates!"

Slowly they came into view through the clouds of spray, swimming into half-vividness and then fading again into fog, but growing ever closer—gates that towered up from the torrent, up and up for a hundred feet, constructed of metal that had never been stained or corroded by the unceasing drive of the water. Silvery-white they were, shot with pale bluish gleams. On their center was a Phœnix, huge as three men's height, red as the fiery heart of a ruby, yellow as the golden rivers that wash Cathay. Crest proudly raised, the stupendous effigy seemed to stare down upon Syra River—at the three on the barge. And the current drove the craft remorselessly toward the gates.

"Gods!" Elak said tonelessly, his voice lost in the thunder of the waters. "The river goes under the gates! We'll be dragged down——"

Esarra gripped his arm. "The bracelet! Let the

Phœnix see——"

Uncomprehendingly Elak let the girl lift his bare arm till the Phœnix bracelet gleamed distinctly through the mists. Was it merely his fancy that a brief, flashing ray of light seemed to leap out between bracelet and the image on the gates? If so, what followed was certainly not imagination. The gates opened. Silently they parted, disclosing glowing depths beyond them, and the barge raced through unharmed. Briefly it surged and, rocked with the current, and then steadied as the gates closed once more. It was oddly silent now. They were in a cavern, glowing with weird brilliance. Violet gleams played over the walls.

Without warning came the inexplicable. There was a flashing, swift movement, and abruptly the barge was surrounded by a transparent, circular wall that seemed to be rising from the waters all around. Elak looked about warily, ready to drag out his rapier at the first sign of danger.

The glass wall lifted. It drew together above the barge, forming a dome. What slight trace of sound had drifted through the Phœnix Gates from the bellowing river was lost completely. Deathly silence fell.

Elak said, "I don't like this. It's like a prison. Princess, what——"

Esarra shrugged slim shoulders. "Assurah knows! But the kings of Sarhaddon have traveled this road longer than men remember." Her gaze went to where Phrygior's body lay beneath the great jeweled canopy. There was a little sob in her voice as she went on, "The legends say that the first king of Sarhaddon came from the land of the Phœnix, and his offspring must return there after death. So——"

"'Ware!" Lycon yelped. "'Ware, Elak!"

Imperceptibly the water beneath the barge had drained away till the craft rested on a shell of crystal. Now Elak saw that they were within a huge transparent sphere—and a shudder of movement shook it as Lycon cried warning. One shudder—and the globe dropped. Instantly deep blackness blanketed them. There was no sense of motion; yet Elak felt strangely certain that the sphere was dropping—dropping—into unknown depths. A giddiness assailed him. He felt Esarra's soft body flung against him, and his arms tightened about her protectively. Then the weird feeling of movement, almost extra-sensory in its inexplicable certainty, grew stronger; from the Phœnix bracelet on his wrist alien magic flowed through him. The darkness lightened. He saw Lycon and Esarra peering around blindly, and knew that they were still blind.

The crystal sphere was dropping down a metallic shaft, the sides of which were merely a blurred gleaming as the speed increased. Briefly a flash of violent red burned Elak's eyeballs, and then came a blaze of pure, deadly white that sent him flat on his face, fists clenched against his agonized eyes. The sickening giddiness grew stronger—stronger yet——

And gratefully Elak let his mind sink into the black pit of unconsciousness that gaped for him.

He slept. . . .

NOW it seemed to Elak that he dreamed, or so he thought; for, though his eyes were closed, he clearly saw what occurred around him. There was at first only a thick shroud of fog, swirling slowly in drab grayness; and very slowly this mist faded and was gone. In its place was a cold, blue emptiness that seemed to stretch into infinite distances.

But it was not the sky, despite the gleaming points of light that swam into view like stars. That Elak knew. For the glowing specks grew brighter and larger, and he saw that they resembled flowers, many-petaled—yet no flowers of earth. With a cold and dreadful certainty he knew that they were alive.

They watched him, hanging motionless in the blue vastness, until the grip of nightmare clutched Elak. Nothing existed but these malefic flowers, it seemed, and they seemed to press toward him with avid hunger; they strained against the blueness that held them back. It was impossible to judge their size. They might have been small as a man's hand, and very close; or unimaginably huge and far away. They waited. . . .

Now the dream changed. A woman came into Elak's range of vision, slim and dark and vital as a black flame. Red as her lips was the gown she wore, and her eyes and long tresses were midnight black. With slow footsteps she came to stand beside Elak, and in her hand, he saw, she bore a strangely-filigreed chalice. Thin steam ascended from it.

She bent over Elak. The gray mists swirled back, blinding, confusing. Out of the fog loomed the woman's face, arrogantly handsome; her pale hand, and the goblet it bore. She lifted it to Elak's mouth. A cloying fragrance crept into his nostrils, and involuntary repugnance shuddered through him. The liquor's aroma was subtly sweet. A drop of the fluid touched his lips, and a hot pang raced through every atom of his body.

"Tyrala!"

On the word the woman drew back, hell-flames flaring in her eyes. She whirled to face a figure who came slowly through the mists.

It was a man, small but delicately proportioned, clad in tight-fitting silver garments, and, seeing him, Elak was reminded of the Northmen's god Baldur. The fineness of his beardless face was at variance with a certain assured strength in the dark, lazily amused eyes.

He said again, "Tyrala, your haste is ill-advised. I had not known of this man's arrival."

The woman stood rigid, clutching the chalice with white fingers. She hesitated, asked, "Since when have you stooped to interesting yourself in my slaves, Ithron?"

The man's smile was malicious. "But is he one of yours? The men of Nyrvana are pale and yellow-haired, even as myself. This one is dark and lean as a wolf. Moreover, he wears a certain sign. . . ."

Tyrala glanced at the bracelet on Elak's wrist. For a moment fear shone in her eyes, but she said nothing.

The man, Ithron, chuckled. "And I think there were others from above, too. Have you forgotten the pact? We two rule over Nyrvana—we two, not you alone. Shall we not judge these intruders—*together?*"

"Aye," Tyrala said presently, though her face was somber and menacing. "As you will. . . ."

Now the fog closed down again, and darkened into blackness. For a space Elak was unconscious, and he awoke slowly, with an unfamiliar, nauseating taste on his tongue. He sat up, spitting and cursing. From near by came the sound of Lycon's snores.

The two were lying on low tapestried couches set side by side in the center of a great windowless room. Hangings of red samite hid the walls. From the ceiling was suspended a silvern lamp that cast a vague yellowish radiance. Otherwise the chamber was empty.

Elak got heavily to his feet and kicked Lycon off his couch. "Wake up!" he commanded. "We might have had our throats slit as you slept, drunken little dog."

"More mead," murmured the drunken little dog, still apparently engrossed in vinous dreams. "Alas, the cup is empty. . . ."

Elak hauled his companion upright by the scruff of the neck. "I said 'wake up'," he grunted. "We're in some wizard's den or other, and your sword may be needed. I see you've still got it." He glanced down with satisfaction at the slim rapier at his own belt.

Lycon opened mildly disapproving eyes. "Our throats are safe, for a while anyhow. They had plenty of time to kill you, if they'd wanted to, last night."

"What d'you mean?"

"That I woke up to find myself alone in here. I hammered on the door and swore in seven languages, but vainly. So, as there was nothing better to do, I went to sleep again."

"Where's the princess?" Elak asked suddenly. Lycon shrugged.

"How should I know? Wait till somebody opens the door, Elak. Then we can use our blades. Until then——" He left the sentence unfinished. A low throbbing musical note sounded, and simultaneously a slit widened in the farther wall.

A man stood in the gap, yellow-haired, slightly built, wearing a loose robe of scarlet. He was unarmed. He lifted his arm in a beckoning gesture.

Elak's hand was on his rapier hilt as he moved forward. "Where are we?" he asked shortly. "Where's——"

"You will come with me," the other said. Elak paused at the expression in the man's blue eyes. They seemed, somehow, withdrawn, as though they looked upon invisible things. No hint of curiosity stirred in their depths. Vaguely, absently, the man looked at Elak, and he said again, "Come."

Lycon swaggered to the threshold. "Lead on," he commanded. "But you'd best play no tricks.

My sword's sharp!"

The red-robed one turned, led the way along a corridor of white stone, windowless and door-less. Elak and Lycon followed, down the passage, up a winding staircase, lit with the cool pallor of hanging lamps, and down a sloping hall to a door of bronze. A gong clanged, peremptory, harsh. The portals opened.

Beyond the threshold was a great room, high-ceilinged, paved with strangely figured mosaic. Blue smoke drifted up from censers. At the farther end of the room was a dais, and upon it—two thrones.

A throne of gleaming metal, red as sunset-clouds, black-cushioned. And one of pale silver. In the silver seat was a man Elak recognized, small and blond, with lazily amused eyes. In the red throne sat a woman.

Tyrala! Elak did not need to see the goblet on a pedestal at her right hand to recognize her. The black eyes watched enigmatically; slim white figures and ivory shoulders gleamed against the blaze of crimson that was Tyrala's robe.

Above the thrones and between them, high on the wall, was a phœnix, delicately carved. Coils of incense slid past the jutting beak.

ELAK'S guide gestured him on. Slowly the two men walked toward the dais. As they paused before it Elak caught a flash of movement from the corner of his eye; he turned to see Esarra hurrying toward them, while another of the slim, yellow-haired men stood watchfully beside an open door.

"Elak!" The girl's face was white against the clustering chestnut curls; she clung to Elak, trembling a little. A silver gown had replaced the shredded night-dress, and there were silver slippers on the princess's small feet.

"Elak!" she said breathlessly. "I was afraid——"

Now Esarra saw the two upon the thrones. She swung to face them, shrinking against Elak's protective arm about her waist.

The red-clad woman, Tyrala, glanced aside at her companion. She spoke in an undertone. The man nodded. He leaned forward.

"Have no fear," he said. "You have suffered no injury as yet—is that not so?"

Now Elak remembered his vision. He said, "Perhaps we have you to thank for that—Ithron."

The woman caught her breath. Ithron's eyebrows lifted.

"Perhaps," was his only comment. "However, strangers come to Nyrvana seldom. The Kings of Sarhaddon—yes. They are of the Phœnix blood. But they come only after death, and not for many ages—aye, longer than you think!—have living men come from above."

"I don't understand you," Elak said. "Where are we? Last I remember was falling down a hole in some damned cavern—are we underground?"

"Aye," Ithron nodded. "You are in Nyrvana. Far and far is this land from the world above; Nyrvana is within a cave, but a cave so vast you could not span its breadth or height with your eyes."

Esarra whispered, "The land of the gods! Where Assurah dwells——" She looked up at the sculptured Phœnix.

"And we rule under Assurah," Ithron said, "Tyrala and I. Before the Phœnix slept, he gave us this charge: to rule Nyrvana and to guard—guard——" He hesitated, glanced at Tyrala. The woman's baleful gaze dwelt on Elak.

"They are here for judgment," she said. "Well? Let us judge!"

"Why are you here?" Ithron asked.

Esarra pulled free from Elak. Standing erect before the dais, regal head raised proudly, she told her story. And as she spoke, Tyrala's gaze grew darker and more ominous, while startled amazement, crept into Ithron's eyes.

"So Xandar rules Sarhaddon," the girl finished. "And he has slain my father. The law of the Phœnix has been broken. Baal-Yagoth has been freed from his chains——"

"Now by Assurah!" Ithron whispered—and his pale eyes were wide now, and blazing as he glared at the enthroned woman beside him. "By Assurah and Iod! This is your work, Tyrala!"

Tyrala sprang up, her slim fingers flexing into claws. She spat words at the man.

"Aye—my work! And what of that? It has been long since Assurah ruled, and he has no power now. Shall I rule over this land of shadows for ever, with these pallid slaves of yours to serve me—to drink my wine——"

Elak saw a touch of horror in Ithron's face as he glanced at the chalice beside Tyrala's throne.

The woman went on bitterly,

"And if I have called on Baal-Yagoth—what then, my lord Ithron? Who are you to halt me? Serve Assurah then, if you will—rule over Nyrvana! But I have made a pact with a priest of Sarhaddon, and for him I have freed Baal-Yagoth from his chains. Soon now I shall go to the outer world, where there are strong men— men with flame and life blazing within them, like this one here"—she flung out her hand toward Elak—"and they shall taste my wine!"

"Stop!" Ithron was facing the woman now, his face grim and hard. "You dare—under the very symbol of Assurah——"

"Aye—I dare! Nor can you thwart me, Ithron. Now I warn you—stay here. Rule Nyrvana. But if you think to meddle with my plans, you may taste my wine yourself!"

Laughing, Tyrala swept down from the dais, across the room and through open doors of bronze. Ithron turned, flung up his arms at the carven Phœnix on the wall. His voice was a rolling thunder.

"Assurah! Waken! Let your wrath pour down upon this harlot and utterly destroy her!"

The incense drifted up. . . .

"Lord of Nyrvana—waken! Baal-Yagoth is risen from his prison and hangs like a shadow over all the world. Smite him with your lightnings; rend him with your iron beak!

"Assurah—god of Sarhaddon! *Waken!*"

3. Duel of Gods

The night is gone and the sword is drawn
And the scabbard is thrown away!
—John G. Neihardt.

VERY slowly the wall behind the thrones began to move. It slid up, the Phœnix rising with it, and revealed a hazy depth beyond, dimly litten with silver radiance. Ithron turned.

"You three—follow."

He moved forward confidently. Elak hesitated, felt Essara tug at his arm. Warily he went toward the gap where the wall had been. Lycon trailed them. His sword brushed the pedestal beside Tyrala's throne, set the goblet rocking. He glanced at it and shuddered.

"Ishtar! I would not taste that wine——"

They stood in glowing haze. The wall dropped behind them. Nothing existed now but silvery fog; somehow Elak had a weird feeling that they stood on the very brink of a gulf that fell away to abysmal depths.

At their feet lay an open coffin. In it was King Phrygior, his dead face relaxed and peaceful. He wore a white robe, and an unsheathed sword rested on his breast.

Esarra dropped to her knees beside the sarcophagus. She whispered something Elak did not hear. Her brown curls fell forward, hiding the cameo face.

Ithron touched the coffin; it slid forward and was gone. The silver mists brightened. Far below came the rolling of deep thunder.

And behind them—the clash of arms! A

woman's voice, commanding, angry.

Ithron turned swiftly, gripped Elak's arm. "Your bracelet! Hold it—thus——" He lifted Elak's wrist. "Stay, here! Tyrala is mad. But her madness gives her strength; I must keep her at bay till Assurah wakes——"

He was gone. A deep-throated roar came faintly to Elak's ears. Dimly he heard Ithron's voice.

But nothing existed but the mist, and two shadows beside him—Esarra and Lycon, waiting . . . and Elak stood with his arm raised, the Phœnix bracelet shining. . . .

Queer tingles darted through his wrist, ran down into his shoulder, racing into every nerve of his body. Flood of power poured into him, shaking the citadel of his mind with its alien strength. . . .

The fog alternately darkened and lightened; the muttering of thunder grew louder. And dimly he heard Tyrala's voice raised in a cry of triumph from the throneroom beyond the wall.

"I have won, my lord Ithron! None can waken Assurah now. And you—you shall taste my wine!"

The thunder bellowed ominously. The fog brightened with a blaze of silver radiance, and before him Elak saw something rise up, a cyclopean shadow, almost formless, yet with a suggestion of sweeping wings and a beaked, upthrust head. . . .

He heard Esarra cry out, felt Lycon drop to his knees, breath rasping in his throat. From the

Phœnix bracelet a tide of primal magic raced through him. The colossal shadow waited in the mist.

Elak felt words rising to his lips without will of his own. He heard himself crying,

"Assurah! Baal-Yagoth is risen! He has burst his chains—"

Elak was never to understand what happened in the next amazing moment. The power that the bracelet had given him was nothing to the inconceivable flood that crashed down on him from the risen god—flood of strange magic, blinding and deafening him, flaming through his brain like lightning. And dimly he heard a voice within his mind,

"I give you strength. Go Forth and slay!"

Forthwith the tide lifted Elak and bore him weightless back; he had a vague impression of walls and rooms flickering past like segments of a dream, and yet he knew, somehow, that Esarra and Lycon kept pace with him, shoulder to shoulder. Something was in his mind, and Elak's fingers closed about the hilt of a sword—a blade of flame, white and terrible. All about him the very air shook with unimaginable power. . . .

Elak's vision cleared; he stood in a room and remembered—the room of his dream, where he had first seen Tyrala. The walls were blue as infinity, and in that clear depth hung the glowing flowerthings he had already seen. Avidly they waited with a horrible air of expectation in their attitude, seemingly watching the horror before them.

A muffled drumming throbbed out; shrill insane flutings piped weirdly. There were monstrously misshapen beings that squatted on
scaled haunches, demoniac toad-like creatures
whose flaming eyes dwelt on the two figures that
danced before an altar.

Tyrala—and Ithron! Both nude, Ithron's pale
body in strange contrast to the dark vividness of
the witch-woman—and Ithron dancing, whirling
like a weightless leaf in Tyrala's grasp. An empty
goblet lay on the stones. Ithron had tasted the
dreadful wine!

The two figures moved in a swift, grotesque
saraband, to the tune of the evil drumming and
the pipes. The flower-things in the walls waited.
And as Tyrala and Ithron danced, the strength
seemed to be draining from the man—the life itself—pouring as though sucked by evil vampir-
ism into the body of the witch.

Ithron grew shrunken, paper-white, skeletal.
And Tyrala's vivid body seemed to drink in life—
whirling and swaying with increased energy.
Sparks danced eerily in her streaming black
hair. Her eyes were pools of lambent radiance.

"Strike!" a voice whispered in Elak's mind.

He scarcely seemed to move, yet the flaming
sword in his hand swung up. From its blade
poured a cascade of light-flings, crackling, flashing, veiling the room with light. Through the
blaze he heard Tyrala's scream, knife-edged,
keening with an agony beyond life. . . .

And other cries came, thin, utterly horrible.
He knew that the glowing flower-things were dy-

ing. . . .

THE curtain of light faded. And now nothing existed within the chamber but an altar, blackened and twisted; the walls were burned and blank, and there were mounds of dust on the floor.

The power caught Elak again, lifting him. He caught a momentary glimpse of a broad vista spread far beneath him, a land of sluggish rivers and dark forests stretching into the distance—and it was gone. Brief blackness, and then a flash of metallic walls sliding past, a shaft up which he sped with frightful rapidity, knowing Esarra and Lycon were beside him. . . .

A cavern now, and high gates. A river, under the warm radiance of the sun, tumbling through a craggy gorge. Then a valley—and Sarhaddon, the castles and walls of Sarhaddon, lay beneath him, and he was slanting down through empty air. . . .

Down he swept, through gates and walls and barriers, until he stood in the throneroom of Sarhaddon's kings. On the great carven chair, ornate with gems and precious metals, sat Xandar the priest, his twisted body hung with royal robes. A circlet of gold crowned the bald head. The scarred half of the priest's face was deftly disguised with paints that could not hide the frightful deformity.

A girl lay before the throne, strapped to an engine of torture. Her body was reddened with sword-cuts. She was screaming as cords slowly wrenched her limbs apart.

147

Around the room stood nobles and priests. On almost every face Elak saw thinly-hidden horror and disgust. One man turned away, and Xandar saw him.

"Ho, you Chemoch!" he roared. "Are you daintier than your king? Would you share this maiden's couch?"

White-faced, the man looked again at the tortured girl. Yet his hand closed convulsively on his sword-hilt.

And then—the voice whispered again in Elak's mind.

"Slay!"

Elak lifted his blade. A great cry went up within the throneroom; the crowd surged back against the tapestried walls. If they had not seen Elak before—he was surely visible now!

The monster on the throne thrust out clawing hands. He bellowed,

"Baal-Yagoth! Yagoth!"

A cloudy veil swept down over the priest, hiding him in shadow like a shroud. A foul, miasmic stench was strong in Elak's nostrils. He swung the sword.

Lightnings blazed out crashing. They thundered down on the priest, enveloping him in flame. They licked at his armor of black fog, and drew back—impotent!

The air was choked with that charnel smell. The darkness crept out from the priest, fingering toward Elak. Again he lifted his sword.

Again the lightnings flared. And this time Elak moved forward, confidently, doggedly, slashing with blade of fire at the dark tendrils that crept in toward him. As he neared Xandar a cold revulsion shuddered through Elak's flesh. He sensed the nearness of an alien thing, a being so evil that it could exist only in the blackness of the pit.

Lightning and shadow clashed, and the castle rocked with thunderous conflict. The priest roared insane blasphemy.

THE blackness coalesced into a tenebrous cloud. Out of it rose a head, malefic and terrible, with serpent eyes of ancient evil. A flattened head that swayed and arose on shimmering scaled coils

The head of Baal-Yagoth!

It swung down at Elak. He countered desperately with his sword—felt himself driven back.

The shadow of cyclopean wings filled the throneroom with rushing winds. Something, unseen yet tangible, dropped toward that monstrous head. A blinding flare of consuming light crashed out, and for a brief moment Elak saw a gleam of blood-red feathers, eyes golden as the moon, and a striking silver beak.

And the shadow surrounding Xandar faded and was gone. The rearing serpenthead had vanished. Only the priest stood before the throne, stripped of his magic and his power, contorted lips wide in a despairing shriek. His face was a Gorgon mask, seared and blackened into a charred cindery horror.

Eyes of insane rage glared at Elak. The priest

sprang forward, hands clawing for Elak's throat.

Once more, and for the last time, the alien voice whispered within Elak's brain.

"Strike!"

Sword of flame screamed through the air. Bone and brain and flesh split under that blow, and for a second Xandar stood swaying, cloven in half from skull to navel, blood spurting in a red tide. A moment the priest stood, and crashed down at Elak's feet dead in a widening crimson pool.

From the court a great cry went up—of triumph and thanksgiving. Elak felt the sword plucked from his hand; it was a flash of light in the air—and then was gone. He stood alone before the throne of Sarhaddon.

The magic had fled. Power of the Phœnix and evil spell of Baal-Yagoth alike were vanished. The nobles pressed forward, shouting.

Elak turned, saw Esarra cutting the last of the cords that bound Xandar's victim to her rack. A guardsman lifted the sobbing girl, bore her out. Esarra obeyed Elak's gesture.

He led her to the throne, seated her in it, and on her slender wrist clasped the Phœnix bracelet he took from his own arm. Elak swung to face the room. His rapier came out, was lifted.

And a hundred swords were unsheathed, shimmering together, at his shout,

"Esarra of Sarhaddon!"

"Esarra!" roared the nobles.

They dropped to their knees, heads bent, paying homage to the girl. But Elak felt a soft hand on his shoulder as he knelt, and looked up into Esarra's eyes. The girl whispered,

"Elak—you will stay in Sarhaddon?"

Slowly he nodded, and Esarra sank back on her throne, a little smile curving her red lips, as the nobles arose and came forward one by one, sword-hilts extended for her touch. Elak made his way through the group, looking for Lycon He found him at last investigating the contents of a drinking-horn.

"We stay in Sarhaddon—for a while anyhow," he told the little man.

"As you will," Lycon said, smiling wisely. He glanced toward the throne. "No doubt you'll be content enough for a few moons. As for me"—he buried his round face in the horn and gulped noisily—"as for me," he finished, wiping his mouth with a pudgy hand, "I hear good reports of the royal wine-cellars. And may the gods blast me if I don't get the keys to 'em before sunset!"

"Through the room a cry rose and mounted,
wordless, fearful."

DRAGON MOON

Out of the dark—out of the unknown—came Karkora . . . rotting the souls of the kings of Cyrena. For Karkora, the Pallid One, was a creature more loathsome than anything on earth. It was beyond good or evil, a Presence from the Outside—a shadow of which the "altar fires had whispered."

1. Elak of Atlantis

Of great limbs gone to chaos,
    A great face turned to night—
Why bend above a shapeless shroud
Seeking in such archaic, cloud
        Sight of strong lords and light?
                —Chesterton.

THE wharf-side tavern was a bedlam. The great harbor of Poseidonia stretched darkly to the southeast, but the waterfront was a blaze of bright lanterns and torches. Ships had made port today, and this tavern, like the others, roared with mirth and rough nautical oaths. Cooking-smoke and odor of sesame filled the broad low room, mingled with the sharp tang of wine. The swarthy seamen of the south held high carnival tonight.

In a niche in the wall was an image of the patron god, Poseidon of the sunlit seas. It was noticeable that before swilling liquor, nearly every man spilled a drop or two on the floor in the direction of the carved god.

A fat little man sat in a corner and muttered under his breath. Lycon's small eyes examined the tavern with some distaste. His purse was, for a change, heavy with gold; so was that of Elak, his fellow adventurer. Yet Elak preferred to drink and wench in this brawling, smelly tavern, a prediliction that filled Lycon with annoyance and bitterness. He spat, muttered under his breath, and turned to watch Elak.

The lean, wolf-faced adventurer was quarreling with a sea captain whose huge, great-muscled body dwarfed Elak's. Between the two a tavern wench was seated, her slanted eyes watching the men slyly, flattered by the attention given her.

The seaman, Drezzar, had made the mistake of underestimating Elak's potentialities. He had cast covetous eyes upon the wench and determined to have her, regardless of Elak's prior claim. Under other circumstances Elak might have left the slant-eyed girl to Drezzar, but the captain's words had been insulting. So Elak remained at the table, his gaze wary, and his rapier loosened in its scabbard.

He watched Drezzar, noting the sunburnt, massive face, the bushy dark beard, the crinkled scar that swept down from temple to jawbone, blinding the man in one gray eye. And Lycon, called for more wine. Steel would flash soon, he knew.

Yet the battle came without warning. A stool was overturned, there was a flare of harsh oaths, and Drezzar's sword came out, flaming in the lamplight. The wench screamed shrilly and fled, having little taste for bloodshed save from a distance.

Elak crouched catlike, his rapier motionless in his hand. A glint of angry laughter shone in the cold eyes.

Drezzar feinted; his sword swept out in a treacherously low cut that would have disemboweled Elak had it reached its mark. But the smaller man's body writhed aside in swift, flowing motion; the rapier shimmered. Its point gashed Drezzar's scalp.

They fought in silence. And this, more than anything else, gave Elak the measure of his opponent. Drezzar's face was quite emotionless. Only the scar stood out white and distinct. His blinded eye seemed not to handicap him in the slightest degree.

Lycon waited for a chance to sheathe his steel in Drezzar's back. Elak would disapprove, he knew, but Lycon was a realist.

Elak's sandal slipped in a puddle of spilled

liquor, and he threw himself aside desperately, striving to regain his balance. He failed. Drezzar's lashing sword drove the rapier from his hand, and Elak went down, his head cracking sharply on an overturned stool.

The seaman poised himself, sighted down his blade, and lunged. Lycon was darting forward, but he knew he could not reach the killer in time.

And then—from the open door came the inexplicable. Something like a streak of flaming light lashed through the air, and at first Lycon thought it was a thrown dagger. But it was not. It was—flame!

White flame, darting and unearthly! It gripped Drezzar's blade, coiled about it, ripped it from the seaman's hand. It blazed up in blinding fiery light, limning the room in starkly distinct detail. The sword fell uselessly to the floor, a blackened, twisted stump of melted metal.

Drezzar shouted an oath. He stared at the ruined weapon, and his bronzed face paled. Swiftly he whirled and fled through a side door.

The flame had vanished. In the door a man stood—a gross, ugly figure clad in the traditional brown robe of the Druids.

Lycon, skidding to a halt, lowered his sword and whispered, "Dalan!"

Elak got to his feet, rubbing his head ruefully. At sight of the Druid his face changed. Without a word he nodded to Lycon and moved toward the door.

The three went out into the night.

2. Dragon Throne.

Now we are come to our Kingdom,
And the Crown is ours to take
With a naked sword at the Council board,
And under the throne the snake,
Now we are come to our Kingdom!
—Kipling.

"I BRING you a throne," Dalan said, "but you must hold it with your blade."

They stood at the end of a jetty, looking out at the moonlit harbor waters. The clamor of Poseidonia seemed far away now.

Elak stared at the hills. Beyond them, leagues upon leagues to the north, lay a life he had put behind him. A life he had given up when he left Cyrena to gird on an adventurer's blade. In Elak's veins ran the blood of the kings of Cyrena, northernmost kingdom of Atlantis, And, but for a fatal quarrel with his stepfather, Norian, Elak would have been on the dragon throne even then. But Norian had died, and Elak's brother, Orander, took the crown.

Elak said, "Orander rules Cyrena. Do you ask me to join a rebellion against my brother?" An angry light showed in the adventurer's cold eyes,

"Orander is dead," the Druid said quietly. "Elak, I have a tale to tell you, a tale of sorcery and black evil that has cast its shadow over Cyrena. But first—" He fumbled in his shapeless brown robe and drew forth a tiny crystal sphere. He cupped it in his palm, breathed upon it. The clear surface clouded, misted—and the fog seemed to permeate the entire globe. The Druid held a ball of whirling gray cloud in his hand.

Within the sphere a picture grew, microscopic but vividly distinct. Elak peered closely. He saw a throne, and a man who sat upon it.

"South of Cyrena, beyond the mountains, lies Kiriath," Dalan said. "Sepher ruled it. And now Sepher still sits upon his throne, but he is no longer human."

In the globe the face of Sepher sprang out in startling clarity. Involuntarily Elak drew back, his lips thinning. At a casual glance Sepher seemed unchanged, a blackbearded, bronzed giant with the keen eyes of a hawk, but Elak knew that he looked upon a creature loathsome beyond anything on earth. It was not evil, as he knew it, but a thing beyond good and evil as it was beyond humanity or deity. A Presence from Outside had touched Sepher and taken Kiriath's king for its own. And Elak knew this was the most horrible being he had ever seen.

Dalan hid the crystal. He said coldly, "Out of the unknown has come a being named Karkora. What he is I know not. I have cast the runes, and they say little to me. The altar fires have whispered of a shadow that will come upon Cyrena, a shadow that may spread over all Atlantis. Karkora, the Pallid One, is not human, nor is he a demon. He is—alien, Elak."

"What of my brother?" the adventurer asked.

"You have seen Sepher," Dalan said. "He is possessed, a vessel of this entity called Karkora.

Ere I left Orander, he, too, had—changed."

A muscle twitched in Elak's brown cheek. The Druid went on.

"Orander saw his doom. Day by day the power of Karkora over him increased, and the soul of your brother was driven further into the outer dark. He died—by his own hand."

Elak's face did not change expression. But for minutes he was silent, a deep sorrow in his gray eyes.

Lycon turned to look out across the sea.

The Druid went on, "Orander sent a message to you, Elak. You, in all Atlantis, are of the royal line of Cyrena. Yours, therefore, is the crown. It will not be easy to hold. Karkora is not defeated. But my magic will aid you."

Elak said, "You offer me the dragon throne?"

Dalan nodded.

"The years have changed me, Dalan. I have gone through Atlantis a vagabond and worse. I put my birthright behind me and forgot it. And I'm not the same man who went from Cyrena years ago," Elak said softly, laughing a little bitterly, and looking over the jetty's edge at his face reflected in the dark swell of the water. "Only a king may sit on the dragon throne. For me—it would be a jest. And a sorry one."

"You fool!" the Druid whispered—and there was rage in the sibilant sound. "Blind, mad fool! Do you think the Druids would offer Cyrena to the wrong man? Blood of kings is in your veins, Elak. It is not yours to deny. You must obey."

"Must?" The word was spoken lightly, yet Lycon felt a tenseness go through him, tightening his muscles. "Must?" Elak asked.

"The decision is mine, Druid. By Mider! The throne of Cyrena means much to me. Therefore I shall not sit in it!"

Dalan's toad face was gargoylish in the moonlight. He thrust his bald, glistening head forward, and his thick, stubby fingers twisted.

"Now am I tempted to work magic on you, Elak," he said harshly. "I am no—"

"I have given you my answer."

The Druid hesitated. His somber eyes dwelt on Elak. Then, without a word, he turned and went lumbering off into the night. His footsteps died.

Elak remained staring out at the harbor. His cheeks were gray, his mouth a tortured white line. And he whirled, abruptly, and looked at the hills of Poseidonia.

But he did not see them. His gaze went beyond them, far and far, probing through all Atlantis to the kingdom of the north—Cyrena, and the dragon throne.

3. The Gates of Dream

Churel and ghoul and Djinn and sprite
Shall bear us company tonight,
For we have reached the Oldest Land
Wherein the powers of Darkness range.
—Kipling.

ELAK'S sleep that night was broken by dreams—

flashing, disordered visions of many things. He stared up at the white moonlit ceiling of the apartment. And—it was changed. The familiar room was gone. Light still existed, but it was oddly changed—grayish and unreal. Unearthly planes and angles slipped past Elak, and in his ears a low humming grew. This changed to a high-pitched, droning whine, and died away at last.

The mad planes reassembled themselves. In his dream Elak saw a mighty crag upthrust against cold stars—colossal against a background of jagged mountain peaks. Snow dappled them, but the darkness of the crag was unbroken. On its top was a tower, dwarfed by distance.

A flood seemed to lift Elak and bear him swiftly forward. In the base of the crag, he saw, were great iron gates. And these parted and swung aside, yawning for him as he moved through.

They shut silently behind him.

And now Elak became conscious of a Presence. It was stygian black; yet in the tenebrous darkness there was a vague inchoate stirring, a sense of motion that was unmistakable.

Without warning Elak saw—the Pallid One!

A white and shining figure flashed into view. How tall it was, how close or distant, the man could not tell. Nor could he see more than the bare outline. A crawling, leprous shimmer of cold light rippled over the being; it seemed little more than a white shadow. But a shadow—

three-dimensional, alive!

The unearthly terror of Karkora, the Pallid One!

The being seemed to grow larger. Elak knew he was watched, coldly and dispassionately. His senses were no longer dependable. It did not seem as though he beheld Karkora with his eyes alone—he was no longer conscious of his body.

He remembered Dalan, and Dalan's god. And he cried silently upon Mider for aid.

The shuddering loathing that filled him did not pass, but the horror that tore at his mind was no longer as strong. Again he cried to Mider, forcing himself to concentrate on the Druid god.

Once more Elak called out to Mider. And, silently, eerily, a wall of flame rose about him, shutting off the vision of Karkora. The warm, flickering fires of Mider were a protective barrier—earthly, friendly.

They closed in—drew him back. They warmed the chill horror that froze his mind. They changed to sunlight—and the sunlight was slanting in through the window, beside which Elak lay on his low bed, awake and shuddering with reaction.

"By the Nine Hells!" he cursed, leaping up swiftly. "By all the gods of Atlantis! Where's my rapier?" He found it, and whirled it hissing through the air. "How can a man battle dreams?"

He turned to Lycon, slumbering noisily nearby, and kicked the small man into wakefulness.

"Hog-swill," said Lycon, rubbing his eyes. "Bring another cup, and swiftly, or I'll—eh? What's wrong?"

ELAK was dressing hastily. "What's wrong? Something I didn't expect. How could I know from Dalan's words the sort of thing that's come to life in Atlantis?" He spat in disgust, "That leprous foulness shall never take the dragon throne!"

He slammed his rapier into its scabbard. "I'll find Dalan. I'll go back with him. To Cyrena."

Elak was silent, but deep in his eyes was a black horror and loathing. He had seen the Pallid One. And he knew that never in words could he hope to express the burning foulness of alien Karkora.

But Dalan had vanished. It was impossible to find the Druid in teeming Poseidonia. And at last Elak gave up hope and determined to take matters into his own hands. A galley called Kraken was leaving that day, he learned, and would beat up the western coast. In fact, by the time Elak had hired a boatman to take him and Lycon to the vessel, the galley's oars were already dipping into the swells.

Elak's cockleshell gained its side, and he clambered over the gunwale, hoisting Lycon after him. He tossed a coin to the boatman and saw the man depart.

THE sweating backs of slaves were moving rhythmically under the lash of the overseers.

One of these came forward at a run, his bronzed face angry.

"Who are you?" he hailed. "What do you seek on the Kraken?"

"Take us to your captain," Elak said shortly, His hand touched the heavy purse at his belt, and coins jingled. The overseer was impressed.

"We're putting to sea," he said. "What do you want?"

"Passage to Cyrena," Lycon snapped. "Be—"

"Bring them here, Rasul," a gruff voice broke in. "They are friends. We'll give them passage to Cyrena—aye!"

And Drezzar, Elak's opponent in the tavern brawl, hastened along the poop toward them, teeth gleaming in his bushy beard.

"Ho!" he yelled at a nearby group of armed seamen. "Seize those two! Take them—alive!" "You dog," Drezzar said with cold rage. He stood before Elak and lifted his hand as though to strike the captive.

Elak said stoically, "I want passage to Cyrena. I'll pay well for it."

"So you will," Drezzar grinned, and ripped off Elak's purse. He opened it and ran golden coins through his thick fingers. "You'll work for it, too. But you'll not reach Cyrena."

"Two more oarsmen for you, Rasul. Two more slaves. "See that they work!"

He turned and strode away. Unresisting, Elak was dragged to a vacant oar and chained there, Lycon shackled beside him. His hands fell in well-worn grooves on the polished wood.

Rasul's whip cracked. The overseer called, "Pull! Pull!"

The Kraken sped seaward. And, chained to his oar, straining at the unaccustomed toil, Elak's dark wolf-face bore a smile that was not pleasant to see.

4. The Ship Sails North

Orpheus has harped her,
Her prow has sheared the spray,
Fifty haughty heroes at her golden oarlocks
    sway,
White the wave before her flings,
Bright from shore she lifts and swings,
Wild he twangs the ringing strings—
Give way! Give way!
                                                    —Benet.

THEY drove down along the coast and the southern tip of Atlantis. Then the galley crept northwest, up the long curve of the continent, and all the while the days were cloudless and fair, and the skies blue as the waters of the Ocean Sea.

Elak bided his time until the Kraken dropped anchor one afternoon at an uninhabited island, to replenish the water supply. Drezzar went ashore with a dozen others, leaving only a few men in charge of the ship. This was apparently safe enough, with the slaves chained. Moreover, Drezzar had the only keys. But, at sunset, Elak nudged Lycon awake and told him to keep

167

watch.

"What for?" Lycon's voice was surly. "Do you—" He broke off, staring, as Elak took a tiny twisted bit of metal from his sandal and inserted it delicately in the lock of his ankle-cuff. "Gods!" Lycon cursed. "You had that all the time—and you waited till now!"

"These locks are easy to pick," Elak said. "What? Of course I waited! We've only a few enemies aboard now, instead of more than a dozen. Keep watch, I tell you."

Lycon obeyed. Footsteps creaked upon the deck occasionally, and there were lanterns here and there on the ship, but their illumination was faint enough. The lapping of water against the hull drowned the soft scrape and click as Elak worked. Presently he sighed in satisfaction and opened the cuff.

Metal clicked and scraped. Elak was free. He turned to Lycon—and then hurrying footsteps sounded on the raised deck. Rasul, the overseer, ran up, dragging his long whip. He peered down—and dragged out his sword, cursing. With the other hand he swept the whip in a great singing blow, smashing down on Elak's unprotected shoulders.

Lycon acted. In one swift motion he flung himself forward, guarding Elak; the lash ripped skin and flesh from Lycon's side. And then Elak's sinewy hand closed on the tough hide; he pulled mightily—pulled it from Rasul's grasp.

"Ho!" the overseer shouted. "Ho! To me!" His voice roared out over the dark sea. His long sword was a pale flickering light in the glow of the lanterns.

Two more men, armed, came running up behind Rasul. They spread out and closed in on Elak. He grinned unpleasantly, as a wolf smiles. The whip was coiled in his hand.

It sprang out suddenly, like a striking snake. The fanged, vicious tip hissed shrilly. In the dimness the lash was difficult to see, impossible to dodge. Rasul roared in pain.

"Slay him!" the overseer shouted.

The three ran in, and Elak gave way, his wrist turning as he swung the whip. A thrown dagger brought blood from the Atlantean's shoulder. And a man staggered back, screaming shrilly, clawing at his eyes that were blinded by the tearing rip of the lash.

"Slay me, then," Elak whispered, cold laughter in his eyes. "But the dog's fangs are sharp, Rasul."

He caught a glimpse of Lycon, bent above his bonds, busily manipulating the bit of metal that would unlock them. Voices called from the shore, Rasul shouted a response, and then ducked and gasped as the whip shrieked through the dark air.

"'Ware my fangs, Rasul!" Elak smiled mirthlessly.

And now the two—Rasul and his companion—were in turn giving way. Step by step Elak forced them back, under the threat of the terrible lash. They could not guard against it, could not see it. Out of the gloom it would come striking, swift as a snake's thrust, leaping viciously at their eyes. The slaves were awake and straining in their chains, calling encouragement to Elak. The man who had been blinded made a misstep and fell among the rowers. They surged up over him; lean hands reached and clawed in the lantern-light. He screamed for a time, and then made no further sound.

Lycon's voice rose, shrill and peremptory, above the tumult.

"Row!" he yelped. "Row, slaves! Ere Drezzar returns—row for your freedom!" Alternately he cursed and threatened and cajoled them, and worked at his bonds with flying fingers.

Elak heard a whisper at his side, saw a slave thrusting a sword at him, hilt-first—the blade the blinded one had dropped. Gratefully he seized it, hurling the whip away. The feel of the cool, leather-bound hilt was grateful. Tide of strength surged up Elak's arm from the sharp steel.

It was not his rapier—but it would do.

"My fangs, Rasul," he said, laughing—and ran in. His two opponents spread out, but he had foreseen that move. He turned his back on Rasul, cut at the other, and almost in the same motion whirled and leaped past, dodging a thrust by a hair's-breadth. And now Rasul only faced him. The other man was down, tearing at a throat sliced through to the spine.

Lycon shouted, "Row, slaves! For your lives!"

The long oars clacked and moved in confusion; then habit stepped in, and rhythmically, slowly, the blades dug into the sea. Lycon yelled a chant, and the slaves kept time to it. Gradually the galley gained way.

On the deck swords flamed and clashed. But Elak was not fated to slay Rasul. The overseer stumbled, dropped to one knee—and hands reached for him out of the dark. Shouting, he was dragged down among the slaves. Voices rose to a yelping crescendo of hate. Rasul screamed— and was silent.

Lycon leaped up, free from his chains. He cursed the rowers; their momentary inattention to their duty had caused confusion. An oar, caught among others, splintered and broke. The butt bent like a bow, snapped back, and smashed a slave's face to bloody ruin. From overside came cries and commands.

THE face of Drezzar rose above the rail, hideous, contorted, the scar flaming red. He gripped his sword between his teeth. After him armed men came pouring.

Lycon, a captured blade bare in his hand, ran toward them, yelling objurgations at the slaves. The oars moved again, tore at the sea, sent the galley through the waves once more. A slave had long since cut the anchor-rope.

A dozen armed men, swords gleaming, were ringed about Lycon, who, his back against the mast, was valiantly battling and cursing in lurid oaths. A few steps away Drezzar came catlike, and murder was in his eyes. He saw Elak stir, and ran in, blade ready.

Elak did not stoop to recover his sword. He sprang forward, under the sweep of the steel, which Drezzar had not expected. The two men went down together, rolling on the blood-slippery deck.

Drezzar tried to reverse the sword in his hand and stab Elak in the back. But Elak's supple body writhed aside, and simultaneously his lean, sinewy fingers closed on Drezzar's, above the hilt of the blade.

Drezzar tried to turn the blow, but could not. Elak continued his enemy's thrust. And the sword went smoothly into Drezzar's belly, without pausing till it grated against the backbone.

"My fangs, Drezzar," Elak said very softly, and with no expression on his wolf-face—and then drove the sword further in till it pinned the captain, like a beetle, to the deck. Drezzar's mouth opened; a roaring exhalation of breath, fraught with ghastly agony, seemed torn out of the man. His hands beat the deck; his body doubled up and arched like a bow.

He coughed blood, gnashed his teeth till they splintered and cracked—and so died.

Elak sprang up. He saw a heavy iron key hanging at Drezzar's belt. This he tore away and cast down among the slaves. A grateful clamor came in response.

Lycon called frantically for aid. Elak responded. But now the outcome of the battle was a foregone conclusion. One by one the freed slaves passed the iron key to their neighbors and came springing up to add their numbers to

Elak's cause. And, presently, the last of the ship's masters lay dead on deck, and the oarsmen—no longer in chains, no longer slaves—sent the galley plunging through the dark sea to the north.

5. Aynger of Amenalk

For the man dwelt in a lost land
  Of boulders and broken men . . .
                    —Chesterton.

THEY came to a forbidding, bleak coast loomed high above the galley. The cold winds of Autumn filled the sails and let the weary oarsmen rest. The sea turned smoothly gray, surging in long, foamless swells under a blue-gray sky. The sun gave little heat. The crew turned gratefully to the ship's stock—oil and wine and woven stuff, finding warmth and comfort in it.

But Elak was chafed by inaction. He longed to reach Cyrena; endlessly he paced the decks, fingering his rapier and pondering on the mystery of the thing called Karkora. What was this Pallid One? Whence had it come? These problems were insoluble, and remained so till, one night, Elak dreamed.

He dreamed of Dalan. The Druid priest seemed to be standing in a forest glade; before him a fire flickered redly. And Dalan said:

"Leave your ship at the red delta. Seek Aynger of Amenalk. Tell him you seek the throne of Cyrena!"

There was no more. Elak awoke, listening to the creaking of the galley's timbers and the whisper of waves against the side. It was nearly dawn. He rose, went on deck, and searched the horizon under a shielding palm.

To the right, breaking the gray cliffs, was a gap. Beyond it—an island. And on the island a castle loomed, part of the rock, it seemed, growing from it.

The galley swept on. And now Elak saw that a river ran between the broken cliffs. At its mouth was a delta, made of reddish sand.

So, in the cold, lowering dawn, Elak and Lycon left the galley. Willing oarsmen rowed them to shore. The two climbed the northern cliff and stood staring around. Inland the plateau stretched unbroken by tree or bush, windswept and desolate. To the west lay the Ocean Sea, chill and forbidding.

"Perhaps this Aynger of your dream dwells in that castle," Lycon said, pointing and shivering. "One of the men told me this is Kiriath. To the north, beyond the mountains, lies Cyrena."

Elak said somberly, "I know. And Sepher rules over Kiriath—Sepher, whom Karkora has taken for his own. Well—come on.

They set out along the edge of the cliff. The wind blew coldly, and brought to them a thin, high piping that seemed to come out of nowhere. Sad, mournful, weird, it murmured half-heard in the air about the two.

And across the plateau a man came—a great gray man, roughly clad, with unkempt hair and iron-gray beard. He played upon a set of pipes, but put these away as he saw Elak and Lycon. He came closer and halted, with folded arms, waiting.

The man's face might have been chipped from the rough rocks of this land. It was harsh and strong and forbidding, and the cool gray eyes were like the sea.

"What do you seek here?" he asked. His voice was deep and not at all unpleasant.

Elak hesitated. "Aynger. Aynger of Amenalk. Do you know of him?"

"I AM Aynger."

For a heartbeat there was silence. Then Elak said, "I seek the throne of Cyrena."

Laughter sprang into the gray eyes. Aynger of Amenalk reached out a huge hand and gripped Elak's arm, squeezing it painfully. He said, "Dalan sent you! Dalan!"

Elak nodded.

"But it is not me you seek. It is Mayana—the daughter of Poseidon. You must seek her there." He pointed to the distant castle on the island. "Her power alone can aid you. But first—come."

He led the way to the cliff's edge. A perilous, narrow path led down the jagged face; Aynger started along it with sure-footed ease, and Elak and Lycon followed more gingerly. Far below, the breakers tore upon the rocks; sea-birds called shrilly.

The path ended at a cave-mouth. Aynger entered, beckoning to the others. The cavern widened into a high-arched chamber, obviously Aynger's home. He gestured to a heap of furs, and gave each of his guests a great horn of mead.

"So. Dalan sent you. I had wondered. Orander is dead. Once the Pallid One has set his seal on a man, there is escape in death alone."

"Karkora," Elak said musingly. "What is he? Do you know, Aynger?"

"You must seek your answer from Mayana, on the isle. Only she knows. Mayana—of the seas. Let me tell you." The gray eyes grew bright with dream. A softness crept into the deep voice. "This land, on the western shore, is Amenalk. Not Kiriath. Once, long ago, Amenalk stretched far to the east. We were a great people then. But invaders came conquering, and now only this bit of land is left to us. Yet it is Amenalk. And I dwell here because in my veins runs the blood of kings."

Aynger flung back his gray, tousled head. "And for ages the castle on the isle had existed. None dwelt there. There were legends that even before the Amenalks held this land, an ancient sea-people made it their home. Sorcerers they were, warlocks and magicians. But they died and were forgotten. So, in time, my own people were scattered through Kiriath, and I dwelt here alone.

"Sepher ruled, well and wisely. One night he walked alone on the cliffs of Amenalk, and when he returned to his palace, he brought a bride with him. The bride was Mayana. Some say he found her in the island castle. Some say she rose from the waves. I think she is not human. She is one of the old sea-race—

"A shadow fell on the land. Out of the dark, out of the unknown, came Karkora. He took Sepher for his own. Mayana fled here, and dwells now in the castle, protected by her sorcery. And Karkora rules."

AYNGER'S gray beard jutted; his eyes were lambent pools. He said, "My people were a Druid race. We worshipped great Mider, as I do now. And I tell you that Karkora is a foulness and a horror—an evil that will spread through all the world if the Druids fail to destroy him. Mayana holds his secret. Mayana knows. You must go to her on her isle. For myself—" A mighty hand clenched. "I have king's blood, and my people live, though in bondage. I shall go through Kiriath and gather men. I think you will need armies, ere you sit on Cyrena's dragon throne. Well, I have an army for you, and for Mider."

Aynger reached behind him, brought out a huge war-hammer, bound with thongs. Laughter touched his grim face.

"We shall fight in the old way, woad-painted, without armor. And I think Helm-Breaker will taste blood again. If you get aid from Mayana—well. But with you or without you, man of Cyrena, Amenalk will go forth to battle!"

The great gray man towered against the cavemouth, a grim, archaic figure, somehow strong with primeval menace. He stood aside, pointing.

"Your way lies there, to the isle. Mine lies inland. When we meet again, if we do, I shall have an army to give you."

Silently Elak moved past Aynger and went up the cliff path. Lycon trailed him. On the windy, treeless plateau he stood unmoving, while the gray giant passed him without a word and strode away, his warhammer over one muscular shoulder, beard and hair flying in the wind.

Aynger grew small in the distance. Elak nodded to Lycon.

"I think we have a strong ally there. We'll need him. But now—this Mayana. If she can solve the riddle of Karkora, I'll find her though I have to swim."

"You won't have to," Lycon said, wiping his mouth. "Gods, that mead was good! There's a bridge to the isle—see? A narrow one, but it will serve. Unless she's set a dragon to guard it."

6. Mayana

By the tall obelisks, all seaweed-girt,
    Drift the pale dead of long and long ago,
Lovers and kings who may not more be hurt,
    Wounded by lips or by the dagger's blow.
                    —The Sunken Towers.

FROM the cliff edge a narrow bridge of rock jutted, a natural formation worn by wind and rain. It ended on a jagged ledge, at the back of which a black hole gaped. Elak said, "Lycon, wait here. I must take this road alone."

The little man disagreed profanely. But Elak was firm.

"It will be safer. So we won't both fall into the same trap. If I'm not back by sundown, come after me—you may be of aid then." Lycon could not help but realize the truth of this. He shrugged fat shoulders.

"Very well. I'll wait in Aynger's cave. His mead was potent; I'm anxious to sample more. Luck, Elak."

Nodding, the Atlantean started along the bridge. He found it safer not to look down, but the surging roar of the breakers sounded disquietingly from beneath. Sea-birds mewed and called. The wind tore at his swaying body.

But at last he was across, and felt the firm stability of the rocky ground under his sandals. Without a backward glance he entered the cave-mouth. Almost immediately outside sounds dimmed and quieted.

The road led down—a natural passage, seemingly, that turned and twisted in the rock. Sand was gritty underfoot, with bits of shell here and there. For a time it was dark, and then a greenish, vague luminous glow appeared, apparently emanated by the sand on which he trod.

It was utterly silent.

Still the tunnel led down, till Elak's feet felt moisture beneath him. He hesitated, staring around. The rocky walls were dewed and sweating. A dank, salty odor was strong in his nostrils. Loosening his rapier in its scabbard, he went on.

The green glow brightened. The passage turned; Elak rounded the corner, and stood motionless, staring. Before him a vast cavern opened.

It was huge and terrifyingly strange. Low-roofed, stalactites hung in myriad shapes and colors over the broad expanse of an underground lake. The green shining was everywhere. The weight of the island above seemed to press down suffocatingly, but the air, despite a salt seasmell, was fresh enough.

At his feet a sandy half-moon of a beach reached down to the motionless surface of the water. Further out, he could see far down vague shadows that resembled sunken buildings—fallen peristyles and columns, and far away, in the center of the lake, was an island.

Ruined marble crowned it. Only in the center a small temple seemed unharmed; it rose from shattered ruins in cool, white perfection. All around it the dead and broken city lay, to the water's edge and beyond. A submerged, forgotten metropolis lay before Elak.

Silence, and the pale green expanse of the waveless lake.

Softly Elak called, "Mayana." There was no response.

Frowning, he considered the task before him. He felt an odd conviction that what he sought lay in the temple on the islet, but there was no way of reaching it save by swimming. And there was something ominous about the motionless green of the waters.

Shrugging, Elak waded out. Icy chill touched his legs, crept higher about his loins and waist. He struck out strongly. And at first there was no difficulty; he made good progress.

But the water was very cold. It was salt, and this buoyed him up somewhat; yet when he glanced at the islet it seemed no nearer. Grunting, Elak buried his face in the waters and kicked vigorously.

His eyes opened. He looked down. He saw, beneath him, the sunken city.

Strange it was, and weird beyond imagination, to be floating above the wavering outline of these marble ruins. Streets and buildings and fallen towers were below, scarcely veiled by the luminous waters, but possessing a vague, shadowy indistinctness that made them half-unreal. A green haze clothed the city. A city of shadows

And the shadows moved and drifted in the tideless sea. Slowly, endlessly, they crept like a stain over the marble. They took shape before Elak's eyes.

Not sea-shapes—no. The shadows of men walked in the sunken metropolis. With queer, drifting motion the shadows went to and fro. They met and touched and parted again in strange similitude of life.

Stinging, choking cold filled Elak's mouth and nostrils. He spluttered and struck out, realizing that he was far beneath the surface, that, unconsciously holding his breath, he had drifted into the depths. He fought his way up.

It was oddly difficult. Soft, clinging arms

seemed to touch him; the water darkened. But his head broke the surface, and he drank deeply of the chill air. Only by swimming with all his strength could he keep from sinking. That inexplicable drag pulled him down.

He went under. His eyes were open, and he saw, far below, movement in the sunken city. The shadow-shapes were swirling up, rising, spinning like autumn leaves—rising to the surface. And shadows clustered about Elak, binding him with gossamer fetters. They clung feathery and tenacious as spider-webs.

The shadows drew him down into the shining depths.

He struck out frantically. His head broke water once more; he saw the islet, closer now.

"Mayana!" he called. *"Mayana!"*

RUSTLING movement shook the shadows. A ripple of mocking laughter seemed to go through them. They closed in again, dim, impalpable, unreal. Elak went under once more, too exhausted to fight, letting the shadows have their will with him. Only his mind cried out desperately to Mayana, striving to summon her to his aid.

The waters brightened. The green glow flamed emerald-bright. The shadows seemed to pause with odd hesitation, as though listening.

Then suddenly they closed in on Elak. They bore him through the waters; he was conscious of swift movement amid whirling green fire.

The shadows carried him to the islet, bore

him up as on a wave, and left him upon the sands.

The green light faded to its former dimness. Choking, coughing, Elak clambered to his feet. He stared around.

The shadows had vanished. Only the motionless lake stretched into the distance. He stood amid the ruins of the islet.

Hastily he staggered away from the water's marge, clambering across broken plinths and fallen pillars, making his way to the central temple. It stood in a tiny plaza, unmarred by time, but stained and discolored in every stone.

The brazen door gaped open. Unsteadily Elak climbed the steps and paused at the threshold. He looked upon a bare room, lit with the familiar emerald glow, featureless save for a curtain, on the further wall, made of some metallic cloth and figured with the trident of the seagod.

There was no sound but Elak's hastened breathing. Then, abruptly, a low splashing came from beyond the curtain. It parted.

Beyond it was green light, so brilliant it was impossible to look upon. Silhouetted against the brightness for a moment loomed a figure—a figure of unearthly slimness and height. Only for a second did Elak see it; then the curtain swung back into place and the visitant was gone.

Whispering through the temple came a voice, like the soft murmur of tiny, rippling waves. And it said:

"I am Mayana. Why do you seek me?"

7. Karkora

And I saw a beast coming up out of the sea, having ten horns and seven heads, and on his horns ten diadems, and upon his heads names of blasphemy . . . and the dragon gave him his power, and his throne, and great authority.
—Revelations 13:1.

ELAK'S wet hand crept to his rapier. There had been no menace in the whisper, but it was strangely—inhuman. And the silhouette he had seen was not that of any earthly woman.

Yet he answered quietly enough, no tremor in his voice:

"I seek the dragon throne of Cyrena. And I come to you for aid against Karkora."

There was silence. When the whisper came again, it had in it all the sadness of waves and wind.

"Must I aid you? Against Karkora?"

"You know what manner of being he is?" Elak questioned.

"Aye—I know that well." The metallic curtain shook. "Seat yourself. You are tired—how are you named?"

"Elak."

"Elak, then—listen. I will tell you of the coming of Karkora, and of Erykion the sorcerer. And of Sepher, whom I loved." There was a pause; then the low whisper resumed.

"Who I am, what I am, you need not know, but you should understand that I am not entirely human. My ancestors dwelt in this sunken city. And I—well, for ten years I took human shape and dwelt with Sepher as his wife. I loved him. And always I hoped to give him a son who would some day mount the throne. I hoped in vain, or so I thought.

"Now in the court dwelt Erykion, a wizard. His magic was not that of the sea, soft and kindly as the waves, but of a darker sort. Erykion delved in ruined temples and pored over forgotten manuscripts of strange lore. His vision went back even before the sea-folk sprang from the loins of Poseidon, and he opened the forbidden gates of Space and Time. He offered to give me a child, and I listened to him, to my sorrow.

"I shall not tell you of the months I spent in strange temples, before dreadful altars. I shall not tell you of Erykion's magic. I bore a son—dead."

The silver curtain shook; it was long before the unseen speaker resumed. "And this son was frightful. He was deformed in ways I cannot let myself remember. Sorcery had made him inhuman. Yet he was my son, my husband's son, and I loved him. When Erykion offered to give him life, I agreed to the price he demanded—even though the price was the child himself."

" 'I shall not harm him,' Erykion told me. 'Nay, I shall give him powers beyond those of any god or man. Some day he shall rule this world and others. Only give him to me, Mayana.' And I hearkened.

"Now of Erykion's sorcery I know little. Something had entered into the body of my son while I bore him, and what this thing was I do not know. It was dead, and it awoke. Erykion awoke it. He took this blind, dumb, maimed man-child and bore it to his home in the depths of the mountains. With his magic he deprived it of any vestige of the five senses. Only life remained, and the unknown dweller within.

"I remembered something Erykion had once told me. 'We have in us a sixth sense, primeval and submerged, which can be very powerful once it is brought to light. I know how to do that. A blind man's hearing may become acute; his power goes to the senses remaining. If a child, at birth, be deprived of all five senses, his power will go to this sixth sense. My magic can insure that.'" So Erykion made of my man-child a being blind and dumb and without consciousness, al-most; for years he worked his spells and opened the gates of Time and Space, letting alien powers flood through. This sixth sense within the child grew stronger. And the dweller in his mind waxed great, unbound by the earthly fetters that bind humans. This is my son—my man-child—Karkora, the Pallid One!"

AND silence. And again the whisper resumed.

"Yet it is not strange that I do not entirely hate and loathe Karkora. I know he is a burning horror and a thing that should not exist; yet I gave him birth. And so, when he entered the mind of Sepher, his father, I fled to this my cas-tle. Here I dwell alone with my shadows. I strove to forget that once I knew the fields and skies and hearths of earth. Here, in my own place, I forgot.

"And you seek me to ask aid." There was anger in the soft murmur. "Aid to destroy that which came from my flesh!"

Elak said quietly, "Is Karkora's flesh—yours?"

"By Father Poseidon, no! I loved the human part of Karkora, and little of that is left now. The Pallid One is—is—he has a thousand frightful powers, through his one strange sense. It has opened for him gateways that should remain always locked. He walks in other worlds, beyond unlit seas, across the nighted voids beyond earth. And I know he seeks to spread his dominion over all. Kiriath fell to him, and I think Cyrena. In time he will take all Atlantis, and more than that."

Elak asked, "This Erykion, the wizard—what of him?"

"I do not know," Mayana said. "Perhaps he dwells in his citadel yet, with Karkora. Not for years have I seen the sorcerer."

"Cannot Karkora be slain?"

There was a long pause. Then the whisper said, "I know not. His body, resting in the citadel, is mortal, but that which dwells within it is not. If you could reach the body of Karkora— even so you could not slay him."

"Nothing can kill the Pallid One?" Elak asked.

"Do not ask me this!" Mayana's voice said with angry urgency. "One thing, one talisman exists—and this I shall not and cannot give you."

"I am minded to force your talisman from you," Elak said slowly, "if I can. Yet I do not wish to do this thing."

FROM beyond the curtain came a sound that startled the man—a low, hopeless sobbing that had in it all the bleak sadness of the mournful sea. Mayana said brokenly:

"It is cold in my kingdom, Elak—cold and lonely. And I have no soul, only my life, while it lasts. My span is long, but when it ends there will be only darkness, for I am of the sea-folk. Elak, I have dwelt for a time on earth, and I would dwell there again, in green fields with the bright cornflowers and daisies gay amid the grass—with the fresh winds of earth caressing me. The hearth-fires, the sound of human voices, and a man's love—my Father Poseidon knows how I long for these again."

"The talisman," Elak said.

"Aye, the talisman. You may not have it."

Elak said very quietly, "What manner of world will this be if Karkora should rule?"

There was a shuddering, indrawn breath. Mayana said, "You are right. You shall have the talisman, if you should need it. It may be that you can defeat Karkora without it. I only pray that it may be so. Here is my word, then: in your hour of need, and not until then, I shall send you the talisman. And now go. Karkora has an earthly vessel in Sepher. Slay Sepher. Give me your blade, Elak."

Silently Elak unsheathed his rapier and extended it hilt-first. The curtain parted. Through it slipped a hand.

A hand—inhuman, strange! Very slender and pale it was, milk-white, with the barest suggestion of scales on the smooth, delicate texture of the skin. The fingers were slim and elongated, seemingly without joints, and filmy webs grew between them.

The hand took Elak's weapon and withdrew behind the curtain. Then it reappeared, again holding the rapier. Its blade glowed with a pale greenish radiance.

"Your steel will slay Sepher now. And it will give him peace." Elak gripped the hilt; the unearthly hand made a quick archaic gesture above the weapon.

"So I send a message to Sepher, my husband. And—Elak—kill him swiftly. A thrust through the eye into the brain will not hurt too much."

Then, suddenly, the hand thrust out and touched Elak upon the brow. He was conscious of a swift dizziness, a wild exaltation that surged through him in hot waves. Mayana whispered:

"You shall drink of my strength, Elak. Without it, you cannot hope to face Karkora. Stay with me for a moon—drinking the sea-power and Poseidon's magic."

"A moon—"

"Time will not exist. You will sleep, and while you sleep strength will pour into you. And when you awake, you may go forth to battle—strong!"

The giddiness mounted; Elak felt his senses leaving him. He whispered, "Lycon—I must give him a message—"

"Speak to him, then, and he will hear. My sorcery will open his ears."

Dimly, as though from far away, Elak heard Lycon's startled voice.

"Who calls me? Is it you, Elak? Where—I see no one on this lonely cliff."

"Speak to him!" Mayana commanded, And Elak obeyed.

"I am safe, Lycon. Here I must stay for one moon, alone. You must not wait. I have a task for you."

There was the sound of a stifled oath. "What task?"

"Go north to Cyrena. Find Dalan, or, failing that, gather an army. Cyrena must be ready when Kiriath marches. Tell Dalan, if you find him, what I have done, and that I will be with him in one moon. Then let the Druid guide your steps. And—Ishtar guide you, Lycon."

Softly came the far voice: "And Mother Ishtar be your shield. I'll obey. Farewell."

Green darkness drifted across Elak's vision.

Dimly, through closing eyes, he vaguely saw the curtain before him swept aside, and a dark silhouette moving forward—a shape slim and tall beyond human stature, yet delicately feminine withal. Mayana made a summoning gesture— and the shadows flowed into the temple.

They swept down upon Elak, bringing him darkness and cool, soothing quiet. He rested and slept, and the enchanted strength of the sea-woman poured into the citadel of his soul.

8. The Dragon's Throne

Dust of the stars was under our feet, glitter of
   stars above—
Wrecks of our wrath dropped reeling down as we
   fought and we spurned and we strove.
Worlds upon worlds we tossed aside, and scattered them to and fro,
The night that we stormed Valhalla, a million
   years ago!
                                            —Kipling.

THE moon waxed and waned, and at last Elak
awoke, on the further shore, by the cavern
mouth that led to the upper world. The underground mere lay silent at his feet, still bathed in
the soft green glow. In the distance the islet was,
and he could make out the white outline of the
temple upon it. The temple where he had slept
for a month. But there was no sign of life. No
shadows stirred in the depths beneath him. Yet
within himself he sensed a secret well of power
that had not been there before.

   Pondering, he retraced his steps through the
winding passage, across the rock bridge to the
high ramp of the plateau. The plain was deserted. The sun was westering, and a cold wind
blew bleakly from the sea.

   Elak shrugged, His gaze turned north, and
his hand touched the rapier-hilt.

   "First, a horse," he grunted. "And then—
Sepher! A blade for the king's throat!"

   So within two hours a mercenary soldier lay

dead, his blood staining a leathern tunic, and Elak galloped north on a stolen steed. Hard and fast he rode, through Kiriath, and whispers were borne to his ears on the gusting winds. Sepher was no longer in his city, they said. At the head of a vast army he was sweeping north to the Gateway, the mountain pass that led to Cyrena. From the very borders of Kiriath warriors were coming in answer to the king's summons; mercenaries and adventurers flooded in to serve under Sepher. He paid well and promised rich plunder—the sack of Cyrena.

A trail of blood marked Elak's path. Two horses he rode to death. But at last the Gateway lay behind him; he had thundered through Sharn Forest and forded Monra River. Against the horizon towered a battlemented castle, and this was Elak's goal. Here Orander had ruled. Here was the dragon throne, the heart of Cyrena.

Elak rode across the drawbridge and into the courtyard. He cast his mount's reins to a gaping servitor, leaped from the horse, and raced across the yard. He knew each step of the way. In this castle he had been born.

And now the throne room, vast, high-ceilinged, warm with afternoon sunlight. Men were gathered there. Princes and lords of Cyrena. Barons, dukes, minor chieftains. By the throne—Dalan. And beside him, Lycon, round face set in unaccustomed harsh lines, for once sober and steady on his feet.

"By Mider!" Lycon roared. "Elak! *Elak!*"

The Atlantean pushed his way through the murmuring, undecided crowd. He came to stand beside the throne. His hand gripped Lycon's shoulder and squeezed painfully. The little man grinned.

"Ishtar be praised," Lycon murmured. "Now I can get drunk again."

Dalan said, "I watched you in the crystal, Elak. But I could not aid. The magic of the Pallid One battled my own. Yet I think you have other magic now—sea-sorcery." He turned to the mob. His lifted arms quieted them.

"This is your king," Dalan said.

Voices were raised, some in approbation, some in angry protest and objection. A tall, lean oldster shouted, "Aye—this is Zeulas, returned once more. This is Orander's brother."

"Be silent, Hira," another snapped. "This scarecrow Cyrena's king?"

Elak flushed and took a half-step forward. Dalan's voice halted him.

"You disbelieve, Gorlias?" he asked. "Well—d'you know of a worthier man? Will you sit on the dragon throne?"

Gorlias looked at the Druid with an oddly frightened air; he fell silent and turned away. The others broke into a renewed chorus of quarreling.

Hira silenced them. His lean face was triumphant. "There's one sure test. Let him take it."

He turned to Elak. "The lords of Cyrena have fought like a pack of snarling dogs since Orander's death. Each wanted the throne. Baron

Kond yelled louder than the rest. Dalan offered him the dragon throne, in the name of Mider, if he could hold it."

FROM the others a low whisper went up—uneasy, fearful. Hira continued:

"Kond mounted the dais a month ago and sat on the throne. And he died! The fires of Mider slew him."

"Aye," Gorlias whispered. "Let this Elak sit upon the throne!"

A chorus of assent rose. Lycon looked worried.

He murmured, "It's true, Elak. I saw it. Red fire came out of nowhere and burned Kond to a cinder."

Dalan was silent, his ugly face impassive. Elak, watching the Druid, could not read a message in the shallow black eyes.

Gorlias said, "If you can sit on the throne, I'll follow you. If not—you'll be dead. Well?"

Elak did not speak. He turned and mounted the dais. For a moment he paused before the great throne of Cyrena, his gaze dwelling on the golden dragon that writhed across its back, the golden dragons on the arms. For ages the kings of Cyrena had ruled from this seat, ruled with honor and chivalry under the dragon. And now Elak remembered how, in Poseidonia, he had felt himself unworthy to mount the throne.

Would the fires of Mider slay him if he took his dead brother's place?

Silently Elak prayed to his god, "If I'm unworthy," he told Mider, with no thought of irreverence, but as one warrior to another, "then slay me, rather than let the throne be dishonored, Yours is the judgment."

He took his place on the dragon throne.

Silence fell like a pall on the great room. The faces of the crowd were intent and strained, Lycon's breath came fast. The Druid's hands, hidden under the brown robe, made a quick, furtive gesture; his lips moved without sound.

RED light flashed out above the throne. Through the room a cry rose and mounted, wordless, fearful. The fires of Mider flamed up in glaring brilliance and cloaked Elak!

They hid him in a twisting crimson pall. They swirled about him, blazing with hot radiance.

They swept into a strange, fantastic shape—a coiling silhouette that grew steadily more distinct.

A dragon of flame coiled itself about Elak!

And suddenly it was gone. Lycon was gasping oaths. The others were milling about in a confused mob. Dalan stood motionless, smiling slightly.

And on the dragon throne Elak sat unharmed! No breath of fire had scorched or blistered him; no heat had reddened his skin. His eyes were blazing; he sprang up and unsheathed his rapier. Silently he lifted it.

There was a clash of ringing blades. A forest of bright steel lifted. A great shout bellowed out.

The lords of Cyrena swore allegiance to their

king!

Now, however, Elak found that his task had scarcely begun. The armies of Sepher were not yet in Cyrena; the king of Kiriath was waiting beyond the mountain barrier till he had gathered his full strength. But he would march soon, and Cyrena must by then be organized to resist him.

"Karkora didn't invade Kiriath," Elak said to Dalan one day as they rode through Sharn Forest. "He invaded the mind of the king instead. Why does he depend on armies to conquer Cyrena?"

Dalan's shapeless brown robe flapped against his horse's flanks, "Have you forgotten Orander? He tried there, and failed. Then there was no single ruler here. If he'd stolen the mind of Kond or Gorlias he'd still have had the other nobles against him. And conquer Cyrena he must, for it's the stronghold of Mider and the Druids. Karkora knows he must destroy us before he can rule this world and others, as he intends. So he uses Sepher and Kiriath's army. Already he's given orders to slaughter each Druid."

"What of Aynger?" Elak demanded.

"A message came from him today. He has gathered his Amenalks in the mountains beyond the Gateway. They wait for our word. Barbarians, Elak—but good allies. They fight like mad wolves."

Cyrena rose to arms. From steading and farm, castle and citadel, city and fortress, the iron men came streaming. The roads glittered with bright steel and rang to the clash of horses' hoofs. The dragon banners fluttered in the chill winds of winter.

Rise and arm! In the name of Mider and the Dragon, draw your blade! So the messengers called; so the word went forth. Rise against Kiriath and Sepher!

The defending swords of Cyrena flashed bright. They thirsted for blood.

And Sepher of Kiriath rode north against the Dragon.

9. The Hammer of Aynger

And a strange music went with him,
  Loud and yet strangely far;
The wild pipes of the western land,
Too keen for the ear to understand,
Sang high and deathly on each hand
When the dead man went to war.
                              —Chesterton.

THE first snows of winter lay white on the Gateway. All around towered the tall, frosted peaks of the mountain barrier, and a bitter wind gusted strongly through the pass. Within a month deep snow and avalanches would make the Gateway almost impassable.

The sky was cloudless, of chill pale blue. In the thin air everything stood out in startling clarity; voices carried far, as did the crunching of snow underfoot and the crackle of rocks deep-bitten by the iron cold.

The pass was seven miles long, and narrow in

only a few spots. For the most part it was a broad valley bounded by the craggy cliffs. Canyons opened into it.

Dawn had flamed and spread in the east. The sun hung above a snow-capped peak. South of a narrow portion of the Gateway part of Cyrena's army waited. Behind them were reinforcements. Upon the crags were archers and arbalesters, waiting to rain death upon the invaders. Steel-silver moved against a background of white snow and black grim rocks.

Elak was astride a war-horse upon a small hillock. Hira rode up, gaunt old face keenly alert, joy of battle in the faded eyes. He saluted swiftly.

"The bowmen are placed and ready," he said. "We've got rocks and boulders into position to crush Sepher's army, should it get too far."

Elak nodded. He wore chain-armor, gold encrusted, with a close-fitting helm of gleaming steel. His wolf face was taut with excitement, and he curbed the steed as it curvetted.

"Good, Hira. You are in command there. I trust your judgment."

As Hira departed Dalan and Lycon arrived, the latter flushed and unsteady in his saddle. He gripped a drinking-horn and swilled mead from it occasionally. His long sword slapped the horse's flank.

"The minstrels will make a song of this battle," he observed. "Even the gods will eye it with some interest."

"Don't blaspheme," Dalan said, and turned to Elak. "I've a message from Aynger. His savage

"I spent months in strange temples. His magic was not that of the sea, soft and kindly as the waves, but of a darker sort."

Amenalks wait in that side canyon—" The Druid flung out a pointing hand—"and will come when we need them."

"Aye," Lycon broke in, "I saw them. Madmen and demons! They've painted themselves blue as the sky and are armed with scythes and flails and hammers, among other things. And they're playing tunes on their pipes and bragging, each louder than the other. Only Aynger sits silent, fondling his Helm-Breaker. He looks like an image chipped out of gray stone."

At the memory Lycon shivered and then

gulped the rest of the mead. "Faith," he said sadly, "the horn's empty. Well, I must get more." And off he went, reeling in the saddle.

"Drunken little dog," Elak remarked. "But his hand will be steady enough on the sword."

Far away a trumpet shouted shrilly, resounding among the peaks. Now the foreguard of Sepher's army was visible as a glitter of steel on calques and lifted spearheads. Along the pass they came, steadily, inexorably, in close battle formation. The trumpet sang and skirled.

In response drums of Cyrena snarled answer. They rose to a throbbing, menacing roar. Cymbals clashed resoundingly. The banners of the dragon flung out stiffly in the cold blast.

Kiriath rode without a standard. In silence, save for the clashing of metallic hoofs and the angry screaming of the trumpet, they came, a vast array that flooded into the valley. Pikeman, archers, knights, mercenaries—on they came, intent on conquest and plunder. Elak could not see Sepher, though his gaze searched for the king.

And slowly the invaders increased their speed, almost imperceptibly at first, and then more swiftly till through the Gateway Kiriath charged and thundered, lances lowered, swords flashing. The trumpet shouted urgent menace.

Dalan's gross body moved uneasily in his saddle. He unsheathed his long blade.

Elak looked around. Behind him the army waited. Everything was ready.

The king of Cyrena rose in his stirrups. He

lifted his rapier and gestured with it. He shouted:

"Charge! Ho—the Dragon!"

WITH a roar Cyrena swept forward down the pass. Closer and closer the two vast forces came. The drums roared death. From the icy peaks the clamor resounded thunderously.

A cloud of arrows flew. Men fell, screaming. Then, with a crash that seemed to shake the mountainous walls of the Gateway, the armies met.

It was like a thunderclap. All sanity and coherence vanished in a maelstrom of red and silver-steel, a whirlpool, an avalanche of thrusting spears, speeding arrows, slashing blades. Elak was instantly surrounded by foes. His rapier flew swift as a striking snake; blood stained its length. His horse shrieked and fell hamstrung to the ground. Elak leaped free and saw Lycon charging to the rescue. The little man was wielding a sword almost as long as himself, but his pudgy fingers handled it with surprising ease. He lopped off one man's head, ruined another's face with a well-placed kick of his steel-shod foot, and then Elak had leaped astride a riderless steed.

Again he plunged into the fray. The brown bald head of Dalan was rising and falling some distance away; the Druid roared like a beast as his sword whirled and flew and bit deep. Blood soaked the brown robe. Dalan's horse seemed like a creature possessed; it screamed shrilly, blowing through red, inflamed nostrils, snapped viciously and reared and struck with knife-edged hoofs. Druid and charger raged like a burning pestilence amid the battle; sweat and blood mingled on Dalan's toad face.

Elak caught sight of Sepher. The ruler of Kiriath bronzed, bearded giant towered above his men, fighting in deadly silence. Smiling wolfishly, Elak drove toward the king.

From the distance came the thin high wailing of pipes. Out of the side canyon men came pouring—barbarous men, half naked, their lean bodies smeared blue with woad. The men of Aynger! At their head ran Aynger himself, his gray beard flying, brandishing the hammer HelmBreaker. The gray giant leaped upon a rock, gesturing toward the forces of Kiriath.

"Slay the oppressors!" he bellowed. "Slay! Slay!"

The weird pipes of the Amenalks shrilled their answer. The blue-painted men swept forward—

From the ranks of Sepher an arrow flew. It sped toward Aynger. It pierced his bare throat and drove deep—deep!

The Amenalk leader bellowed; his huge body arced like a bow. Blood spouted from his mouth.

A battalion charged out from the ranks of Kiriath. They sped toward the Amenalks, lances lowered, pennons flying.

Aynger fell! Dead, he toppled from the rock into the lifted arms of his men. The pipes skirled. The Amenalks, bearing their leader, turned and fled back into the valley!

Cursing, Elak dodged a shrewd thrust, killed his assailant, and spurred toward Sepher. The hilt of his rapier was slippery with blood. His body, under the chain armor, was a mass of agonizing bruises; blood gushed from more than one wound. His breath rasped in his throat. The stench of sweat and gore choked him; he drove over ground carpeted with the writhing bodies of men and horses.

Down the valley Dalan fought and bellowed his rage. The battle-thunder crashed on the towering crags and sent deafening echoes through the Gateway.

Still the trumpets of Kiriath called; still the drums and cymbals of Cyrena shouted their defiance.

And still Sepher slew, coldly, remorselessly, his bronzed face expressionless.

Kiriath gathered itself and charged. The forces of Cyrena were forced back, fighting desperately each step of the way. Back to the narrowing of the pass they were driven.

High above the archers loosed death on Kiriath.

With ever-increasing speed Sepher's army thrust forward. A gust of panic touched the ranks of Cyrena. A dragon banner was captured and slashed into flying shreds by keen blades.

Vainly Elak strove to rally his men. Vainly the Druid bellowed threats.

The retreat became a rout. Into the narrow defile the army fled, jammed into a struggling, fighting mob. An orderly retreat might have saved the day, for Kiriath could have been trapped in the narrow pass and crippled by boulders thrust down by the men stationed above.

As it was, Cyrena was helpless, waiting to be slaughtered.

Kiriath charged.

QUITE suddenly Elak heard a voice. In through the mountains. Above the call of trumpets came the thin wailing of pipes. Louder it grew, and louder.

From the side canyon the blue barbarians of Amenalk rushed in disorderly array. In their van a group ran together with lifted shields. Upon the shields was the body of Aynger!

Weirdly, eerily, the ear-piercing skirling of the pipes of Amenalk shrilled out. The woad-painted savages, mad with blood-frenzy, raced after the corpse of their ruler.

Dead Aynger led his men to war!

The Amenalks fell on the rear of the invaders. Flails and scythes and blades swung and glittered, and were lifted dripping red. A giant sprang upon the shield-platform, astride the body of Aynger. In his hand he brandished a war-hammer.

"Helm-Breaker!" he shouted. "He—Helm-Breaker!"

He leaped down; the great hammer rose and fell and slaughtered. Casques and helms shattered under the smashing blows; the Amenalk wielded Helm-Breaker in a circle of scarlet death about him.

"Helm-Breaker! Ho—slay! Slay!"

Kiriath swayed in confusion under the on-slaught. In that breathing-space Elak and Dalan rallied their army. Cursing, yelling, brandishing steel, they whipped order out of chaos. Elak snatched a dragon banner from the dust, lifted it high.

He turned his horse's head down the valley. One hand lifting the standard, one gripping his bared rapier, he drove his spurs deep.

"Ho, the Dragon!" he shouted. *"Cyrena! Cyrena!"*

Down upon Kiriath he thundered. Behind him rode Lycon and the Druid. And after them the remnants of an army poured. Hira led his archers from the cliffs. The arbalasters came bounding like mountain goats, snatching up swords and spears, pouring afoot after their king.

"Cyrena!"

The drums and cymbals roared out again. Through the tumult pierced the thin, weird calling of the pipes.

"Helm-Breaker! Slay! Slay!"

And then madness—a hell of shouting, scarlet battle through which Elak charged, Dalan and Lycon beside him, riding straight for the bushy beard that marked Sepher. On and on, over screaming horses and dying men, through a whirlpool of flashing, thirsty steel, thrusting, stabbing, hacking

The face of Sepher rose up before Elak.

The bronzed face of Kiriath's king was impassive; in his cold eyes dwelt something inhuman. Involuntarily an icy shudder racked Elak. As he paused momentarily the brand of Sepher whirled up and fell shattering in a great blow.

Elak did not try to escape. He poised his rapier, flung himself forward in his stirrups, sent the sharp blade thrusting out.

The enchanted steel plunged into Sepher's throat. Simultaneously Elak felt his back go numb under the sword-cut; his armor tore raggedly. The blade dug deep into the body of the war-horse.

The light went out of Sepher's eyes. He remained for a heart-beat upright in his saddle. Then his face changed.

It darkened with swift corruption. It blackened and rotted before Elak's eyes, Death, so long held at bay, sprang like a crouching beast.

A foul and loathsome thing fell forward and tumbled from the saddle. It dropped to the bloody ground and lay motionless. Black ichor oozed out from the chinks of the armor; the face that stared up blindly at the sky was a frightful thing.

And without warning darkness and utter silence dropped down and shrouded Elak.

10. The Black Vision

And the devil that deceived them was cast into the lake of fire and brimstone, where are also the beast and the false prophet; and they shall be tormented day and night for ever and ever.

—Revelations 20:10.

HE FELT again the dizzy vertigo that presaged the coming of Karkora. A high-pitched, droning whine rang shrilly in his cars; he felt a sense of swift movement. A picture came.

Once more he saw the giant crag that towered amid the mountains. The dark tower lifted from its summit. Elak was drawn forward; iron gates opened in the base of the pinnacle. They closed as he passed through.

The high whining had ceased. It was cimmerian dark. But in the gloom a Presence moved and stirred and was conscious of Elak.

The Pallid One sprang into view.

He felt a sense of whirling disorientation; his thoughts grew inchoate and confused. They were slipping away, spinning into the empty dark. In their place something crept and grew; a weird mental invasion took place. Power of Karkora surged through Elak's brain, forcing back the man's consciousness and soul, thrusting them out and back into the void. A dreamlike sense of unreality oppressed Elak.

Silently he called upon Dalan.

Dimly a golden flame flickered up, far away. Elak heard the Druid's voice whispering faintly, out of the abyss.

"Mider—aid him, Mider—"

Fires of Mider vanished. Elak felt again the sense of swift movement. He was lifted—

The darkness was gone. Gray light bathed him. He was, seemingly, in the tower on the summit of the crag—the citadel of Karkora. But the place was unearthly!

The planes and angles of the room in which Elak stood were warped and twisted insanely. Laws of matter and geometry seemed to have gone mad. Crawling curves swept obscenely in strange motion; there was no sense of perspective. The gray light was alive. It crept and shimmered. And the white shadow of Karkora blazed forth with chill and dreadful radiance.

Elak remembered the words of Mayana, the sea-witch, as she spoke of her monstrous son Karkora.

"He walks in other worlds, beyond unlit seas, across the nighted voids beyond earth."

Through the whirling chaos a face swam, inhuman, mad, and terrible. A man's face, indefinably bestialized and degraded, with a sparse white beard and glaring eyes. Again Elak recalled Mayana's mention of Erykion, the wizard who had created the Pallid One.

"Perhaps he dwells in his citadel yet, with Karkora. Not for years have I seen the sorcerer."

If this were Erykion, then he had fallen victim to his own creation. The warlock was insane. Froth dribbled on the straggling beard; the mind and soul had been drained from him.

He was swept back and vanished in the grinding maelstrom of the frightful lawless geometrical chaos. Elak's eyes ached as he stared, unable to stir a muscle. The shadow of the Pallid

One gleamed whitely before him.

The planes and angles changed; pits and abysses opened before Elak. He looked through strange gateways. He saw other worlds, and with his flesh shrinking in cold horror he stared into the depths of the Nine Hells. Frightful life swayed into motion before his eyes. Things of inhuman shape rose up out of nighted depths. A charnel wind choked him.

The sense of mental assault grew stronger; Elak felt his mind slipping away under the dread impact of alien power. Unmoving, deadly, Karkora watched—

"Mider," Elak prayed. "Mider—aid me!"

The mad planes swept about faster, in a frantic saraband of evil. The dark vision swept out, opening wider vistas before Elak. He saw unimaginable and blasphemous things, Dwellers in the outer dark, horrors beyond earth-life—

The white shadow of Karkora grew larger. The crawling radiance shimmered leprously. Elak's senses grew dulled; his body turned to ice. Nothing existed but the now gigantic silhouette of Karkora; the Pallid One reached icy fingers into Elak's brain.

The assault mounted like a rushing tide. There was no aid anywhere. There was only evil, and madness, and black, loathsome horror.

QUITE suddenly Elak heard a voice. In it was the murmur of rippling waters. He knew Mayana spoke to him by strange magic.

"In your hour of need I bring you the talisman against my son Karkora."

The voice died; the thunder of the seas roared in Elak's ears. A green veil blotted out the mad, shifting planes and angles. In the emerald mists shadows floated—the shadows of Mayana.

They swept down upon him. Something was thrust into his hand—something warm and wet and slippery.

He lifted it, staring. He gripped a heart, bloody, throbbing—alive!

The heart of Mayana! The heart beneath which Karkora had slumbered in the womb! The talisman against Karkora!

A shrill droning rose suddenly to a skirling shriek of madness, tearing at Elak's ears, knifing through his brain. The bleeding heart in Elak's hand drew him forward. He took a slow step, another.

About him the gray light pulsed and waned; the white shadow of Karkora grew gigantic. The mad planes danced swiftly.

And then Elak was looking down at a pit on the edge of which he stood. Only in the depths of the deep hollow was the instability of the surrounding matter lacking. And below was a shapeless and flesh-colored hulk that lay inert ten feet down.

It was man-sired and naked. But it was not human. The pulpy arms had grown to the sides; the legs had grown together. Not since birth had the thing moved by itself. It was blind, and had no mouth. Its head was a malformed grotesquerie of sheer horror.

Fat, deformed, utterly frightful, the body of Karkora rested in the pit.

The heart of Mayana seemed to tear itself from Elak's hand. Like a plummet it dropped, and fell upon the breast of the horror below.

A shuddering, wormlike motion shook Karkora. The monstrous body writhed and jerked.

From the bleeding heart blood crept out like a stain. It spread over the deformed horror. In a moment Karkora was no longer flesh-colored, but red as the molten sunset.

And, abruptly, there was nothing in the pit but a slowly widening pool of scarlet. The Pallid One had vanished.

Simultaneously the ground shook beneath Elak; he felt himself swept back. For a second he seemed to view the crag and tower from a distance, against the background of snow-tipped peaks.

The pinnacle swayed; the crag rocked. They crashed down in thunderous ruin.

Only a glimpse did Elak get; then the dark curtain blotted out his consciousness. He saw, dimly, a pale oval. It grew more distinct. And it was the face of Lycon bending above Elak, holding a brimming cup to the latter's lips.

"Drink!" he urged. "Drink deep!"

Elak obeyed, and then thrust the liquor away. He stood up weakly.

HE WAS in the pass of the Gateway. Around him the men of Cyrena rested, with here and there a blue-painted warrior of Amenalk. Corpses littered the ground. Vultures were already circling against the blue.

Dalan was a few paces away, his shallow black eyes regarding Elak intently. He said, "Only one thing could have saved you in Karkora's stronghold. One thing—"

Elak said grimly, "It was given me. Karkora is slain."

A cruel smile touched the Druid's lipless mouth. He whispered, "So may all enemies of Mider die."

Lycon broke in, "We've conquered, Elak. The army of Kiriath fled when you killed Sepher. And, gods, I'm thirsty!" He rescued the cup and drained it.

Elak did not answer. His wolf face was dark; in his eyes deep sorrow dwelt. He did not see the triumphant banners of the dragon tossing in the wind, nor did he envision the throne of Cyrena that waited. He was remembering a low, rippling voice that spoke with longing of the fields and hearth-fires of earth, a slim, inhuman hand that had reached through a curtain—a seawitch who had died to save a world to which she had never belonged.

The shadow was lifted from Atlantis; over Cyrena the golden dragon ruled under great Mider. But in a sunken city of marble beauty the shadows of Mayana would mourn for Poseidon's daughter.

PRINCE RAYNOR

Someone flung a shield. Kialeh

lifted his blade to parry.

CURSED BE THE CITY

This is the tale they tell, O King: that ere the royal banners were lifted upon the tall towers of Chaldean Ur, before the Winged Pharaohs reigned in secret Aegyptus, there were mighty empires far to the east. There in that vast desert known as the Cradle of Mankind—aye, even in the heart of the measureless Gobi—great wars were fought and high palaces thrust their minarets up to the purple Asian sky. But this, O King, was long ago, beyond the memory of the oldest sage; the splendor of Imperial Gobi lives now only in the dreams of minstrels and poets....
The Tale of Sakhmet the Damned.

CHAPTER I
The Gates of War

IN THE gray light of the false dawn the prophet had climbed to the cuter wall of Sardopolis, his beard streaming in the chill wind. Before him, stretching across the broad plain, were the gay tents and pavilions of the besieging army, emblazoned with the scarlet symbol of the wyvern, the winged dragon beneath which King Cyaxares of the north waged his wars.

Already soldiers were grouped about the catapults and scaling- towers, and a knot of them gathered beneath the wall where the prophet stood. Mocking, rough taunts were voices, but for a time the whitebearded oldster paid no heed to the gibes. His sunken eyes, beneath their snowy penthouse brows, dwelt on the far distance, where a forest swept up into the mountain slopes and faded into blue haze.

His voice came, thin piercing.

"Wo, wo unto Sardopolis! Fallen is Jewel of Gobi, fallen and lost forever, and all its glory gone! Desecration shall come to the altars, and the streets shall run red with blood. I see death for the king and shame for his people. . . ."

For a time the soldiers beneath the wail had been silent, but now, spears lifted, they interrupted with a torrent of half-amused mockery. A bearded giant roared:

"Come down to us, old goat! We'll welcome you indeed!"

THE prophet's eyes dropped, and the shouting of the soldiers faded into stillness. Very softly the ancient spoke, yet each word was clear and distinct as a sword-blade.

"Ye shall ride through the streets of the city in triumph. And your king shall mount the silver throne. Yet from the forest shall come your doom; an old doom shall come down upon you, and none shall escape. He shall return—*He*—the mighty one who dwelt here once. . . ."

The prophet lifted his arms, staring straight into the red eye of the rising sun. *"Evohe! Evohe!"*

Then he stepped forward. Two steps and plunged. Straight down, his beard and robe streaming up, till the upthrust spears caught him, and he died.

And that day the gates of Sardopolis were burst in by giant battering-rams, and like an unleashed flood the men of Cyaxares poured into the city, wolves who slew and plundered and tortured mercilessly. Terror walked that day, and a haze of battle hung upon the roofs. The defenders were hunted down and slaughtered in the streets without mercy. Women were outraged, their children impaled, and the glory of Sardopolis faded in a smoke of shame and horror. The last glow of the setting sun touched the scarlet wyvern of Cyaxares floating from the tallest tower of the king's palace.

Flambeaux were lighted in their sockets, till the great hall blazed with a red fire, reflected from the silver throne where the invader sat. His black beard was all bespattered with blood and grime, and slaves groomed him as he sat among his men, gnawing on a mutton-bone. Yet, despite the man's gashed and broken armor and the filth that besmeared him, there was something unmistakably regal about his bearing. A king's son was Cyaxares, the last of a line that had sprung from the dawn ages of Gobi when the feudal barons had reigned.

But his face was a tragic ruin.

Strength and power and nobility had once dwelt there, and traces of them still could be seen, as though in muddy water, through the mask of cruelty and vice that lay heavy upon Cyaxares. His gray eyes held a cold and passionless stare that vanished only in the crimson blaze of battle, and now those deadly eyes dwelt on the bound form of the conquered king of Sardopolis, Chalem.

In contrast with the huge figure of Cyaxares Chalem seemed slight; yet, despite his wounds, he stood stiffly upright, no trace of expression on his pale face.

A strange contrast! The marbled, tapestried throne-room of the palace was more suitable to gay pageantry than this grim scene. The only man who did not seem incongruously out of place stood beside the throne, a slim, dark youth, clad in silks and velvets that had apparently not been marred by the battle. This was Necho, the king's confidant, and, some said, his familiar demon. Whence he had come no one knew but of his evil power over Cyaxares there was no doubt.

A little smile grew on the youth's handsome face. Smoothing his curled dark hair, he leaned close and whispered to the king. The latter nodded, waved away a maiden who was oiling his beard, and said shortly:

"Your power is broken, Chalem. Yet are we

merciful. Render homage, and you may have your life."

For answer Chalem spat upon the marble flags at his feet.

A curious gleam came into Cyaxares' eyes. Half inaudibly he murmured, "A brave man. Too brave to die. . . ."

Some impulse seemed to pull his head around until he met Necho's gaze. A message passed in that silent staring. For Cyaxares took from his side a long, bloodstained sword; he rose, stepped down from his dais—and swung the brand.

CHALEM made no move to evade the blow. The steel cut through bone and brain. As the dead man fell, Cyaxares stood looking down without a trace of expression. He wrenched his sword free.

"Fling this carrion to the vultures," he commanded.

From the group of prisoners near by came an angry oath. The king turned to face the man who had dared to speak. He gestured.

A pair of guards pushed forward a tall, well-muscled figure, yellow-haired, with a face strong despite its youth, now darkened with rage. The man wore no armor, and his torso was criss-crossed with wounds.

"Who are you?" Cyaxares asked with ominous restraint, the sword bare in his hand.

"King Chalem's son—Prince Raynor."

"You seek death?"

Raynor shrugged. "Death has come close to

me today. Slay me if you will. I've butchered about a dozen of your wolves, anyway, and that's some satisfaction."

Behind Cyaxares came a rustle of silks as Necho moved slightly. The king's lips twitched beneath the shaggy beard. His face was suddenly hard and cruel again.

"So! Well, you will crawl to my feet before the next sun sets." He gestured. "No doubt there are torture vaults beneath the palace. Sudrach!"

A brawny, leather-clad man stepped forward and saluted. "You have heard my will. See to it."

"If I crawl to your feet," Raynor said quietly, "it'll be to hamstring you, bloated toad."

The king drew in his breath with an angry sound. Without another word he nodded to Sudrach, and the torturer followed Raynor as he was conducted out. Then Cyaxares went back to his throne and mused for a time, till a slave brought him wine in a gilded chalice.

But the liquor had no power to break his dark mood. At last he rose and went to the dead king's apartments, which the invaders had not dared to plunder for fear of Cyaxares' wrath. Above the silken couch a gleaming image hung from its standard—the scarlet wyvern, wings spread, barbed tail stiffly upright. Cyaxares stood silently staring at it for a space.

He did not turn when he heard Necho's soft voice. The youth said, "The wyvern has conquered once again."

"Aye," Cyaxares said dully. "Once again, through vileness and black shame. It was an evil day when we met, Necho."

Low laughter came. "Yet you summoned me, as I remember. I was content enough in my own place, till you sent your summons."

Involuntarily the king shuddered. "I would Ishtar had sent down her lightnings upon me that night."

"Ishtar? You worship another god now.

Cyaxares swung about, snarling. "Necho, do not push me too far! I have still some power—"

"You have all power," the low voice said. "As you wished."

For a dozen heart-beats the king made no answer. Then he whispered, "I am the first to bring shame upon our royal blood. When I was crowned I swore many a vow on the tombs of my fathers—and for a time I kept those vows. I ruled with truth and chivalry—"

"And you sought wisdom."

"Aye. I was not content. I sought to make my name great, and to that end I talked with sorcerers—with Bleys of the Dark Pool."

"Bleys," Necho murmured. "He was learned, in his way. Yet—he died."

The king's breathing was unsteady. "I know. I slew him—at your command. And you showed me, what happened thereafter."

"Bleys is not happy now," Necho said softly. "He served the same master as you. Wherefore—" The quiet voice grew imperious. "Wherefore live! For by our bargain I shall give you all power on earth, fair women and treasure beyond imagination. But when you die—you shall serve me!"

The other stood silent, while veins swelled on his swarthy forehead. Suddenly, with a bellowing, inarticulate oath, he snatched up his sword. Bright steel flamed through the air—and rebounded, clashing. Up the king's arm and through all his body raced a tingling shock, and simultaneously the regal apartment seemed to darken around him. The fires of the flambeaux darkened. The air was chill—and it whispered.

Steadily the room grew blacker. Now all was midnight black, save for a shining figure that stood immobile, blazing with weird and unearthly radiance. Little murmurs rustled through the deadly stillness. The body of Necho shone brighter, blindingly. And he stood without movin or speaking, till the king shrank with a shuddering cry, his blade clattering on the marble.

"No!" he half sobbed. "For *His* mercy—*no!*"

"He has no mercy," the low voice came, bleak and chill. "Therefore worship me, dog whom men call king. *Worship me!*"

And Cyaxares worshiped. . . .

CHAPTER II
Blood in the City

PRINCE RAYNOR was acutely uncomfortable. He was stretched upon a rack, staring up at the dripping stones of the vault's roof, and Sudrach, the torturer, was heating iron bars on the hearth. A great cup of wine stood nearby, and occasionally Sudrach, humming under his breath, would reach for it and gulp noisily. "A thousand pieces of gold if you help me escape," Raynor repeated without much hope.

"What good is gold to a flayed man?" Sudrach asked. "That would be my fate if you escaped. Also, where would you get a thousand golden pieces?"

"In my apartment," Raynor said. "Safely hidden."

"You may be lying. At any rate, you'll tell me where this hiding place is when I burn out your eyes. Thus I'll have the gold—if it exists—without danger to myself."

Raynor made no answer, but instead tugged at the cords that bound him. They did not give. Yet Raynor strained until blood throbbed in his temples, and was no closer to freedom when he relaxed at last.

"You'll but wear yourself out," Sudrach said over his shoulder. "Best save your strength. You'll need it for screaming." He took an iron bar from the fire. Its end glowed redly, and Raynor watched the implement with fascinated horror. An unpleasant way to die. . . .

But as the glowing bar approached Raynor's chest there came an interruption. The iron door was flung open, and a tall, huge-muscled black entered. Sudrach turned, involuntarily lifting the bar as a weapon. Then he relaxed, his eyes questioning.

"Who the devil are you?" he grunted.

"Eblik, the Nubian," said the black, bowing. "I bear a message from the king. I lost my way in this damned palace, and just now blundered to my goal. The king has two more prisoners for your hands."

"Good!" Sudrach rubbed his hands. "Where are they?"

"In the—" The other stepped closer. He fumbled in his belt.

Then, abruptly, a blood-reddened dagger flashed up and sheathed itself in flesh. Sudrach bellowed, thrust out clawing hands. He doubled up slowly, while his attacker leaped free, and then he collapsed upon the dank stones and lay silent, twitching a little.

"The gods be praised!" Raynor grunted. "Eblik, faithful servant, you come in time!"

Eblik's dark, gargoylish face was worried. "Let me—" He slashed the cords that bound the prisoner. "It wasn't easy. When we were separated in the battle, master, I knew Sardopolis would fall. I changed clothes with one of Cyaxares' men— whom I slew—and waited my chance to escape. It was by the merest luck that I heard you had offended the king and were to be tortured. So—" He shrugged.

Raynor, free at last, sprang up from the rack, stretching his stiffened muscles. "Will it be easy to escape?"

"Perhaps. Many are drunk or asleep. At any rate, we can't stay here."

The two slipped cautiously out into the corridor. A guard lay dead, weltering in his blood, not far away. They hurried past him, and silently threaded their way through the palace, more than once dodging into passages to evade detection.

"If I knew where Cyaxares slept, I'd take my chances on slitting his throat," Raynor said. "Wait! This way!"

At the end of a narrow hall was a door which, pushed open, showed a moonlit expanse of garden. Eblik said, "I remember—I entered this way. Here—" He dived into a bush and presently emerged with a sword and a heavy battle-ax; the latter he thrust in his girdle. "What now?"

"Over the wall," Raynor said, and led the way. The high rampart was not easy to scale, but a spreading tree grew close to it, and eventually the two had surmounted the barrier. As Raynor dropped lightly to the ground he heard a sudden cry, and, glancing around, saw a group of men, armor gleaming in the moonlight, racing toward him. He cursed softly.

Eblik was already fleeing, his long legs covering the yards with amazing speed. Raynor followed, though his first impulse was to wait and give battle. But in the stronghold of Cyaxares such an action would have been suicidal.

Behind the pair the pursuers bayed menace. Swords came out flashing. Raynor clutched his comrade's arm, dragged him into a side alley, and the two sped on, frantically searching for a hiding-place. It was Eblik who found sanctuary five minutes later. Passing the blood-smeared, corpse-littered courtyard of a temple, he gasped a hasty word, and in a moment both Raynor and Eblik were across the moonlit stretch and fleeing into the interior of the temple.

From a high roof hung a golden ball, dim in the gloom. This was the sacred house of the Sun, the dwelling place of the primal god Ahmon. Eblik had been here before, and knew the way. He guided Raynor past torn tapestries and overthrown censers, and then, halting before a golden curtain, he listened. There was no sound of pursuit.

"Good!" the Nubian warrior said. "I've heard of a secret way out of here, though where it is I don't know. Maybe we can find it."

HE drew the curtain aside, and the two entered the sanctuary of the god. Involuntarily Raynor whispered a curse, and his brown fingers tightened on his rapier hilt.

A small chamber faced them, with walls and floor and ceiling blue as the summer sky. It was empty, save for a single huge sphere of gold in the center.

Broken upon the gleaming ball was a man.

From the wall a single flambeau cast a flickering radiance on the twisted, bloodstained body, on the white beard that was dappled with blood. The man lay stretched across the globe, his hands and feet impaled with iron spikes that had been driven deeply into the gold.

Froth bubbled on his lips. His hoary head rolled; eyes stared unseeingly. He gasped, "Water! For the love of Ahmon, a drop of water!"

Raynor's lips were a hard white line as he sprang forward. Eblik helped him as he pried the spikes free. The tortured priest moaned and bit at his mangled lips, but made no outcry. Presently he lay prostrate on the blue floor. With a muttered word, Eblik disappeared, and came back bearing a cup which he held to the dying man's mouth.

The priest drank deeply. He whispered, "Prince Raynor! Is the King safe?"

Swiftly Raynor answered. The other's white head rolled.

"Lift me up—swiftly!"

Raynor obeyed. The priest ran his hands over the golden sphere, and suddenly, beneath his probing fingers, it split in half like a cloven fruit, and in its center a gap widened. A steep staircase led down into hidden depths.

"The altar is open? I cannot see well. Take me down there. They cannot find us in the hidden chamber."

Raynor swung the priest to his shoulders and without hesitation started down the steps, Eblik behind him. There was a low grating as the altar swung back, a gleaming sphere that would halt and baffle pursuit. They were in utter darkness. The prince moved cautiously, testing each step before he shifted his weight. At last he felt the floor level beneath his feet.

SLOWLY, a dim light began to grow, like the first glow of dawn. It revealed a bare stone vault, roughly constructed of mortised stones, strangely at variance with the palatial city above. In one wall a dark hole showed. On the floor was a circular disk of metal, its center hollowed out into a cup. Within this cup lay a broken shard of some rock that resembled gold-shot marble, half as large as Raynor's hand. On the shard were carved certain symbols the prince did not recognize, and one that he did—the ancient looped cross, sacred to the sun-god.

He put the priest down gently, but nevertheless the man moaned in agony. The maimed hands clutched at air.

"Ahmon! Great Ahmon . . . give me more water!"

Eblik obeyed. Strengthened, the priest fumbled for and gripped Raynor's arm.

"You are strong. Good! Strength is needed for the mission you must undertake."

"Mission?"

The priest's fingers tightened. "Aye; Ahmon guided your steps hither. You must be the messenger of vengeance. Not I. I have not long to live. My strength ebbs. . . ."

He was silent for a time, and then resumed, "I have a tale to tell you. Do you know the legend of the founding of Sardopolis? How, long ago, a very terrible god had his altar in this spot, and was served by all the forest dwellers . . . till those who served Ahmon came? They fought and prisoned the forest god, drove him hence to the Valley of Silence, and he lies bound there by strong magic and the seal of Ahmon. Yet there was a prophecy that one day Ahmon would be overthrown, and the bound god would break his fetters and return to his first dwelling place, to the ruin of Sardopolis. The day of the prophecy is at hand!"

The priest pointed. "All is dark. Yet the seal should be there—is it not?"

Raynor said, "A bit of marble—"

"Aye—the talisman. Lift it up!" The voice was now peremptory. Raynor obeyed.

"I have it."

"Good. Guard it well. Lift the disk now."

Almost apprehensively the prince tugged the disk up, finding it curiously light. Beneath was nothing but a jagged stone, crudely carved with archaic figures and symbols. A stone—yet Raynor knew, somehow, that the thing was horribly old, that it had existed from the dawn ages of Gobi.

"The altar of the forest god," said the priest. "He will return to this spot when he is freed. You must go to the Reaver of the Rock, and give him the talisman. He will know its meaning. So shall Ahmon be avenged upon the tyrant. . . ."

Suddenly the priest surged upright, his arms lifted, tears streaming from the blind eyes. He cried, *"Ohé—ohé!* Fallen forever is the House of Ahmon! Fallen to the dust. . . ."

He fell, as a tree falls, crashing down upon the stones, his arms still extended as though in worship. So died the last priest of Ahmon in Gobi.

Raynor did not move for a while. Then he bent over the lax body. A hasty examination showed him that the man was dead, and shrugging, he thrust the marble shard into his belt.

ELAK OF ATLANTIS

"I suppose that's the way out," he said, pointing to the gap in the wall, "though I don't like the look of it. Well—come on."

He squeezed himself into the narrow hole, cursing softly, and Eblik followed.

CHAPTER III
The Reaver of the Rock

WITH slow steps Cyaxares paced his apartment, his shaggy brows drawn together in a frown. Once or twice his hand closed convulsively on his sword-hilt, and again the secret agony within him made him groan aloud. But not once did he glance at the scarlet symbol of the wyvern that hung above his couch.

Going to a window, he looked down over the city, and then his gaze went out to the plain and the distant, forested mountains. He sighed heavily.

A voice said, "You may well look there, Cyaxares. For there is your doom, unless you act swiftly."

"Is it you, Necho?" the king asked heavily. "What new shamefulness must I work now?"

"Two men go south to the Valley of Silence. They must be slain ere they reach it."

"Why? What aid can they get there?"

Necho did not answer at first. His voice was hesitant when he said, "The gods have their own secrets. There is something in the Valley of Silence that can send all your glory and power crashing down about your head. Nor can I aid you then. I can only advise you now and if you follow my advice—well. But act I cannot and must not, for a reason which you need not know. Send out your men therefore, with orders to overtake those two and slay them—swiftly!"

"As you will," the king said, and turned to summon a servitor.

"SOLDIERS follow us," Eblik said, shading his eyes with a calloused hand. He was astride a rangy dun mare, and beside him Raynor rode on a great gray charger, red of nostril and fiery of eye. The latter turned in the saddle and looked back.

"By the gods!" he observed. "Cyaxares has sent half an army after us. It's lucky we managed to steal these mounts."

The two had reined their horses at the summit of a low rise in the forest. Back of them the ground sloped to the great plain and the gutted city of Sardopolis; before them jagged mountains rose, covered with oak and pine and fir. The Nubian licked dry lips, said thirstily, "The fires of all hells are in my belly. Let's get out of this wilderness, where there's nothing to drink but water."

"The Reaver may feed you wine—or blood," Raynor said, "Nevertheless, our best chance is to find this Reaver and seek his aid. A mercenary once told me of the road."

He clapped his heels against the charger's flanks, and the steed bounded forward. In a moment the ridge had hidden them from the men of Cyaxares. So the two penetrated deeper and deeper into the craggy, desolate wilderness, a place haunted by wolves and great bears and, men whispered, monstrous, snake-like cock-adrills.

They went by snow-peaked mountains that lifted white cones to the blue sky, and they fled along the brink of deep gorges from which the low thunder of cataracts rose tumultuously. And always behind them rode the pursuers, a grim and warlike company, following slowly but relentlessly.

But Raynor used more than one stratagem. Thrice he guided his charger up streams along which the wise animal picked its way carefully; again he dislodged an avalanche to block the trail. So it came about that when the two rode down into a great, grassy basin, the men of Cyaxares were far behind.

On all sides the mountains rose. Ahead was a broad, meadow-like valley, strewn with thickets and green groves. Far ahead the precipice rose in a tall rampart, split in one place into a narrow canyon.

To the right of the gorge lifted a great gray rock, mountain-huge, bare save for a winding trail that twisted up its surface to a castle upon the summit. Dwarfed by distance, the size of the huge structure could yet be appreciated—a castle of stone, incongruously bedecked with fluttering, bright banners and pennons.

Raynor pointed. "He dwells there. The Reaver of the Rock."

"And here comes danger," Eblik said, whipping out his battle-ax. "Look!"

From a grove of nearby trees burst a company of horsemen, glittering in the afternoon sunlight, spears lifted, casques and helms agleam. Shouting, they rode down upon the waiting pair. Raynor fingered his sword-hilt, hesitating.

"Put up your blade," he directed Eblik. "We come in friendship here."

The Nubian was doubtful. "But do they know that?"

Nevertheless he sheathed his sword and waited till the dozen riders reined in a few paces away. One spurred forward, a tall man astride a wiry black.

"Are you tired of life, that you seek the Reaver's stronghold?" he demanded. "Or do you mean to enter in his service?"

"We bear a message," Raynor countered. "A message from a priest of Ahmon."

"We know no gods here," the other grunted.

"Well, you know warfare, or I've misread the dents in your armor," Raynor snapped. "Sardopolis is fallen! Cyaxares has taken the city and slain the king, my father, Chalem of Sardopolis."

TO0 his amazement a bellow of laughter burst from the troop. The spokesman said, "What has that to do with us? We own no king but the Reaver. Yet you shall come safely before him, if that is your will. It were shameful to battle a dozen to two, and the rags you wear aren't worth the taking."

Eblik started like a ruffled peacock. "By the gods, you have little courtesy here! For a coin I'd slit your weasand!"

The other rubbed his throat reflectively, grinning. "You may have a trial at that later, if you wish, my ragged gargoyle. But come, now, for the Reaver is in hall, and tonight he rides forth on a raid."

With a nod Raynor spurred his horse forward, the Nubian at his side, and, surrounded by the men of the Reaver, they fled across the valley to the castle. Thence they mounted the steep, dangerous path up the craggy ramp, till at last they crossed a drawbridge and dismounted in a courtyard.

So they took Raynor before the Reaver of the Rock.

A great, shining, red-cheeked man he was, with grizzled gray beard and a crown set rakishly askew on tangled locks. He sat before a blazing fire in a high-roofed stone hall, an iron chest open at his feet. From this he was taking jewels and golden chains and ornaments that might have graced a king's treasury, examining them carefully, and making notes with a quill pen upon a parchment on his lap.

He looked up; merry eyes dwelt on Raynor's flushed face and touseled yellow hair.

"Well, Samar, what is it now?"

"Two strangers. They have a message for you—or so they say."

Suddenly the Reaver's face changed. He

leaned forward, spilling treasure from his lap. "A message? Now there is only one message that can ever come to me . . . speak, you! Who sent you?"

RAYNOR stepped forward confidently. From his belt he drew the broken shard of marble, and extended it.

"A priest of Ahmon bade me give you this," he said. "Sardopolis is fallen."

For a heartbeat there was silence. Then the Reaver took the shard, examining it carefully. He murmured, "Aye. So my rule passes. For long and long my fathers held the Rock, waiting for the summons that never came. And now it has come."

He looked up. "Go, all of you, save you two. And you, Samar—wait, for you should know of this."

The others departed. The Reaver shouted after them, "Summon Delphia!"

He turned to stare into the fire. "So I, Kialeh, must fulfill the ancient pledge of my ancestors. And invaders are on my marches. Well—"

There came an interruption. A girl strode in, dark head proudly crcct, slim figure corseted in dinted armor. She went to the Reaver, flung a blazing jewel in his lap.

"Is this my guerdon?" she snarled. "Faith o' the gods, I took Ossan's castle almost single-handed. And my share is less than the share of Samar here!"

"You are my daughter," the Reaver said quietly. "Shall I give you more honor, then, in our free brotherhood? Be silent. Listen."

Raynor was examining the girl's face with approval. There was beauty there, wild dark lawless beauty, and strength that showed in the firm set of the jaw and the latent fire of the jet eyes. Ebony hair, unbound, fell in ringlets about steel-corseleted shoulders.

The girl said, "Well? Have you had your fill of staring?"

"Let be," the Reaver grunted. "I have a tale for all of you . . . listen." His deep voice grew stronger. "Ages on ages ago this was a barbarous land. The people worshipped a forest-god called—" his hand moved in a queer quick sign— "called Pan. Then from the north came two kings, brothers, bringing with them the power of the sun-god, Ahmon. There was battle in the land then, and blood and reddened steel. Yet Ahmon conquered.

"The forest-god was bound within the Valley of Silence, which lies beyond my castle. The two kings made an agreement. One was to rule Sardopolis, and the other, the younger, was to rear a great castle at the gateway of the Valley of Silence, and guard the fettered god. Until a certain word should come. . . ."

The Reaver weighed a glittering stone in his hand. "For there was a prophecy that one day the rule of Ahmon should be broken. Then it was foretold that the forest-god should be freed, and should bring vengeance upon the destroyers of Sardopolis. For long and long my ancestors have guarded the Rock—and I, Kialeh, am the last. Ah," he sighed. "The great days are over indeed. Never again will the Reaver ride to rob and plunder and mock at gods. Never—what's this?"

A man-at-arms had burst into the hall, eyes alight, face fierce as a wolf's. "Kialeh! An army is in the valley!"

"By Shaitan!" Raynor cursed. "Cyaxares' men! They pursued us—"

The girl, Delphia, swung about. "Gather the men! I'll take command—"

Suddenly the Reaver let out a roaring shout. "No! By all the gods I've flouted—*no!* Would you grudge me my last battle, girl? Gather your men, Samar—but I command!"

Samar sprang to obey. Delphia gripped her father's arm. "I fight *with* you, then."

"I have another task for you. Guide these two through the Valley of Silence, to the place you know. Here—" he thrust the marble shard at the prince. "Take this. You'll know how to use it when the time comes."

Then he was gone, and curtains of black samite swayed into place behind him.

Raynor was curiously eying the girl. Her face was pale beneath its tan, and her eyes betrayed fear. Red battle she could face unflinchingly, but the thought of entering the Valley of Silence meant to her something far more terrible. Yet she said, "Come. We have little time."

Eblik followed Raynor and Delphia from the hall. They went through the harsh splendor of the castle, till at last the girl halted before a blank stone wall. She pressed a hidden spring. A section of the rock swung away, revealing the dimlit depths of a passage.

Delphia paused on the threshold. Her dark eyes flickered over the two.

"Hold fast to your courage," she whispered—and her lips were trembling. "For now we go down into Hell . . ."

CHAPTER IV
The Valley of Silence

YET at first there seemed nothing terrible about the valley. They entered it from a cavern that opened on a thick forest, and, glancing around, Raynor saw tall mountainous ramparts that made the place a prison indeed. It was past sunset, yet already a full moon was rising over the eastern cliffs, outlining the Reaver's castle in black silhouette.

They entered the forest.

Moss underfoot deadened their footsteps. They walked in dim gloom, broken by moonlit traceries filtered through the leaves. And now Raynor noted the curious stillness that hung over all.

There was no sound. The noise of birds and beasts did not exist here, nor did the breath of wind rustle the silent trees. But, queerly, the prince thought there was a sound whispering through the forest, a sound below the threshold of hearing, which nevertheless played on his taut nerves.

"I don't like this," Eblik said, his ugly face set and strained. His voice seemed to die away with uncanny swiftness.

"Pan is fettered here," Delphia whispered. "Yet is his power manifest. . . ."

Soundlessly they went through the soundless forest. And now Raynor realized that, slowly and imperceptibly, the shadowy whisper he had sensed was growing louder—or else his ears were becoming more attuned to it. A very dim murmur, faint and far away, which yet seemed to have within it a multitude of voices. . . .

The voices of the winds . . . the murmur of forests . . . the goblin laughter of shadowed brooks. . . .

It was louder now, and Raynor found himself thinking of all the innumerable sounds of the primeval wilderness. Bird-notes, and the call of beasts. . . .

And under all, a dim, powerful motif, beat a wordless shrilling, a faint piping that set the prince's skin to crawling as he heard it.

"It is the tide of life," Delphia said softly. "The heart-beat of the first god. The pulse of earth."

For the first time Raynor felt something of the primal secrets of the world. Often he had walked alone in the forest, but never yet had the hidden heart of the wilderness reached fingers into his soul. He sensed a mighty and very terrible power stirring latent in the soil beneath him, a thing bound inextricably to the brain of man by the cords of the flesh which came up, by slow degrees, from the seething oceans which once rolled unchecked over a young planet. Unimaginable eons ago man had come from the earth, and the brand of his mother-world was burned deep within his soul.

Afraid, yet strangely happy, as men are sometimes happy in their dreams, the prince motioned for his companions to increase their pace.

The forest gave place to a wide clearing, with shattered white stones rearing to the sky. Broken plinths and peristyles gleamed in the moonlight. A temple had once existed here. Now all was overgrown with moss and the with slow-creeping lichen.

"Here," the girl said in a low whisper. "Here. . . ."

In the center of a ring of fallen pillars they halted. Delphia pointed to a block of marble, on which a metal disk was inset. In a cuplike depression in the metal lay a broken bit of marble.

"The talisman," Delphia said. "Touch it to the other."

Silence . . . and the unearthly tide of hidden life swelling and ebbing all about them. Raynor took the amulet from his belt, stepped forward, fighting down his fear. He bent above the disk—touched marble shard to marble—

As iron to lodestone, the two fragments drew together. They coalesced into one. The jagged line of breakage faded and vanished.

Raynor held the talisman—complete, unbroken!

Now, quite suddenly, the vague murmurings mounted into a roar—gay, jubilant, triumphant! The metal disk shattered into fragments. Beneath it the prince glimpsed a small carved stone, the twin of the one beneath the temple of Ahmon.

Above the unceasing roar sounded a penetrating shrill piping.

Delphia clutched at Raynor's arm, pulled him back. Her face was chalk-white.

"The pipes!" she gasped. "Back—quickly! To see Pan is to die!"

Louder the roar mounted, and louder. In its bellow was a deep shout of alien laughter, a thunder of goblin merriment. The chuckle of the shadowed brooks was the crash of cataracts and waterfalls.

The forest stirred to a breath of gusty wind.

"Back!" the girl said urgently. "Back! We have freed Pan!"

Without conscious thought Raynor thrust the talisman into his belt, turned, and, with Delphia and Eblik beside him, fled into the moonlit shadows. Above him branches tossed in a mounting wind. The wild shrieking of the pipes grew louder.

Tide of earth life—rising to a mad paean of triumph!

The wind exulted:

"Free . . . free!"

And the unseen rivers shouted:

"Great Pan is free!"

CLATTERING of hoofs came from the distance. Bleating calls sounded from afar.

The girl stumbled, almost fell. Raynor gripped

at her arm, pulling her upright, fighting the un-reasoning terror mounting within him. The Nu-bian's grim face was glistening with sweat.

"Pan, Pan is free!"

"Evohé!"

The black mouth of a cavern loomed before them. At its threshold Raynor cast a glance be-hind him, saw all the great forest swaying and tossing. His breath coming unevenly, he turned, following his companions into the cave.

"Shaitan!" he whispered. "What demon have I loosed on the land?"

Then it was race, sprint, pound up the wind-ing passage, up an unending flight of stone steps, through a wall that lifted at Delphia's touch—and into a castle shaking with battle. Raynor stopped short, whipping out his sword, staring at shadows flickering in the distance.

"Cyaxares' men," he said. "They've entered."

In the face of flesh-and-blood antagonists the prince was suddenly himself again. Delphia was already running down the corridor, blade out. Raynor and the Nubian followed.

They burst into the great hall. A ring of armed men surrounded a little group who were making their last stand before the hearth. Tow-ering above the others Raynor saw the tangled locks and bristling beard of Kialeh, the Reaver, and beside him his lieutenant Samar. Corpses littered the floor.

"Ho!" roared the Reaver, as he caught sight of the newcomers. "You come in time! In time—to die with us!"

CHAPTER V

Cursed Be the City

GRIM laughter touched Raynor's lips. He drove in, sheathing his sword in a brawny throat, whipped it out, steel singing. Nor were Eblik and Delphia far behind. Her blade and the Nubian's ax wreaked deadly havoc among Cyaxares' soldiers, who, not expecting attack from the rear, were confused.

The hall became filled with a milling, yelling throng, from which one soldier, a burly giant, emerged, shouting down the others.

"Cut them down! They're but three!"

Then all semblance of sanity was lost in a blaze of crimson battle, swinging brands, and huge maces that crashed down, splitting skulls and spattering gray brain-stuff. Delphia kept shoulder to shoulder with Raynor, seemingly heedless of danger, her blade flicking wasplike through the air. And the prince guarded her as best he could, the sword weaving a bright maze of deadly lightnings as it whirled.

The Reaver swung, and his sword crushed a helm and bit deep into bone. He strained to tug it free—and a soldier thrust up at his throat. Samar deflected the blade with his own weapon, and that cost him his life. In that moment of inattention a driven spear smashed through corselet and jerkin and drank deep of the man's lifeblood.

Silent, he fell.

The Reaver went beserk. Yelling, he sprang

over his lieutenant's corpse and swung. For a few moments he held back his enemies—and then someone flung a shield. Instinctively Kialeh lifted his blade to parry.

The wolves leaped in to the kill. Roaring, the Reaver went down, blood gushing through his shaggy beard, staining its iron-gray with red. When Raynor had time to look again, Kialeh lay a corpse on his own hearth, his head amid bright jewels that had spilled from the over-turned treasure-chest.

The three stood together now, the last of the defenders—Raynor and Eblik and Delphia. The soldiers ringed them, panting for their death, yet hesitating before the menace of cold steel. None wished to be the first to die.

And, as they waited, a little silence fell. The prince heard a sound he remembered.

Dim and far away, a low roaring drifted to his ears. And the eerie shrilling of pipes. . .

It grew louder. The soldiers heard it now. They glanced at one another askance. There was something about that sound that chilled the blood.

It swelled to a gleeful shouting, filling all the castle. A breeze blew through the hall, tugging with elfin fingers at sweat-moist skin. It rose to a gusty blast.

In its murmur voices whispered.

"Evohé! Evohe

They grew louder, mad and unchecked. They exulted.

"Pan, Pan is free!"

"Gods!" a soldier cursed. "What devil's work is this?" He swung about, sword ready.

The curtains of samite were ripped away by the shrieking wind. Deafeningly the voices exulted:

"Pan is free!"

The piping shrilled out. There came the clatter of ringing little hoofs. The castle rocked and shuddered.

Some vague, indefinable impulse made Raynor snatch at his belt, gripping the sun-god's talisman in bronzed fingers. From it a grateful warmth seemed to flow into his flesh—and the roaring faded.

He dragged Delphia and the Nubian behind him. "Close to me! Stay close!"

The room was darkening. No—it seemed as though a cloudy veil of mist dropped before the three, guarding them. Raynor lifted the seal of Ahmon.

The fog-veils swirled. Dimly through them Raynor could see the soldiers moving swiftly, frantically, like rats caught in a trap. He tightened one arm about Delphia's steel-armored waist.

Suddenly the hall was ice-cold. The castle shook as though gripped by Titan hands. The floor swayed beneath the prince's feet.

The mists darkened. Through rifts he saw half-guessed figures that leaped and bounded . . . heard elfin hoofs clicking. Horned and shaggyfurred beings that cried jubilantly as they danced to the pipes of Pan. . . .

Faun and dryad and satyr swung in a mad saraband beyond the shrouding mists. Faintly there came the screaming of men, half drowned in the loud shrilling.

"Evohé!" the demoniac rout thundered. "Evohé! All hail, O Pan!"

With a queer certainty Raynor knew that it was time to leave the castle—and swiftly. Already the great stone structure was shaking like a tree in a hurricane. With a word to his companions he stepped forward hesitantly, the talisman held high.

The walls of mist moved with him. Outside the fog-walls the monstrous figures gamboled. But the soldiers of Cyaxares screamed no more.

Through a castle toppling into ruin the three sped, into the courtyard, across the drawbridge, and down the face of the Rock. Nor did they pause till they were safely in the broad plain of the valley.

"The castle!" Eblik barked, pointing. "See? It falls."

And it was true. Down it came thundering, while clouds of ruin spurted up. Then there was only a shattered wreck on the summit of the Rock. . . .

Delphia caught her breath in a little sob. She murmured, "The end of the Reavers for all time. I—I lived in the castle for more than twenty years. And now it's gone like a puff of dust before the wind."

The walls of fog had vanished. Raynor returned the talisman to his belt. Eblik, staring up at the Rock, swallowed uneasily.

"Well, what now?" he asked.

"Back along the way we came," the prince said. "It's the only way out of this wilderness that I know of."

The girl nodded. "Yes. Beyond the mountains lie deserts, save toward Sardopolis. But we have no mounts."

"Then we'll walk," Eblik observed, but Raynor caught his arm and pointed.

"There! Horses— probably stampeded from the castle. And—Shaitan! There's my gray charger. Good!"

So, presently, the three rode toward Sardopolis, conscious of a wierd dim throbbing that seemed to pulse in the air all about them.

AT dawn they topped a ridge and saw before them the plain. All three reined in their mounts, staring. Beneath them lay the city—but changed!

It was a ruin.

Doom had come to Sardopolis in the night. The mighty towers and battlements had fallen, and huge gaps were opened in the walls. Of the king's palace nothing was left but a single tower, from which, ironically, the wyvern banner flew. As they watched, that pinnacle, too, swayed and tottered and fell, and the scarlet wyvern drifted down into the dust of Sardopolis.

On fallen towers and peristyles distant figures moved, with odd, ungainly boundings. Quickly Raynor turned his eyes away. But he could not shut his ears to the distant crying of pipes, gay and pagan, yet with a faintly mournful undertone.

"Pan has returned to his first altar," Delphia said quietly. "We had best not loiter here."

"By all hell, I agree," the Nubian grunted, digging his heels into his steed's flanks. "Where now, Raynor?"

"Westward, I think, to the Sea of Shadows. There are cities on its shore, and galleys to take us to a haven. Unless—" He turned questioning eyes on Delphia.

She laughed, a little bitterly. "I cannot stay here. The land is sunk back into the pit. Pan rules. I go with you."

The three rode to the west. They skirted, but did not enter, a small grove where a man lay in agony. It was Cyaxares, a figure so dreadfully mangled that only sheer will kept him alive. His face was a bloody mask. The once-rich garments were tattered and filthy. He saw the three riders, and raised his voice in a weak cry which the wind drowned.

Beside the king a slim, youthful figure lounged, leaning idly against an oak-trunk. It was Necho.

"Call louder, Cyaxares," he said. "With a horse under you, you can reach the Sea of Shadows. And if you succeed in doing that, you will yet live for many years."

Again the king cried out. The wind took his voice and shredded it to impotent fragments.

Necho laughed softly. "Too late, now. They

are gone."

CYAXARES let his battered head drop, his beard trailing in the dirt. Through shredded lips he muttered, "if I reach the Sea of Shadows . . . I live."

"True. But if you do not, you die. And then—" Low laughter shook the other.

Groaning, the king dragged himself forward. Necho followed.

"A good horse can reach the Sea of Shadows in three days. If you walk swiftly, you may reach it in six. But you must hurry. Why do you not rise, my Cyaxares?"

The king spat out bitter oaths. In agony he pulled himself forward, leaving a trail of blood on the grass . . . blood that dripped unceasingly from the twin raw stumps just above his ankles.

"The stone that fell upon you was sharp. Cyaxares, was it not?" Necho mocked. "But hurry! You have little time. There are mountains to climb and rivers to cross. . . ."

So, in the trail of Raynor and Eblik and Delphia, crept the dying king, hearing fainter and ever fainter the triumphant pipes of Pan from Sardopolis. And presently, patient as the silent Necho, a vulture dipped against the blue and took up the pursuit, the beat of its wings distinctly audible in the heavy, stagnant silence. . . .

And Raynor and Delphia and Eblik rode onward toward the sea. . . .

*The amulet bore
six signs*

THE CITADEL OF DARKNESS

Black Arts and Necromancy Flourish in Ancient
Forests When a Prince Pits Himself Against
Astrological Gods!

*Hearken, O King, while I tell of high dooms
and valorous men in the dim mists of long-passed
aeons—aye, long and long ago, ere Nineveh and
Tyre were born and ruled and crumbled to the
dust. In the lusty youth of the world Imperial
Gobi, Cradle of Mankind, was a land of beauty
and of wonder and of black evil beyond imagination. And of Imperial Gobi, mistress of the Asian
Seas, nothing now remains but a broken shard, a
shattered stone that once crowned an obelisk—
nothing is left but a thin high wailing in the wind,
a crying that mourns for lost glories. Hearken
again, O King, while I tell you of my vision and
my dream. . . .*
        —The Tale of Sakhmet the Damned.

255

CHAPTER I
The Sign of the Mirror

FOR six hours the archer had lain dying in the great oak's shadow. The attackers had not troubled to strip him of his battered armor—poor stuff compared to their own forged mail, glittering with brilliant gems. They had ridden off with their loot, leaving the wounded archer among the corpses of his companions. He had lost much blood, and now, staring into the afternoon dimness of the forest, he knew death was coming swiftly.

Parched lips gaped as the man gasped for breath. Once more he tried to crawl to where a goatskin canteen lay upon the glossy, motionless flank of a fallen war-horse. And again he failed. Sighing, he relaxed, his fevered cheek against the cool earth.

Faintly a sound came to the archer's ears—the drumming of hoofs. Were the raiders returning? One hand gripped the bow that lay beside him; weakly he strove to fit an arrow to the string.

TWO horses cantered into view—a great gray charger and a dun mare. On the latter rode a tall, huge-muscled black man, his gargoylish face worried and anxious.

The gray's rider seemed small beside the Nubian, but his strong frame was unwearied by hours in the saddle. Under yellow, tousled hair was a hard young face, bronzed and eagle eyed.

He saw the shambles beneath the oak, reined in his steed.

"By Shaitan!" he snapped. "What devil's work is this?"

The dying man's fingers let the bow fall.

"Prince Raynor—water!" he gasped.

Raynor leaped to the ground, snatched a goatskin, and held it to the archer's lips.

"What's happened?" he asked presently. "Where's Delphia?"

"They—they took her."

"Who?"

"A band of warriors took us by surprise. We were ambushed. We fought, but—they were many. I saw them ride south with Delphia."

The archer of a sudden looked oddly astonished. His hand reached out and gripped the bow that lay beside him.

"Death comes," he whispered, and a shudder racked him. His jaw fell; he lay dead.

Raynor stood up, a hard, cold anger in his eyes. He glanced up at the Nubian, who had not dismounted.

"We also ride south," he said shortly. "It was a pity we fell behind, Eblik."

"I don't think so," Eblik observed. "It was an act of providence that your horse should go lame yesterday. Had we been trapped with the others, we'd have died also."

Raynor fingered his sword-hilt. "Perhaps not. At any rate, we'll have our chance to cross blades with these marauding dogs."

"So? I think—"

"Obey!" Raynor snapped, and vaulted to the saddle. He set spurs to the horse's flanks, galloped past the heap of bodies beneath the oak. "Here's a trail. And it leads south."

Grunting his disapproval, the Nubian followed.

"You may have been Prince of Sardopolis," he muttered, "but Sardopolis has fallen."

That was true. They were many days' journey from the kingdom where Raynor had been born, and which was no longer a home for him. Three people had fled from doomed Sardopolis— Raynor, his servant Eblik, and the girl Delphia— and in their flight they had been joined by a few other refugees.

And now the last of the latter had been slain, here in unknown country near the Sea of Shadows that lay like a shining sapphire in Imperial Gobi. When Raynor's horse had gone lame the day before, he and Eblik had fallen behind for an hour that stretched into a far longer period—and now the archers were slain and Delphia herself a captive.

The two rode swiftly; yet when night fell they were still within the great forest that had loomed above them for days. Raynor paused in a little clearing.

"We'll wait here till moonrise," he said. "It's black as the pit now."

Dismounting, the prince stretched weary muscles. Eblik followed his example. There was a brook near by, and he found water for the horses. That done, he squatted on his haunches, a grim black figure in the darkness.

"The stars are out," he said at last, in a muffled tone.

Raynor, his back against a tree-trunk, glanced up. "So they are. But it's not moonrise yet."

The Nubian went on as though he had not heard. "These are strange stars. I've never seen them look thus before."

"Eh?" The young prince stared. Against the jet curtain of night the stars glittered frostily, infinitely far away. "They look the same as always, Eblik."

But—did they? A little chill crept down Raynor's spine. Something cold and indefinably horrible seemed to reach down from the vast abyss of the sky—a breath of the unknown that brooded over this primeval wilderness.

The same stars—yes! But why, in this strange land, were the stars dreadful?

"You're a fool, Eblik," Raynor said shortly. "See to the horses."

The Nubian shivered and stood up.

"I wish we had never come into this black land," he murmured, in an oddly subdued voice. "It is cold here—too cold for midsummer."

A low whisper came out of the dark.

"Aye, it is cold. The gaze of the Basilisk chills you."

"Who's that?" Raynor snarled. He whirled, his sword bare in his hand. Eblik crouched, great hands flexing.

Quiet laughter sounded. A shadow stepped

from behind an oak trunk. A giant figure moved forward, indistinct in the gloom.

"A friend. Or at least, no enemy. Put up your blade, man. I have no quarrel with you."

"No?" Raynor growled. "Then why slink like a wolf in the dark?"

"I heard the noise of battle. I heard strange footsteps in the forest of Mirak. These called me forth."

A glimmer of wan, silvery light crept through the trees. The moon was rising. Its glow touched a great billow of white hair; shaggy, tufted eyebrows, a beard that rippled down upon the newcomer's breast. Little of the man's face could be seen. An aquiline beak of a nose jutted out, and sombre dark eyes dwelt on Raynor. A coarse gray robe and sandals covered the frame of a giant.

"Who are you?"

"Ghiar, they call me."

"What talk is this of a—Basilisk?" Eblik asked softly.

"Few can read the stars," Ghiar said. "Yet those who can know the Dwellers in the Zodiac. Last night the sign of the Archer was eclipsed by the Fish of Ea. And this night the Basilisk is in the ascendancy." The deep voice grew deeper still; organ-powerful it rolled through the dark aisles of the forest. "Seven signs hath the Zodiac! The Sign of the Archer and the Sign of the Fish of Ea! The Sign of the Serpent and that of the Mirror! The Basilisk, and the Black Flower—and the Sign of Tammuz which may not be drawn.

Seven signs—and the Basilisk rules tonight."

MEETING the brooding stare of those dark eyes, Raynor felt a nameless sense of unease.

"My business is not with the stars," half-angrily he said. "I seek men, not mirrors and serpents."

The tufted eyebrows lifted.

"Yet the stars may aid you, stranger, as they have aided me," Ghiar rumbled. "As they have told me, for example, of a captive maid in Malric's castle."

Raynor tensed. "Eh?"

"Baron Malric rules these marshes. His men captured your wench, and she is his prisoner now."

"How do you know this?" Raynor snapped.

"Does that matter? I have certain powers—powers which may aid you, if you wish."

"This is sorcery, Prince," Eblik muttered. "Best run your blade through his hairy gullet."

Raynor hesitated, as though almost minded to obey. Ghiar shrugged.

"Malric's castle is a strong one; his followers are many. You alone cannot save the girl. Let me aid you."

Raynor's laugh was hotly scornful. "You aid me, old man? How?"

"Old? Aye, I am older than you think. Yet these oaks, too, are ancient, and they are strong with age. Let me tell you a secret. Malric fears the stars. He was born under the Sign of the Fish of Ea, which serves the Sign of the Black

261

Flower. I, too, was born under the Sign of the Fish of Ea, but to me has been given power to rule, not to serve. The baron knows my power, and in my name you may free the girl."

Eblik broke in. "What would you gain by this?"

For a moment Ghiar was silent. The cold wind ruffled his white beard and tugged at his gray robe.

"What would I gain? Perhaps vengeance. Perhaps Baron Malric is my enemy. What does that matter to you? If I give you my aid, that should be enough."

"True," Raynor said. "Though this smacks of sorcery to me. However"—he shrugged—"Shaitan knows we need help, if Malric be as strong as you say."

"Good!" Ghiar's somber eyes gleamed with satisfaction. He fumbled in his robe, brought out a small glittering object. "This amulet will be your weapon."

Raynor took the thing and scrutinized it with interest. The amulet was perhaps as large as his palm, a disc of silvery metal on which figures were graven clockwise.

Six signs the amulet bore.

An arrow and a fish; a serpent and a circle; a flower and a tiny dragonlike creature with a long tail and a row of spines on its back.

In the amulet's center was a jewel—cloudy black, with a gleaming starpoint in its tenebrous heart.

"The Sign of Tammuz," whispered Ghiar.

"Which may not be drawn! Yet by the star in the black opal ye may know him, Tammuz, Lord of the Zodiac!"

Raynor turned the object in his hand. On the amulet's back was a mirror-disc.

Ghiar said warningly, "Do not look too long in the steel. Through the Sign of the Mirror the power of the Basilisk is made manifest, and you may need that power. Show Malric the talisman. Order him, in my name, to free the girl. If he obeys, well. If he refuses"—the deep voice sank to an ominous whisper—"if he refuses, turn the amulet. Let him gaze into the Sign of the Mirror!"

Ghiar's hand lifted; he pointed south. "There is your road. The moon is up. Ride south!"

Raynor grunted, turned to his horse. Silently he vaulted to the saddle and turned the steed's head into the trail. Eblik was not far behind.

Once Raynor turned to look over his shoulder. Ghiar was still standing in the clearing, his shaggy head lifted, motionless as an image.

The warlock stared up at the stars.

CHAPTER II
The Sign of the Basilisk

SO EBLIK and Prince Raynor came to the outlaw's castle, a great gray pile of stone towering above the gloomy forest. They came out of the woods and stood silent for a time, looking across a broad grassy meadow, beyond which the castle brooded like a crouching beast. Red flame of lamps and flambeaux glittered from the mullioned windows. In the gateway light glistened on armor.

"Follow!" Raynor snapped, and spurred forward.

Across the sward they fled, and before the nodding guardsman had sprung to alertness, two muscular figures were almost upon him. Bearded lips opened in a shout that died unuttered. Gleaming steel thrust through a bare throat, slipped free, stained crimson. Choking on his own blood, the guard clawed at the gate and fell slowly, face down, to lie motionless in the moonlight

"One guard," Raynor murmured. "Baron Malric fears few enemies, it seems. Well, that will make our task the easier. Come."

They went through the flagged courtyard and entered the castle itself. A bare sentry-room of stone, with a great oak door in the far wall—a room stacked with weapons, sword and mace and iron war-hook. Raynor hesitated, and then slipped quietly to the door. It was not barred. He pushed it gently open and peered through the crack. Eblik saw his master's figure go tense.

Raynor looked upon the castle's great hall. High-ceilinged it stretched up to oak rafters, blackened with smoke, that crisscrossed like a spider's web far above. The room itself was vast. Rich furs and rugs covered the floor; a long T-shaped table stretched almost from wall to wall. Around it, laughing and shouting in vinous mirth as they fed, were the men of Malric, his outlaw band.

Bearded men, wolf-fierce, gnawing on mutton-bones and swilling from great mugs of heady spiced liquor. At the head of the board, on an ornate throne, sat the baron himself—and he was truly a strange man to lord it over these lawless savages.

For Malric was slim and dark and smiling, with a gayly youthful face, and long hair that fell loosely about his slim shoulders. He wore a simple brown tunic, with loose, baggy sleeves, and his hands were busy twirling a gilded, filigreed chalice. He looked up as two burly outlaws entered, half dragging the slim form of a girl.

IT WAS Delphia. She still wore her dinted armor, and her ebony hair, unbound, fell in ringlets about her pale face. There was beauty in that face, wild and lawless beauty, and fire and strength in the jet eyes. She straightened and glared at Malric.

"Well?" she snapped. "What new insult is this?"

"Insult?" the baron questioned, his voice calm and soft. "I intend none. Will you eat with us?" He motioned to a chair that stood vacant beside him.

"I'd sooner eat with wild dogs," Delphia declared.

And at her words a low, ominous growl rose from the outlaws. One man, a burly fellow with a cast in one eye and a white scar disfiguring his cheek, leaped up and hurried to the girl's side. There he turned to face Malric.

"Have I given you leave to rise, Gunther?" the baron asked gently.

For answer the other growled an oath. "By Shaitan!" he snarled. "You've kept me waiting long enough, Malric. This wench is my own. I captured her, and I'll have her. If she eats with us, she sits beside me!"

"So?" Malric's voice did not change. Ironic laughter gleamed in the dark eyes. "Perhaps you grow tired of my rule, Gunther. Perhaps you wish to sit in my throne, eh?"

The outlaws watched, waiting. A hush hung over the long table. Involuntarily Raynor's hand crept to his swordhilt. He sensed death in the air.

Perhaps Gunther sensed it too. The white scar on his cheek grew livid. He roared an inarticulate oath and whipped out a great blade. Bellowing, he sprang at Malric. The sword screamed through the air.

The baron scarcely seemed to move, so swift was his rising. Yet suddenly he stood facing Gunther, and his slim hand dipped into his loose sleeve and came out with the light glittering on bright metal.

Swift as a snake's striking was Malric's cast. And a lean knife shot through the air and found its mark unerringly. Through eye and thin shell of bone and into soft, living brain it sped. Gunther screamed hoarsely once and his sword missed its target, digging instead into the wood of the table.

The outlaw's body bent back like a drawn

bow. Gunther clawed at his face, his nails ripping away skin and flesh in a death agony.

And he fell, his mail ringing and clashing, to lie silent at Malric's feet.

The baron seated himself, sighing. Once more his fingers toyed with the gilded chalice. Seemingly he ignored the shout of approbation that thundered up from the outlaws.

But after a moment he glanced up at Delphia. He gestured, and the two guards dragged her forward.

Watching at the door, Raynor decided that it was time to act. Madness, perhaps, walking into a den of armed enemies. But the prince had changed his opinion. He had developed a queer, inexplicable confidence in Ghiar's talisman. He found the disc in his belt, cupped it in his palm, and with a word to Eblik kicked open the door and stepped into the hall.

Ten steps he took before he was discovered. Ten steps, with the Nubian at his heels, great battle-ax ready.

Then the wolves saw him and sprang up, shouting.

Simultaneously Malric called an order. His voice penetrated knife-keen through the tumult, and silence fell. The baron sat motionless, a little frown between his eyes, watching the two interlopers.

"Well?" he demanded. "Who are you?" And he cast a swift glance at Delphia, whose slight start had been betraying.

"My name matters little," Raynor said. "I

bring you a message from a certain Ghiar."

"Ghiar!"

A repressed whisper shuddered through the outlaws. There was fear in it, and bitter hatred.

"What is this message?" Malric demanded.

"That you free this girl."

THE baron's youthful face was bland.

"Is that all?" he asked.

Raynor was conscious of a feeling of disappointment. He had expected some other reaction—what, he did not know. But Malric's calm passivity baffled him.

The baron waited. When no answer came, he made a quick gesture. And up from the board leaped armed men, shouting, blades bared. They poured down upon Raynor and on Eblik crouching behind him, gargoyle face twisted in battle lust.

So this was what came of warlocks' promises! Raynor grinned bitterly, whipped out his sword—and remembered the talisman. What had Ghiar said?

"If he refuses, turn the amulet. Let him gaze into the Sign of the Mirror!"

The foremost man was almost upon him as Raynor flung up his hand, the talisman cupped within it. From the mirror darted a ray of light—needle-thin, blindingly brilliant.

It struck full in the outlaw's face. It probed deep—deep!

Instantly a mask of stark, frightful horror replaced the look of savagery. The man halted, stood frozen and motionless as a statue, his eyes like those of a tortured animal.

Like a soundless whisper in Raynor's brain came the memory of Ghiar's words :

"The gaze of the Basilisk chills you. . . ."

And now from the mirror in the talisman pale bright rays were streaming, cold as white fires, unearthly as the arrows of the fabled Moon-goddess. And like arrows, too, they flamed swiftly through the air, seeking and finding their marks; and one by one Malric's men stiffened and stood frozen.

The last was the baron himself. And then the fires of the talisman died and were gone.

"Delphia!" Raynor cried. The girl was already running toward him, down the length of the hall.

"This is sorcery, Prince," Eblik said. "And it is evil!"

"It aids us, at least," Raynor flung at him, and then turned to meet the girl.

And halted—staring.

A sudden, icy chill had dropped down upon the great hall. The lamps dimmed swiftly and faded into utter darkness.

Through the midnight black Raynor heard Delphia scream. He sprang forward, cursing.

His foot struck a prostrate body. He bent, and searching fingers found a man's bearded chin.

"Delphia!" he shouted.

"Raynor!" she called and her voice seemed to fade and dwindle as though from infinite distances. "Raynor! Help me!"

The prince's sword screamed through the dark. He stumbled forward blindly, seeking to penetrate the jet blackness, and quite suddenly one hand gripped hard, leathery flesh.

He heard an angry voice.

"Thou meddling fool! You dare to lift steel against the Lord of the Zodiac?"

The voice of—Ghiar! Ghiar, the warlock, come now to Malric's castle by some evil sorcery.

"Lift steel?" Raynor questioned furiously. "I'll give you a taste of it, skulking wizard!"

He thrust strongly just as Ghiar pulled free. A pain-filled screech rang out.

But Raynor had lost the wizard in the darkness, and he pushed forward hurriedly, before the oldster could escape.

"Thou fool!" Ghiar's voice whispered, cold with bitter menace. "Blind, rash fool!"

Raynor, groping in the dark, paused suddenly. A strange, greenish glow was beginning to pervade the hall. But its eerie light gave no illumination. Rather, it served only to reveal the source from which it sprang.

A gross and hideous bulk, scaled and shining, loomed above the man. It was shaped like a dragon, and Raynor suddenly remembered the symbol that he had seen on the talisman.

The Sign of the Basilisk!

Only instinct saved the prince then.

He knew, with a dreadful certainty, that to meet the dreadful gaze of the horror would mean death. And before he had time to catch but a flashing glimpse of the Basilisk, Raynor whirled, both hands lifted to his eyes. Through them, darting into the secret fortress of his mind, an icy chill had leaped suddenly—a cold beyond cold, a horror beyond life.

Four strides he took, blinded, his head throbbing with agony. Something soft and heavy caught his foot, and Raynor stumbled and crashed down upon the stones. The world went out in a blanket of merciful oblivion.

CHAPTER III
The Sign of the Black Flower

RAYNOR awoke suddenly. Sun light was slanting down through the high oaks, and a gruff voice was cursing steadily in several outlandish dialects of Gobi. The prince realized that he was being carried on someone's back, and recognized the deep voice as Eblik's.

He wriggled free, dropped to the ground, and the Nubian turned swiftly, his ugly face twisted with delight.

"Shaitan!" he growled. "The gods be praised! So you're alive, eh?"

"Just about," Raynor said wryly. "What's happened?"

"How should I know? When the lights went out back in Malric's castle, I blundered out of the hall in the dark, and when I got back Delphia was gone and you were lying on your face with a bump as large as World-Mountain on your head. So I picked you up and headed east."

"Why east?" Raynor asked. "You have my

thanks, but it might have been better to have remained in the castle. Delphia—"

"She's to the east," Eblik grunted. "At least, our best chance is to go in that direction. I picked up one of Malric's men and brought him with us. He woke up an hour ago, and I choked some information from the dog. Ghiar has a citadel in Mirak Forest, in that direction." He nodded toward the rising sun. "You were cursing the warlock in your sleep, so I guessed a little of what had happened. What now?"

"We go to Ghiar's citadel," Raynor decided. "You did well, Eblik." Swiftly he explained what had happened. "Where are our horses?"

"Shaitan knows. They took fright and ran off. It isn't far, however."

"So? Well, I'm beginning to understand now, Eblik. Ghiar used me as a cat's-paw. Though just how I still cannot understand."

Raynor pondered. No doubt Ghiar had abducted the girl, but why had not the warlock stolen her by means of his magic, without seeking Raynor's aid? Could it be that the wizard had been unable to enter Malric's castle until someone had opened a gateway for him?

The prince had heard of such beings— creatures that could not enter a house unless they were lifted across the threshold, alien things that could never cross running water. Perhaps the amulet itself had given Ghiar power to materialize in the castle.

Reminded of the talisman, Raynor fumbled in his belt and found the disc there. He examined it with renewed curiosity. In the black jewel the star-point glowed with pale brilliance.

"Well, we go east, then," Raynor decided. "Come."

Without further words he set off at a steady, effortless lope that ate up the miles. The giant Nubian paced him easily, swinging his great ax as though in anticipation.

The oak forest stretched far and far, beyond their horizon. Overhead the sun grew hotter, pouring down its rays that would still be blasting upon Gobi when the empire would be not even a memory in the minds of men. But at last, hours later, the trees thinned and the two men found themselves at the top of a long slope that stretched down to the dark waters of a lake.

In the lake's center was an islet. And on the islet—Ghiar's citadel. A citadel of darkness! Blacker than the nighted gulf of Abaddon was the great block of shining stone that towered up to the sky, a single, gigantic, polished oblong of jet, with neither tower nor window to break its grim monotony. No bridge spanned the lake.

The waters were steel-gray; frigid as polar seas they seemed.

On the islet, about the citadel, the ground was carpeted with darkness. The nature of this shadowy stain was a riddle; it was not stone, for now and again a long ripple would shudder across it as the wind sighed past.

The citadel lay in the shelter of a valley, and over all seemed to hang a slumbrous, eerie quiet. No sound stirred, save for the wind's occasional murmuring. And even that was oddly hushed.

Thus might sleep the fabled Elysian Fields, where the dead who have tasted Lethe wander to and fro, with a half-incurious yearning for lost delights, amid the eternal hush of the shadow-land.

With a little shiver Raynor shook off the spell. He strode forward, the Nubian at his side. Eblik said nothing, but his keen barbaric senses guessed that sorcery dwelt in this valley. The black's eyes were distended; his nostrils twitched as though seeking to scent something that dwelt beyond the threshold of his realization.

As the two went down the slope a dim, unreal perfume seemed to rise and drift about them, an odor sensed rather than actually scented. And a drowsy langour made Raynor's eyes heavy.

TRULY dark magic guarded Ghiar's citadel!

They reached the lake's shore. They circled swiftly, and discovered there was no means of crossing to the islet.

"Short of building a raft," Raynor observed, "which would take too long, I see nothing to it but a swim."

"Aye," Eblik assented, readily enough, but his somber eyes dwelt on the motionless gray waters. "Yet it would be well to have our blades ready, Prince."

A dagger hung at Raynor's side; he unsheathed this and gripped it between his teeth.

Without a word he dived into the lake, came up yards away, swimming strongly.

And the water was cold—cold! Frigid beyond anything Raynor had ever known.

The dreadful chill of it lanced deep into his bones, making them grind together with the sheer pain of the unearthly cold.

Looking down, he found that the water was opaque. A uniform dull grayness made it seem as though he was floating on clouds. What mystery might lurk in these hidden depths he could not guess; but at least nothing rose to halt his progress.

The lake was not wide; yet Raynor was curiously exhausted when at last he waded through shallows and on to dry land. Eblik was not far behind. Now, not far away, Ghiar's citadel rose blackly cryptic before them.

And at their feet were—the Black Flowers!

The ground could not be seen, so thickly they grew. A living carpet of velvety darkness they covered the islet, weirdly beautiful, with stems and leaves and soft petals all of the same glossy black.

Ever and anon a soft wind whispered past, and waves rippled across the jet sea.

SAVE for the wind, it was utterly silent. The two men moved forward. The flowers brushed against their ankles, and a soft cloud of disturbed pollen hung like smoke in their wake. And ever the insidious perfume crept into their nostrils—stronger now, vaguely repellent, and redolent of unknown and forbidden things.

His gaze riveted on the citadel, Raynor did not at first realize that he was making little progress. Then he glanced down quickly, or tried to. But his muscles seemed to respond with unwillingness, and it was with a genuine effort that he succeeded in looking down. The black flowers seemed to be swaying toward him; around his feet the smoky darkness hung.

The dim haze fingered up, questing!

Raynor tried to spring forward. His feet kicked up a great cloud of pollen, and it shrouded him like a pall.

He was unconscious of the fact that he had halted and was swaying to and fro, slowly.

Over his vision a dim curtain dropped.

He seemed to fall very slowly.

The black flowers leaned toward him hungrily. A velvet blossom brushed his cheek; another seemed to cup his mouth as though in dreadful simulacrum of a kiss. Raynor breathed the dark perfume of the flower's heart. . . .

Of a sudden veils were lifted, and he saw unimaginable things. A blaze of sound and light and color swirled into being. Trumpets shrilled in his ears, and he heard the thunder of high walls crumbling to ruin. Confused visions of the past came to Raynor, and he lived again, dimly as in a dream, things he remembered and things he had forgotten.

And always the strange, deadly perfume was strong in his nostrils; but he felt no urge to move. The soporific spell of the Lethean flowers held him bound in fetters of dark magic.

It was pleasant to lie here, to rest, and to re-member.

Then a rough hand gripped Raynor's arm; he was lifted, and immediately fell again heavily. From an immense distance came a harsh, de-spairing cry.

The voice of Eblik!

The sound pierced through the mists that shrouded Prince Raynor's brain. The Nubian was in danger, had cried to his master for help. Realization of this gave the prince strength as he battled down the terrible urge to remain mo-tionless, to sleep, and at last Raynor won. The effort left him sweating and exhausted, but abruptly the visions faded and were gone.

He looked upon Ghiar's citadel, and the haunted islet in the lake. With a sobbing curse he staggered upright. At his feet lay the uncon-scious Nubian, and Raynor lifted the black to his shoulders. Then, holding his breath, he plunged forward across the dark sea, even at that mo-ment of mad turmoil feeling an odd sense of sadness at the thought of the jet, velvety beauty he crushed underfoot.

A wind rippled the blooms; they seemed to sigh as in farewell.

The Sign of the Black Flower was conquered!

CHAPTER IV
The Sign of the Serpent

NOW GHIAR'S citadel loomed above them.

Grimly enigmatic it towered there featureless, with no gate or window breaking the dull monotony of its gloomy structure. Sick and dizzy, Raynor plunged on. And, quite suddenly, he realized that he had been wrong. A portal gaped in the high wall just before him.

Had it previously escaped his searching gaze? Perhaps; it was more probable that a hidden door had slid silently aside to admit the interlopers. It was not a comforting thought, for it meant that eyes were invisibly watching Raynor—eyes of the warlock Ghiar.

Nevertheless, the prince sprang over the threshold. Instantly the portal shut behind him. With little hope Raynor turned and attempted to reopen the door, but he failed.

Even if he had succeeded, what then? His path lay into the heart of the citadel. And a dimly lighted passageway stretched slanting down before him. Smiling grimly, Raynor moved on, carrying the unconscious Eblik, who now, however, began to stir and twitch feebly.

In a moment the giant Nubian had regained his senses. With one catlike movement he leaped free, the huge war-ax gripped in his hand. Then, seeing no enemy, he relaxed, grinning somewhat feebly at Raynor.

"We're in the citadel?" he asked. "Shaitan, there's magic in those damned flowers. Sorcery of the pit!"

"Keep your voice down," Raynor said. "Ghiar may have ways of hearing us, and watching us too. But we can't turn back now, and anyway I want to try my sword on Ghiar's ugly neck."

"I'm curious to see if necromancy will armor him against this," said Eblik, with a flash of white teeth, and the ax cleft the air in a deadly blow. The Nubian handled the heavy weapon as though it were light as a javelin.

Warily the two continued along the corridor. The dim light came from no discernible source; it seemed to gleam faintly from the air all about them. The walls and roof and floor were of the same dark stone.

The passage dipped, widened. The two men came out on a little ledge overhanging an abyss. At their feet was a gulf, dropping straight down to a milky, luminous shining far beneath. Nor was it water that lay at the pit's bottom, though it was certainly liquid. It glowed with a wan, eerie light that reflected palely upon the black room arching above.

Here the corridor broadened into a circular cavern. A bridge spanned the abyss. It arched from the ledge's lip, straight and unbroken as Bifrost Bridge that Norsemen say reaches to Valhalla's gate. It stretched to a black wall of rock and ended beneath an arched opening in the stone.

"Our path lies there," Raynor said grimly. "Pray to your Nubian gods, Eblik!"

The prince stepped forward upon the perilous bridge.

It was narrow, terribly so. Giddy vertigo clutched at the man's brain, impelling him to look down. He fought against the dangerous impulse, kept his eyes steadily upon his goal. He felt Eblik's hand grip his shoulder, heard the Nubian gasp : "It draws me! Guide me, Prince—I dare not keep my eyes open."

"Hold fast," Raynor said between clenched teeth. Yet he looked down. He could not help it.

Nausea clutched him. Far below, in the milky slime, dark bodies moved slowly, writhing and squirming in the dimness. What they were Raynor could not tell, but the creatures had a sickeningly human aspect, despite their ambiguous outlines. A blind deformed face stared up; a shocking muzzle gaped; but no sound came.

The things squirmed and flopped their way through the pale liquid, and Raynor knew that his hasty glance down had been an error. He felt stronger than ever the weird compulsion that seemed to tug at him, drawing him, overbalancing him so that he swayed perilously on the giddy bridge.

With a grinding effort he looked again at the bridge's end. Through some secret reservoir of mind he drew strength and will. He stepped forward, slowly, carefully. But he could not banish the thought of the horrors that dwelt below.

Yet at last the two men reached their goal. Sweating and gasping, they stepped to solid footing. And before them the portal in the rock opened enigmatically.

"God!" Eblik groaned. "Must we cross that hell-bridge on our return? If we do return."

But Raynor had crossed the threshold, and

was standing silent before the Snake.

He was in a small cave, high-roofed, dimly lit, and containing nothing but a crude throne of rock directly facing him. On the throne sat a thing that bore a vague resemblance to a man. Staring at it, Raynor was reminded of the creatures he had just seen in the abyss.

Black and hideous and deformed it towered there, a pulpy shapeless thing of darkness, less human than a crudely chiseled idol. The head was worst of all. It was flattened, snakelike, with bulging dull eyes that stared blindly. The lower part of the face was elongated into a muzzle, and the creature was entirely covered with scales.

It sat there motionless, and bound about its brow like a dreadful crown was a snake. Its flattened head was lifted as in the uraeus crown of the Pharaohs, and its wise, ancient gaze dwelt coldly upon Raynor.

He had never seen anything as lovely and as horrible as this serpent.

The scintillant colors in its body flickered, changed, fading as smoke fades from red to violet, emerald green, shining topaz, sun-yellow, all in an intricate design that also shifted and moved strangely. The blinding beauty of the snake struck through Raynor like a sword.

Its eyes held him.

Very horrible were those eyes, alien beyond all imagining. Their gaze was at first tender, almost caressing, like that of a well loved maiden. Strange magic reached out to grip the man.

The eyes of the snake probed into his soul.

He felt nothing, heard nothing, saw nothing but the flood of alien sorcery pouring into his mind from the incredibly ancient eyes of the serpent.

He was unconscious of the fact that Eblik had halted behind him, motionless, paralyzed.

And those passionless bright eyes were not evil—no! They were older than evil; beyond it, above it, as a god is above human motives and ideals.

They spoke of a wisdom beyond earthly understanding.

THEY erased all else from Raynor's consciousness.

The cords that bound him to this earth, the human ties, slipped away slowly. He had not lost his memories of warm hearths, of laughing, fire-lit faces, of sword-play and of the mad high excitement of war. He remembered these things, with a distant, diamond-sharp clarity; but they had lost their significance.

They were unimportant.

They would pass, and be enveloped in the shadow of the ultimate night, and, in the end, they would not matter.

He remembered Eblik the Nubian, the pale proud face of Delphia rose up before him; but he felt no warmth of human kinship or understanding.

All these things were slipping away from him, in a clear, cold wisdom that came from beyond the stars. He envisioned man as a bit of animate clay moving for a little while upon a ball of mud and stone and water that drifted through the void, through the darkness that would finally engulf it.

So the Snake, that ancient one, gave to Raynor its vision. And the serpent uncoiled from the brow of the seated thing, and it slid down and glided across the stones to the prince, and it coiled about his body with a chill and merciless grip. The wise, flattened head lifted, till it was on a level with the man's face. The eyes of the serpent reached into Raynor's brain, into the secret fortress of his soul, and the prince stepped back one pace.

Then another. Slowly, like an automaton, he moved back toward the abyss that gaped behind him. He passed Eblik without seeing the black. For nothing existed but the dark, alien gaze of the serpent, brooding and old—old beyond earthlife!

The pit yawned behind him. Some stirring of human consciousness gave Raynor pause. He stopped, his sluggish thoughts feebly trying to rise free from the frigid ocean that held them motionless. Dimly he heard a cry from Eblik—muffled, faint, scarcely more than a despairing groan.

And that cry again saved him. Raynor could not have saved himself, but he knew that the Nubian called to his master for aid. And the thought of that was a faint, hot flame that rose and waxed brighter and slowly burned away the chill darkness that darkened his mind.

Slowly, slowly indeed, did the prince battle

his way back to life. He swayed there upon the edge of the great gulf, while the serpent watched, and Eblik, after that one moan, was silent. And at last Raynor won.

Tide of life surged through his blood. He uttered a hoarse shout, gripped the cold, muscular body of the serpent, dragged it from his body. He flung the snake from him into the abyss.

A far sighing drifted up, unearthly, distant.

With that the spell lifted. Raynor came back to consciousness, no longer bound by the dark fetters of primeval magic; he swayed and leaped away from the edge of the pit.

He gave an inarticulate cry, somehow triumphant—exulting.

For the Sign of the Serpent was vanquished!

CHAPTER V

The Sign of the Fish of Ea

A MOVEMENT caught Raynor's attention. The hideous image on the throne was moving slightly. Its misshapen black hand lifted; the muzzle gaped and shuddered. From the deformed mouth came a voice, deep as though it burst from the tongue of a corpse. Harsh, half-inarticulate, and muffled, it croaked:

"Mercy! In your mercy, slay me!"

The dull eyes looked upon Raynor. Shrinking a little in revulsion, the prince almost by instinct whipped out his sword. The monster slowly lifted its frightful head.

"Slay me! Slay me!"

"By all the gods," Raynor whispered through white lips, "what manner of being are you?"

"Once human, like you," the harsh voice groaned. "Once I ruled this citadel. Once I was a greater sorcerer than Ghiar."

A black paw beat the throne's side in agony. "Ghiar served me. I taught him the dark lore. And he turned to evil, and overthrew me, and prisoned me here. He set the Serpent to guard me. From my lips even now he learns wisdom. I serve him in ways I may not tell you. My soul roves between the stars to bring him knowledge."

Raynor forced himself to speak. "Know you aught of a girl, a captive of Ghiar's?"

"Aye! Aye! The warlock has need of a maiden once in a decade. Thus he renews his youth. Ghiar is old—death should have taken him centuries ago. But by the young blood of a maiden, and by her young soul, he drinks fresh vigor. He gains strength to work new evil. Follow this road, and you will find the girl."

Raynor made an impulsive gesture. But the horrible voice froze him in mid-stride.

"Hold! You have conquered the Snake. Yet I am still captive, still in agony you cannot imagine. Give me release, I pray you! Slay me!"

Raynor dared not look upon the hideous figure. "You seek death?"

"I should have died centuries ago. Free me now, and I shall aid you when you need aid most. Slay me!"

Raynor's lips tightened in resolution. He

stepped forward, lifted his sword. As the blade swept down the monster croaked:

"Remember! The Sign of Tammuz is Lord of the Zodiac. It is the Master Sign."

Steel put a period to the words. The horror's head leaped from its shoulders; a foul-smelling ichor spurted a foot into the air. The creature toppled to lie motionless on the stones.

"Blood a' Shaitan!" Raynor muttered shakily. "I think we've walked into hell itself."

"Those be true words," said a low voice. "Once again you have saved us, master. But for what? Some worse doom, I think."

Eblik was rubbing his head, shivering. The prince gave a bark of laughter that held no mirth.

"Well, our road is open before us. And a brave man goes to meet his doom, instead of waiting for it to creep up on him. Hold fast to your ax, Eblik."

Raynor skirted the throne and entered a passage that gaped in the wall behind it. Once more the way led downward. It was a monotonous journey between dull walls of black stone.

What had the monster on the throne meant? "The Sign of Tammuz is Lord of the Zodiac." The Master Sign that could not be drawn—the sign of which the jet jewel in Ghiar's amulet was the symbol.

The passage turned and twisted, but always descended. They were far beneath ground level now, Raynor thought. His leg muscles were beginning to ache when at last the way was barred by a door of iron.

It was, however, unfastened, and moved aside at Raynor's cautious push.

He looked into a great circular room. Wan green light illuminated it dimly. The floor was of mosaic, figured in a bizarre design that centered in the Signs of the Zodiac. A golden Archer and a blue Fish; a scarlet Serpent and a black Flower; the Basilisk, all in shining green; and the disc of the Mirror in dull steel-gray.

In the exact center of the room was an immense jewel of jet set into the mosaic. A blindingly bright starpoint glittered deep in the gem's heart.

It was frigidly cold. Looking up, Raynor realized why. The room was roofless. Its shaft probed up through the heart of the huge stone structure, a hollow tube that ended, far above, in a purple-black sky, shot with innumerable stars. The day had ended, and moonless night brooded over the warlock's citadel.

THE stars looked down upon the Signs of the Zodiac.

The walls were hung with curtains of white samite. They parted now, and a slim figure entered. It was Delphia. She moved slowly, her gaze staring blindly before her, the coils of midnight hair clustering about the pale, keen face. Three paces she took, and halted.

"Delphia!" Raynor called, and stepped forward. The girl did not move.

She lifted her head, gazed up at the stars.

There was a queer avidity in her face, a tenseness as though she waited eagerly for something. It was utterly silent—and cold, cold.

Raynor gripped Delphia's arm, shook her
roughly.

"Wake up!" he said urgently. "Are you under
a spell?"

"She has enchantment on her," Eblik
grunted, peering into the girl's eyes. "Let me
carry her, Prince. Once we're out of this evil
place she may awaken."

Raynor hesitated. Before he could speak a
new voice came, softly mocking.

"Nay, let me carry the wench! I shall be gentle."

With an oath Raynor whipped around, his
sword bared. Eblik's war-ax was suddenly in his
hand, quivering like a falcon straining to be released. There, filling the passage by which they
had entered, were a dozen men, fierce-eyed,
grinning with hate and triumph—the outlaws of
Mirak Forest.

At their head stood Baron Malric. His youthful face wore a gay, reckless smile, despite the
fact that he was in the heart of the wizard's
stronghold.

"Hold!" he whispered. "Do not move! For if
you do, I shall slay you." And one slim hand
slipped toward the loose velvet sleeve and the
sharp knife Malric wore strapped to his forearm.

"How the devil did you get here?" Raynor
snarled.

"I followed the path you opened for me. I

swam the lake and crossed the field of the Black Flowers. I tracked you here through the citadel. It was not an easily won victory—no! Of all my men, these few are all that remain. Some sleep amid the Black Flowers. Others died elsewhere. But it does not matter. Ghiar was too reckless when he hired you to steal the girl from my castle. Warlock he may be, but I rule Mirak!"

"Hired me?" Raynor said slowly. "You mistake. Ghiar is my enemy, as he is yours."

MALRIC laughed softly. "Well, it does not matter whether you lie or tell truth. For you and this black shall both die here, and after I have found and slain Ghiar, I shall go back to my castle with the wench."

"After you have slain Ghiar!"

The words whispered out; the samite curtains parted, and a man stepped through. It was the warlock. The dim green light touched the great billow of white beard, the shaggy eyebrows, of the giant. The dark, somber eyes held no emotion.

"You seek me, Malric? I am here. Slay me if you can."

The baron, after a single start, stood motionless. His gaze locked in a silent, deadly duel with the cold stare of the wizard.

Abruptly, without warning, Malric moved. Too fast for eye to follow his hand dipped, came up flashing brought death. Steel flickered through the air. The keen knife drove at Ghiar's throat— and fell blunted, ringing on the stones.

"Mortal fool," the warlock whispered. "You seek to battle the stars in their courses. Malric, I am Lord of the Zodiac. I have power over the Signs that rule men's lives."

The baron moistened his lips. His smile was crooked.

"Is this so? I know something of the Zodiac, Ghiar, and I know you do not rule all the Signs. You yourself, once spoke to me of being born under the Sign of the Fish of Ea. As was I. How can you rule your ruler—or any other Sign? Nor are you Lord of the Stars. There is a certain Sign"—Malric glanced at the great black jewel in the mosaic's center—"Aye, there is Tammuz. He is Lord of the Master Sign."

"Who can call on Tammuz?" Ghiar said coldly. "Once in a thousand years is a man born under his Sign. And only such a man may work the ultimate magic. Aye, I said to you I was born under the Sign of the Fish of Ea, but who are you that I should tell you full truth—as I do now?" The warlock frowned at Raynor. "As for you and your servant, you shall die with the others. Had you been wise, you would not have sought me here. This girl is mine; I need her life to give me renewed youth."

"D'you think I fear a wizard?" Raynor snapped, and sprang. His sword sheared down, screaming through cleft air.

And rebounded, clashing. The weapon dropped from Raynor's nerveless hand, which was paralyzed as though by a strong electric shock. Snarling an oath, the prince tensed to leap, ready to close with the warlock with bare hands.

Ghiar's peremptory gesture halted him.

"Rash fools!" the wizard whispered, a chill and dreadful menace in the sibilant words. "You shall die as no man has died for a thousand years."

His arms lifted in a strange, archaic gesture. A gesture that reached up toward the stars far above, a gesture that summoned!

Bleak and ominous came the warlock's voice.

"Your doom comes. For now I call on the Sign of the Fish of Ea!"

CHAPTER VI
The Sign of Tammuz

THE green light thickened and grew fainter. An eerie, cloudy emerald glow dropped down upon the roofless room. The figure of Ghiar was a dark shadow towering in the dimness. And the deep voice thundered out:

"Ea! Lord of Eridu and E-apsu! Dweller in the house of the watery deep! *Shar-apsi!* By the power of thy Sign I call on the Lord of that which is below, watcher of Aralu, home of the restless dead. Ea, troubler of the great waters, consort of Damkina, Damgal-nunna, rise now from the eternal abyss!"

The green darkness thickened. Raynor, straining his eyes, could see nothing. He made an effort to move, but found he could not. A weird paralysis held him helpless.

He heard a sound, faint and far away. The sound of waters. The tinkling of brooks, the rushing of mighty cataracts, the thunder of tides crashing on basalt cliffs. The noises of the great deep heralded the coming of Ea, Lord of the waters under the earth.

Nothing existed but the glowing emerald fogs. A deeper light began to grow above. The mists poured up toward it.

Thicker they grew, and thicker. They swirled into an inverted whirlpool, rushing up toward the bright green shining in the air, flooding into it, vanishing. Vanishing as though plunging into an abyss that had no bottom!

A figure swam slowly into view, stiff and rigid. One of Baron Malric's wolves. Raynor had a glimpse of a strained, agonized face, and then the man was caught up into the torrent and vanished into the emerald glow. A thin, high scream drifted faintly from afar.

There were others after that. One by one the outlaws were caught up by the tide of alien magic, drawn into the weird whirlpool, swirled into nothingness. All were gone at last save for Malric.

Now the baron came into view. His youthful face was expressionless, but in the wide eyes was a horror beyond life. The bright hair tossed as though the man floated through water.

No sound came from Malric. He drifted up— and vanished!

The tide gripped Raynor. He felt himself lifted weightless, felt himself circling, rising. The shining abyss loomed above him. Desperately he fought to escape from the necromantic spell.

Quite suddenly the green mists were blotted out. Raynor seemed to hang in a black, starless immensity. He was alone in the void of eternal night.

In the distance a white, chill light began to grow. It approached, meteorlike, and Raynor saw a round, oddly familiar object speeding toward him. Soon it hung in the void not far away, and the prince remembered the deformed monster that had sat on the throne above the abyss—the captive of the snake that he had slain. Here was the same misshapen, hideous head, with its glazed eyes and elongated muzzle, all covered with glittering scales.

The Thing spoke.

"My promise, Prince Raynor. You gave me release. And I promised aid when you should need it most. I bring that aid now."

"The amulet," said the monstrous disembodied head.

Abruptly Raynor remembered the talisman Ghiar had given him in Mirak forest, the disc that bore the Signs of the Zodiac on its surface. He did not seem to move, yet the amulet was in his hand, and lifted high. It had changed. The Signs were erased, all but the black jewel in its center. Within the gem the star-point pulsed and waned with supernal brilliance.

"Tammuz is Lord of the Zodiac," the hideous muzzle croaked. "His magic is above magic. He is master of truth. Through him you may cast away the fetters of glamour and sorcery. Once in a thousand years is a man born under this Sign, and only such a man may call on Tammuz. I am that man! I was born under the Master Sign! Ghiar lies—he boasts of that which he is not! And now, to keep my promise and to aid you, I summon the Lord of the Zodiac. I summon—Tammuz!"

Forthwith the black jewel blazed with an icy, incredible light, starkly pitiless and blindingly bright; and the fantastic vision snapped out and vanished. The talisman was snatched from Raynor's hand. He felt firm stone beneath his feet; a cold wind blew on his sweating face.

Once more he was in Ghiar's citadel. He stood in the roofless room of the Zodiac. But no longer was it filled with the green mists.

DELPHIA and Eblik stood motionless; near them towered the warlock. Of Malric and his wolves there was no trace.

Ghiar's beard fluttered in the frigid blast. His deep eyes were hate-filled. And, with a queer, strange certainty, Raynor knew that by the Sign and the power of the real Tammuz, all magic had been stripped from the wizard.

No longer master of dark sorcery, Ghiar was human, vulnerable! Raynor's shout was madly exultant as he sprang. The armor of invulnerability had been torn from Ghiar. But inhuman strength still surged in the giant frame. Huge muscles rolled under the coarse robe.

Ghiar swept out his arm in a bonecrushing

blow. The shock of it made Raynor reel. Shaking his head blindly, he reeled in and closed with the warlock.

The two men crashed down on the stones. Ghiar fell uppermost; his fingers stabbed down at Raynor's eyes. The prince rolled his head aside, and the warlock bellowed with pain as his hand smashed against rock. Abruptly Ghiar thrust himself away, and his mighty body dropped upon Raynor with an impact that drove the breath from the smaller man's lungs.

Weakly the prince drove a blow at the wizard's face. Blood spurted, staining the white beard. Roaring, Ghiar's hands fastened on Raynor's throat. They tightened remorselessly.

The prince rolled aside; he caught Ghiar's body between his legs, locking his feet together. Breath spewed from the warlock's lips in a foul gust. Ghiar bared his teeth in a murderous grin. And his fingers tightened—tightened.

A hot, throbbing agony was in Raynor's skull. He could not breathe. Knifelike pain thrust into his spine. A little more pressure, and his backbone would crack.

Sheer blind madness swept down on the prince then. Like a flood of red waters it poured through him, sweeping away all else but an insane lust to kill—and swiftly.

Raynor's thigh muscles bulged, holding Ghiar's body in a vise between them. The grinding strain of that frightful effort made sweat burst out on the prince's face; yet he knew that this was the crucial time. It was kill or be slain.

Bones cracked and gave sickeningly. There was a sudden softness in the wizard's body. Ghiar gave a frightful, howling shriek that seemed to burst up from the depths of his lungs. Blood spewed from the gaping mouth, frothed over the white beard, fell on Raynor.

The mighty hands released their grip on the prince's throat. Ghiar sprang up in one last convulsive effort. Dying, he thrust up his arms to the cold stars and screamed like a beast.

And he fell, as a tree falls, smashing down on the stones. He lay inert. From him blood crept darkly across the mosaic, touching and then covering the Sign of the Fish of Ea, the Sign under which Ghiar had been born and had ruled.

The warlock was dead. Consciousness left Raynor then. Merciful darkness blanketed him. Nor did he recover until he felt water poured between his lips, felt a cool, soft hand on his brow. He opened his eyes.

ABOVE him sunlight slanted between the branches of an oak. The green, warm daylight of Mirak Forest was all about him. And Delphia knelt at his side, her eyes no longer blinded with sorcery, her face clouded with anxiety.

"Raynor," she said gratefully. "You're alive, thank the gods!"

"Alive?" growled Eblik, coming from behind an oak. "I'd not have carried him here if he hadn't been. How do you feel, Prince?"

"Well enough," Raynor said. "My legs ache like fire, but I'm unharmed, I think. You carried me out of the citadel, Eblik?"

"That he did," Delphia nodded. "And swam the lake with you. The Black Flowers were dead, Raynor, blasted as though by lightning."

"If you can walk, we'd best be moving," Eblik said impatiently.

Raynor stood up, wincing slightly. "True. We'll find horses and leave this accursed forest behind us."

Together he and Delphia set out along the winding path that led through Mirak. Eblik hesitated a moment before he followed. He looked up at the blue, cloudless sky.

"May the gods grant we get out of this wilderness before nightfall," he grunted. "Out of this black forest, and in another land—a land where the stars are less evil."

Gripping his war-ax, he hurried after Delphia and Raynor. And, presently, the three of them were swallowed by the cool, dim aisles of the vast forest.